THE LAST GOOD PLACE

**Other Books in Carolyn Weston's
Krug & Kellog Series**

Poor Poor Ophelia
Susannah Screaming
Rouse the Demon

THE LAST
GOOD PLACE

ROBIN BURCELL

Based on characters created by
Carolyn Weston

Text copyright © 2015 Brash Books LLC

ISBN: 1941298850
ISBN 13: 9781941298855

Published by Brash Books LLC
12120 State Line #253
Leawood, Kansas 66209

www.brash-books.com

AUTHOR'S NOTE

When I was approached by Brash Books to continue Carolyn Weston's Krug & Kellog series of crime novels, I was immediately intrigued. The books were the basis for the seventies TV show *The Streets of San Francisco*. When the TV series hit the air, I was starting high school in South San Francisco. But I can still remember the thrill and excitement I felt seeing Karl Malden and Michael Douglas playing police homicide inspectors and solving crimes just up the road from where I lived.

The pilot for the TV series was adapted directly from Weston's first novel, *Poor Poor Ophelia*, with a couple of important distinctions. Her books took place in Santa Monica, but the setting for TV was changed to San Francisco. And while the characters stayed pretty much the same, their names were changed: the young, college-educated detective Casey Kellog became Steve Keller (Michael Douglas), and his older, school-of-hard-knocks-educated partner Al Krug became Mike Stone (Karl Malden).

The Weston books are wonderful and offer an entertaining reflection of police work in the seventies. But police procedure and technology have advanced so much since then—and for the better. As much fun as it is to visit the past, the hard-bitten Al Krug would have been fired long ago for some of his actions. (Even the television producers must have sensed this, as they toned down Krug's character into the more genteel version that Malden played.) While I wanted to stay true to Weston's vision of Krug, I couldn't ignore my memories of Malden's Lt. Mike Stone. I decided that I could merge the two and keep the essence of both the book version and TV version by moving the series to present day San Francisco. Krug/Stone is still old school, but in my interpretation, he knows when to pull back. He's still a great foil for the young, energetic go-getter, Casey Kellog, who in my new story retains his youthful exuberance and his belief that a college education makes all the difference in the world. And just as in Weston's original books, in my updated version, both men have much to learn about—and from—each other. I hope you enjoy their new adventures.

ONE

Marcie Valentine tugged at the waist of her running pants, zipped up her purple jacket, then grabbed an elastic tie, sweeping her shoulder-length dishwater-blond hair into a ponytail as she hurried down the stairs. Once in the kitchen, she turned the blinds enough to peer out the window over the wooden fence that separated her yard from her neighbor's. Trudy Salvatori, also dressed for running in a navy zip-up hoodie and black capris, sat at her kitchen table drinking a breakfast shake and reading the newspaper.

Perfect.

Marcie backed away from the window, took her cell phone, then called Trudy's number. "Hey," she said when Trudy answered. "Ready for the morning run?"

"Oh…I'm running a bit late this morning. I'll meet you near the bridge trail where we usually stop. Assuming I get out of here in time."

"See you there."

Marcie disconnected, stuffed the phone into her jacket pocket, then leaned against the counter. Even though she knew this was going to happen, even *planned* for it, she was second-guessing herself. She and Trudy had been friends, best friends, ever since Marcie and Devin moved into the house five years back. Just a few months ago, at a Cinco de Mayo party, Trudy announced that she and her husband, Tony, were putting their house on the market because they were divorcing. They'd fallen out of love.

Marcie had been shocked at the time. Not so any longer. No doubt in her mind as to why. Trudy was sleeping with Marcie's husband, Devin. Not that it mattered. At least it wouldn't after today, she thought as she heard Devin moving around upstairs, allegedly getting ready for work. And that was when she wondered if she really wanted this. Just let the Salvatoris move.

Pretend her own husband had never been unfaithful.

Or was she imagining Devin's affair with Trudy? So many little things had seemed odd.

Maybe she couldn't be sure about *those* things. But *this?* Devin suddenly guarding his cell phone, taking business calls after hours when he'd never done so before. The nights he worked overtime that also matched up to Trudy's extended hours at the campaign office…

The proof was there, and so Marcie had decided today was going to be *the* day. Devin belonged to *her*, not Trudy.

But when she went for her keys on the dining-room table, she couldn't find them. Her purse was right there, hanging on the back of the dining-room chair. No keys inside.

A quick and frantic search of the kitchen, then the little table by the front door, made her rethink her plans.

How was it that something like this *always* happened?

She was losing it…

Self-doubt crowded her thoughts, and she stood there in the middle of the kitchen, telling herself that maybe the keys were fate's way of waking her up, making her realize she was going down the wrong path.

No. She'd worked through everything in her mind, planned the entire day accordingly, and she wasn't going to let something that trivial get in the way.

Besides, there was a spare key beneath one of the flowerpots outside the back door.

She didn't need her keys for this to work.

That calmed her, and she walked over to the stairs. "I'm leaving!" she called up to Devin.

"Have a good run!"

Her eye on the stairwell, she opened then closed the front door firmly, not leaving at all—instead, tiptoeing over to listen as Devin moved about in the bedroom above. A moment later, the sound of him talking softly. "She just left...Yeah. Come on up the back porch stairs."

Marcie bit her lip, tempted to race up and stop him now before Trudy got there. But suddenly she heard him in the hallway. And the sound of the gate latch in the side yard startled her. She slipped into the kitchen, shutting herself into the broom closet. Feeling like a fool, she peered through the slats, trying to contain her fury when she saw Trudy walk past the backdoor window, then heard her run up the patio stairs that led to the master bedroom balcony.

Going for a run my ass, she thought, resisting the urge to race up there, confront them both.

She wanted to cry.

She wanted to scream.

But she needed to be smart about this. She'd gone to too much trouble to waste her efforts on raw emotion, and she pulled out her phone then sent the text she'd pretyped into the message: *She's here.*

Waiting was hell. She checked the time on her cell phone, saw it was five past seven. Hearing nothing coming from upstairs, she opened the broom closet, slipped out the back door and around the side of the house.

You want this...

But did she? Was it worth the price?

It was, she decided, keeping close to the house, positioning herself at the garden gate just as her front door opened. She froze, her heart beating as she pressed herself against the side of the house. This was not going as planned. "Careful," she heard Devin say.

"Always am," came Trudy's reply.

And then Marcie heard the front door close and what sounded like Trudy running down the porch stairs and on down the street.

Panicking, she grabbed her phone from her pocket, opened the text function, and typed: *She's leaving!*

No sooner had she hit SEND than she heard the engine of a vehicle from up the street. She opened the gate just wide enough to see a green pickup truck cruise past in the same direction Trudy had taken off, the driver glancing over as though looking at the FOR SALE sign posted by Trudy's driveway.

Unbelievable. He'd assured Marcie that she wouldn't recognize him. No one would ever know he was there.

And he was right. Because the person in that truck looked nothing like the same man.

That still didn't ease her fears.

What if she'd imagined this whole thing? Trudy and Devin's affair? What if Devin somehow found out what she had planned?

She'd been so careful to make sure he didn't notice the missing money.

Wasted money if she didn't go through with this.

She couldn't…

Marcie stared at her phone, the screen still lit from the last text. It would be so easy to call it off. Pretend nothing happened, nothing was wrong.

That was exactly what she was going to do.

She shoved the phone into the pocket of her purple running suit, zipped it, then stepped out, and after waiting long enough to be sure that both Trudy and the truck were long out of sight, she jogged down the hill, telling herself that the best thing to do was get out, act normal. And so she took off at a slow jog just as the neighbor at the end of her street hobbled out his front door, then navigated down his porch stairs. She saw his paper near the sidewalk, jogged over, scooped it up, then brought it to him. *That was normal.*

"Morning," she said, keeping her pace steady, but slow.

He lifted the paper in greeting. "Nice day for a run."

And normally it would have been. A soft breeze carried the faint tang of salt from the bay, and the early autumn sun lit the dew on the grass as though someone had sprinkled diamond dust over it. The beauty was lost on her as she tried to put her husband and Trudy from her mind. Listen to the pace of her shoes on the sidewalk, the feel of the cool air on her face. Get into the rhythm. Run. Just run.

Soon her neighborhood was behind her, and she turned the corner to Lincoln Boulevard, jogging along the bike path, following it through the Presidio, the air thick with the scent of eucalyptus. Eventually she reached the Presidio Promenade trail by the bay, the sandy gravel crunching beneath her as she ran. To her left, the top of the Golden Gate Bridge was hidden in the marine layer, waiting for the sun to burn it off. A gull cried out as it flew past then dove down toward the water. The faint bark of sea lions drifted in from the bay. She turned away, not caring. Ever since she'd suspected Devin and Trudy were having an affair, the world had turned into a darker place. She'd imagined any number of ways to end this thing between them, none of them good. A week ago, she and Trudy had been running right here on this path, and she'd actually contemplated turning toward the bridge, having Trudy follow her, then pushing her right down to the rocks below. Had it not been for the witnesses, she wondered if she would have.

That was when she realized there were far better ways to end this thing between them. She'd come up with what she thought was a good option.

So why was she having second thoughts?

Because she couldn't bear it if she was wrong and Devin somehow found out.

Call it off. It's not worth it.

That was the thought going through her head as she continued down the path and noticed a couple kneeling in the gravel up ahead, their backs to her. They seemed to be tending someone on the ground, and she caught a glimpse of navy-and-black running clothes and then a familiar Nike shoe…

She quickened her pace, raced up to the couple, then stopped beside them.

The man looked up at her. "We just found her like this."

Everything Marcie had so meticulously planned turned into one giant blur. Her heart stopped momentarily then started up again with a thud. It was several seconds before she could think clearly. Realizing this was supposed to be her friend, worried that this couple tending her could read this morning's every guilty thought flitting through her head, she shook herself and tried to think of something appropriate to say. "She's…okay, right?"

"She's been strangled," the man said. "I think she's dead."

TWO

Sergeant Casey Kellog signaled then slowed his unmarked police car at the corner, waiting for traffic to clear, all the while ignoring his partner, Sergeant Al Krug, who was telling him to go straight. "There's a perfectly good parking spot in the fire lane," Al said, then slapped the placard sitting on the dash that read SAN FRANCISCO POLICE OFFICIAL BUSINESS. "That's what this is for."

Casey kept his eye on the traffic, thick with the morning commuters. "Just practicing a little community-oriented policing by not parking in a red zone. It's bad for our image."

"You're killing me with this new-age policing. It's taken us three days to pin this guy down to get his statement, so park out front. Last thing I wanna do is miss him because *you're* worried what the public thinks."

Compromising, Casey pulled into the loading zone instead. Getting a guy like Al to buy into modern-day policing was not an easy task. A widower in his early fifties, Al was as old school as one could get. Right down to the gray fedora he wore whenever he went out. Even so, Casey never stopped trying, and as he pulled the key from the ignition, he said, "It's all about improving public perception."

"Yeah?" Al said, picking up a file folder from between the seats. "My *police* perception tells me if there's an emergency, we're gonna want the car nearby. But if you're all fired up to put some of that newfangled police science to work, see if you can't improve this guy's faulty memory."

"Easy enough. Cognitive interview techniques." He reached into the backseat for his leather portfolio notebook. "I've got a checklist."

"When you're looking at that checklist, wondering why the Vulcan mind meld from your textbooks isn't working? Maybe think about deviating from the script." He handed Casey the file folder, adjusted his hat, then got out. They walked to the corner store, and Al pulled open the glass door. A small bell sounded as they entered.

The clerk, a man about the same age as Al, stood behind the counter, waiting on a white-haired woman who was purchasing milk, juice, and eggs.

"I'm sorry, Mrs. Little," he said. "This card is also declined."

"I don't know why. Can't you try it again?"

"I've tried. Multiple times."

"There must be some mistake. I can bring the money in later when the bank opens."

"If I do that with you, everyone will be expecting it."

"Maybe I have enough here."

She reached into her purse, her hand shaking as she pulled out a few coins and carefully counted.

Casey eyed the groceries, then dug a twenty from his pocket, walking up to the counter and placing it next to her money. "That should cover it."

She looked up at Casey, her eyes glistening. "I can't take that from you."

"Consider it a loan. When you get the money, bring it in."

"Thank you, young man."

The clerk bagged up the items, and the woman left, thanking Casey with every step.

Al held the door for her. As it swung closed, he showed the man his star, saying, "Leo Rivers?"

The man nodded.

"Sergeant Krug. The Boy Scout here is my partner, Sergeant Kellog. He's got a few questions for you about the murder of Danny Watkins."

"I already told the officers everything I know. I didn't see anything."

Al nodded at Casey to take over.

Casey opened his notebook, eyeing his checklist. "What were you doing about an hour before the murder?"

"The same as every other day. Standing here."

"Do you remember anything different about that day?"

"Yes. Someone got murdered."

"I mean before the murder."

"How can anyone remember what happened? It's all a blur."

"Understandable." But no matter what question Casey posed from his cognitive interview checklist, the answer was the same. The man didn't remember. By all accounts, this method should have worked, but after several fruitless minutes, Casey asked, "*Where* exactly were you when the shots were fired?"

"Right here. At this counter. But like I said, I only heard them. I didn't see anything."

"So you *heard* the shots?" Casey asked, losing patience as Al's phone rang. "You've got a clear view of the door. How was it you didn't see who had the gun?"

Rivers shrugged. "It was dark out? I don't remember."

Behind him, Casey could hear Al speaking softly into the phone, saying, "Yeah. Got it…Not much longer. Give me a minute to wrap it up here."

Clearly Al was about to step in. Desperate to get what he needed before that happened, Casey decided the only thing left was to appeal to the clerk's sense of duty. "Mr. Rivers. A man lost his life out there. Right in front of you. He had two young daughters."

"I wish I could help, but if there's nothing else, I have work to do."

"As do we," Al said. Surprisingly, he turned his back on them, looking out the plate-glass window. "Lot of drug deals going on in this neighborhood, Mr. Rivers? I expect there's a lot of violence."

"Too much," Rivers replied.

"Like those two punks there across the street right now." He pointed toward two men, early twenties, standing on the corner. "I'd hate to think they might mistake our visit for, say, a snitchfest."

"A what?" Rivers asked, his gaze flicking in the direction of the men.

"Snitchfest," Al said, then walked over to the door, taking hold of the sign that read CLOSED. He turned it and slapped it against the glass so it faced out to the street. He peered out the window once more, then sauntered to the counter, leaning forward so that his face was mere inches from Rivers's. "Where one party snitches on another, to report drug dealing out in front of their store."

"Why would they think that? I didn't report anything."

"They don't know that, do they? So pick which case you want to be involved in. A murder stemming from a robbery that happened eight days ago, or a drug sting that's gonna go down as soon as I get narcotics out here to set up shop on your doorstep."

Rivers's gaze fixed on the street corner, where one of the men seemed to be watching them. "Maybe I do remember seeing a man with a gun."

Casey poised his pen over the paper. "What was his name?"

"Terrance Pritchett."

"And where do you know him from?"

"He shops in here sometimes. I've seen his name on the welfare debit card."

"What's he drive?"

"Silver Toyota pickup."

"Now, see?" Al smiled. "That's not so hard, is it?" He turned the sign so that it read OPEN again, then held the door for Casey. "Let's go, College Boy."

Casey waited until they were well up the street before saying anything. "What happened to letting me get the information my way?"

"Like I said, sometimes you gotta deviate from the script."

"Deviate is one thing. Veiled threats about retribution from drug dealers?"

"Didn't seem all that veiled to me. Achille's heel, kid. Besides, it got the information we needed a helluva lot faster than you were getting it."

"And we're in a hurry because...?"

"The op center called. Homicide out by the Golden Gate Bridge. Possible Landmark Strangler." He held up his phone, taunting Casey with it. "Unless, of course, you want me to call them back and reassign it?"

"No." Casey definitely wanted that case, and he quickened his pace to the car, Al following. "How long have they been holding it?"

"Half an hour, maybe. And technically it's not ours. Yet. Happened on the trail, so it belongs to the park rangers. They're asking for our assistance."

Casey was simply going to have to convince them to turn it over. He unlocked the doors, and they got in.

Al picked up the radio, keying the mic, giving his call sign. "Five-Henry-three, dispatch."

"Five-Henry-three. Go ahead."

"We're en route to Golden Gate Bridge on a one-eight-seven. Park rangers requesting assistance."

"Ten-four."

Al looked over at Casey. "And that, College Boy, is why we park out front."

THREE

Casey maneuvered through the morning commute en route to the Golden Gate Bridge, occasionally blasting his siren, wishing traffic would miraculously disappear. He took one corner a bit sharp, and Al slapped his hand on the dash. "What's your hurry, Hotshot?"

"You said it's a possible Landmark Strangler victim."

"Who will still be dead no matter how fast you drive. Let's aim to get there in one piece."

Casey slowed, even though he wanted to do otherwise. This would make the fourth murder in the past four months—all near or around famous San Francisco landmarks. And because of the publicity, it had the city in a panic. Even though whoever solved the case would appear the hero in the public's eye, Casey wanted it for a different reason. Not only was he the newest investigator in Homicide, he was the youngest, just shy of thirty. He needed this case to prove his worth—show the rest of the department that he deserved to be there, that his promotion wasn't a sign of favoritism or some lucky break. It was the same reason he'd recently taken the lieutenant's promotional test—something he hadn't shared with anyone, not even Al. It wasn't to promote, but to prove he could do it. To prove he had what it took.

Maybe then it might quiet some of the veteran officers who felt Casey was out of his element, he thought as he parked along the street near the Battery Trail. Al called in their arrival as they walked beneath the pines and eucalyptus down a gravel trail that led toward the bay. Yellow crime-scene tape was strung from tree to tree. The long ends of the bright plastic ribbon whipping about in the gusty wind looked more like party streamers than a barrier to a crime scene. In case there was any confusion—not that anyone expected any—an officer, clipboard in hand, stood guard at the outer perimeter.

Casey and Al stopped to give their names and star numbers, and the officer jotted them down on his crime-scene log, then lifted the tape, allowing them entry. The inner perimeter, also delineated with crime-scene tape, was about twenty-five yards farther in, where another officer stood guard. Casey kept one eye on the gravel path as they walked down to the main crime scene to make sure they didn't trample on anything important.

The coroner investigator, Kevin Melton, was crouched down by the body. He glanced over at them, nodded in greeting, then turned his attention back to the victim, a woman in her early thirties, wearing a navy-blue-and-black jogging suit. Her blond hair was pulled in a low ponytail at the back of her head, covered in dust, as was the blue ball cap, its rim studded with rhinestones.

Al moved closer, leaning in toward the woman for a better look. "What's the word?"

"Won't know until the autopsy," Melton said. "But if I had to guess? Marks on her neck and petechial rash around the face, at least what you can see through the makeup that's disturbed... Factor in that she was killed practically under the Golden Gate Bridge and in view of Alcatraz? It sure looks like another Landmark Strangler case. At least on the surface."

"Just what we need," Al replied. "Can't wait to see the headlines."

Casey tucked his portable radio beneath his arm then opened his portfolio notebook. "Who's our primary officer?" he asked Melton.

"Park ranger." He nodded toward the trail, where a group of people stood, among them the ranger and a female SFPD officer.

"I'll go see what they've got," Casey said.

Al glanced in that direction. "You mean you'll see if you can sweet-talk them out of the case? I'll catch up to you in a few." He went back to conversing with Melton about the state of the body.

Casey snapped his notebook closed then approached the officers. The park ranger looked barely old enough to shave. The patrol officer, a tall woman with long dark hair pulled back into a bun at the nape of her neck, was closer to Casey's age. She looked up as he approached, but her mirrored sunglasses kept him from seeing her expression.

She gave a slight smile. "You must be from Homicide," she said, holding her hand out.

He shook it. "Casey Kellog."

"Becca Windsor. I was in the area when the rangers called for assistance. Our primary is Glenn Powers."

Casey shook hands with the man. "How can we help?" he asked.

"For now," Glenn said, "some guidance."

Hiding his disappointment that he wasn't asking him to take the case outright, he said, "What do you have so far?"

"The couple with the German shepherd found the woman. Mr. and Mrs. Harris. Jogging the opposite direction as our victim just after seven thirty."

"And the other woman? In the purple running clothes?"

"Victim's neighbor," the ranger said. He checked his notes. "Marcie Valentine."

"She was there when it happened?" Casey asked, figuring if so, no way was it a Strangler case.

"Actually no. They were supposed to be jogging together, but plans were changed at the last minute."

Casey eyed the neighbor, who was sitting on a bench, not interacting with the others, staring out into the distance. "You've taken everyone's statements?"

"So far."

"Okay. It's always a good idea to verify things. How about you and Officer Windsor stand by with the neighbor while I do a quick interview with the couple who reported it? Then we can compare facts."

"Okay."

Al joined Casey. "So?"

"Not turning it over to us yet. But we're taking additional statements. To compare."

"That's a start. But if you really want him to reconsider? Offer up a reminder on how much paper work there is."

He and Al walked up to the group then asked the man with the dog if he wouldn't mind answering a few questions first.

"Sure," he said, handing the German shepherd's leash to his wife.

She cocked her head to the side, raising her brows as she nodded toward Casey and Al.

Her husband shook his head. "I get it," he said.

"Get what?" Casey asked as they walked to a spot about twenty yards away, in view of the crime scene, but out of hearing of the other witnesses.

"I'm supposed to tell you that my wife thinks she saw the man who attacked the woman. She's worried that no one's taking her seriously."

"Saw him where?" Casey asked.

"Coming from the direction of the dead woman, right before we found her."

Al reached out and touched Casey's shoulder. "Finish your interview. I'll get a description from her."

Casey turned to a blank page in his notebook. "Where did you see him?"

"I didn't. But she swears she saw the guy coming from the direction of the dead woman. I mean, anyone coming from that way would have to pass her, but—" Mr. Harris glanced back at his wife, then, in a lower voice, he added, "She tends to be imaginative. I mean, who's to say if the guy was involved, right?"

"In these cases, every little detail helps. He could be a witness. So what'd you see?"

"Nothing until we practically tripped over the woman. Well, our dog sort of keyed in on her, otherwise we might have just jogged on by. She was behind that large shrub." He pointed to the bushes near the trail.

"Did you see or hear anything unusual before or after?"

"Me? Nothing. Truth is, I had my mind on a million other things. Running's a new venture for me. More of a fast walk if you want the truth. Heart attack a few months ago. Doctor's orders. Frankly, I was worried more about how much farther to the car."

"Where're you parked?"

He nodded in the direction of the Golden Gate Bridge. "The dirt lot up there," he said, pointing in the direction of the overflow parking. "Have to get here early, before the tourists, if you want to park. We got here about six thirty? Quarter to seven?"

"So you were on your return trip?"

"Running toward the bridge from Crissy Field."

"You see anyone or anything then?"

"Nope. Pretty much deserted except the diehards. No one really until we were on our way back. Usually gets busy after seven. Locals mostly at that hour."

"And this guy your wife saw? What can you tell me about him?"

"Like I said, not a lot. I didn't even realize she said anything until she reminded me after we found the woman. And then it was an I-told-you-so thing."

"Reminded you?"

"Yeah. 'What if it was that guy I saw?'" he replied, using a high-pitched voice to mimic his wife. Then, apparently realizing how petulant he sounded, he added, "Sorry. But since the heart attack, she's nagging me all the time about my health. Half the time I tune her out, so if she mentioned something? I don't remember it."

Casey gave a sympathetic nod, having heard his father say the same thing about his mother numerous times. "And the lady in purple? The neighbor?"

Harris glanced toward her, shaking his head. "What a way to find out about your friend, huh?"

"Where was she when this happened?"

"Not sure, other than she came running up just a few minutes after we found her."

"From where?"

He pointed toward the bridge. "Somewhere in the vicinity of the parking lot? She coulda come from anywhere. I wasn't really paying attention at that point."

Casey handed the man his card. "If you think of anything else, call."

"I will."

A growing crowd gathered at the outside perimeter on both sides of the path, though the CSIs had set up tarps around the body and yellow crime-scene tape strung from tree to tree for a barrier. Even so, a number of onlookers held up cameras or cell phones, recording the scene, probably posting it on social media at that very moment. Casey ignored them, thanked Mr. Harris, and was about to compare notes with the park ranger, when he saw Mrs. Harris jump up from the bench, telling Al, "That's him! The guy I saw!"

Casey looked that direction, saw a man in a blue-and-red hooded sweat shirt look back over his shoulder then take off at a run.

"Al!" Casey said then tossed his portfolio over.

Al caught it, and Casey raced after the suspect, keying his radio. "Five-Henry-fourteen…code thirty-three. Trail at Golden Gate Bridge."

"Five-Henry-fourteen. Confirm, code thirty-three?"

"Affirm…" He tried to keep his voice steady, knowing how jolted it sounded when he ran. "Westbound…One-eighty-seven suspect…WMA, late twenties…brown hair…red-and-blue sweat shirt."

"All units. Clear the air. Code thirty-three."

Casey heard Officer Windsor behind him. The suspect ran up the path, through the trees then on toward the overflow bridge parking lot. He jumped over a low shrub, almost losing his footing when he slid in the gravel lot. Casey followed, closing the distance slightly. The man reached the street, turned right up the hill.

"Suspect heading up Lincoln…toward bridge parking lot," Casey radioed.

"Bridge parking lot," dispatch repeated.

Casey and Windsor reached the lot. Several cars and two tour buses filled the space. No suspect. They split up, taking different routes up to the bridge gift shop, which wasn't yet open for business. They met on the far side, and Casey turned back toward the parking lot but failed to locate anyone who looked like their suspect, certainly no one out of breath. He peered down to the trail below, but it was empty.

Windsor eyed the pedestrians milling about, some walking up the steps or the ramps toward the gift shop and of course the walkway to the Golden Gate. She looked over at Casey, shaking her head.

Great. They lost him, he thought as two patrol cars pulled up in the lot below, red and blue lights flashing. Casey radioed for them to check the underpass and the streets beyond.

The two units took off, tires screeching.

Becca met him on the walkway that gave them a view of the parking lot for the bridge gift shop.

Casey, trying to catch his breath, looked around, saw a group of tourists walking up from the overflow lot. "Anyone take plate numbers down there?"

"First thing. If he had a car and parked it there, we'll know."

"What about up here?"

"It was empty. The locals park below to run on the trail."

It wasn't empty now. He made another sweep of the area then said, "Let's do a last look down by the tour buses."

Which was when Casey noticed a group of art students near the front of one bus. One young man in particular caught Casey's attention. Unlike the others bundled up in coats, he was wearing a dark, short-sleeved T-shirt, and he wasn't carrying a sketch-book. More important, he was breathing hard.

"There!" Casey said.

Casey's legs felt wooden from the first chase. Even so, he closed the distance. Casey reached out, felt the guy's shirt slip from his grasp. The suspect lunged forward. Officer Windsor came from the side of the bus and cut him off. He darted around her, past the two buses, then out the other side, looking back at them as he ran into the street.

He never saw the car coming around the corner.

Just a screech of tires. Then a sickening thud as he bounced from the hood onto the windshield. Someone screamed as he hit the ground.

Casey barely stopped in time. "Son of a…"

He keyed the radio, tried to keep his voice calm. "Four-oh-eight. Roll a four-boy unit code three."

Casey kneeled down to check the man's pulse. A crowd gathered around them, then someone pointed at Casey. "He caught him. He caught the Landmark Strangler."

FOUR

Casey directed a newly arrived park ranger to keep the growing crowd back from the accident scene. The primary ranger, who had called for their assistance, looked a bit sick as he stared at the dead suspect. Al, arriving from the trail, moved beside the man. "You okay?"

The ranger nodded as he leaned forward, his hands on his knees.

"Talk about a cluster," Al told the ranger. "Two deaths in one morning. Paperwork for days, never mind the autopsies. Well, probably not so much on the suspect. We *know* what killed him. But the woman? Definitely gonna have to autopsy her. Always sort of creeps me out when they start peeling the face—"

The ranger turned on his heel and made a beeline toward the restrooms.

Al walked up to Casey. "That should about do it."

"Little harsh on him, don't you think?"

"You wanted the case, didn't you?" Al nodded toward their suspect. "That's the guy who took off?"

"Dumped his sweatshirt somewhere. But pretty sure he is," Casey said, keeping his voice low. "Whether he's the killer or not—"

"Let's hope he is, since he's dead. Makes the investigation a lot easier." Al saw a white news van just down the road, stopped, fortunately, by an officer who was directing the van's driver to back up. "Great. More press."

An ambulance rolled up with the requested motor officers, better known as four-boy units. And all too soon, traffic on the bridge in both directions was at a standstill and probably would be all day because of the murder. The news vans, however, were coming in the back way, avoiding bridge traffic, which meant they'd need to expand the blockades, because it was only going to get worse.

This part of the investigation, at least, was out of their hands and would be handled by the traffic units. Casey only hoped they'd release him from the accident scene soon so he could get back to the case he was supposed to be investigating. Well, assuming the homicide would be turned over to the PD. "You think the ranger's gonna take it?"

"The kid was as green as his uniform. He's probably calling his supe right now to suggest they turn it over. But it can never hurt to check." Al called the op center, asking them to contact the commanding officer for Parks. "Be sure to let them know there are *two* homicides associated with it. And that we'd be glad to take both."

It was less than five minutes later that they received word that Parks was not going to be taking the cases. Casey tried not to appear happy about it when the park ranger reappeared a few minutes later. "Mr. Harris and his wife?" Casey asked Al, worried he had missed them. "Where are they?"

"Sent them home once I took their statements. Of course, had I known you were gonna find the suspect, I might've brought the wife up here for an ID. Save the time of putting together a photo lineup."

Casey eyed the bloodied corpse. "Let's hope *we* can ID him. If he is the Landmark Strangler, I'd like to at least know his name."

Any further discussion was put aside by the arrival of the traffic officers. After Casey gave his statement to them, he turned to Windsor and held out his hand. "Thanks…I appreciate the help, Officer."

"Becca," she said, returning his shake.

"Becca, thank you."

He started to walk away, then stopped, turned toward her. "You, uh, wouldn't be interested in going out for a drink sometime, would you?"

She didn't answer right away. Just looked at him as though trying to decide if he was serious. Or worthy. Or whatever it was females thought about in these situations. Then, "When?"

"Tonight? This weekend? Uh…" God, he sounded like a moron. "What's good for you?"

"Tonight. Drinks after work. Lobby, six."

"Six."

Al grinned widely as he and Casey walked down the hill toward the overflow lot.

"What's so funny?" Casey asked.

"You. Thinking you're gonna get off at six."

"This case is practically writing itself. Why wouldn't I?"

"No reason."

They continued on to the car, Casey thinking about how long it had been since he'd actually had a date. Months, he was sure.

"Earth to College Boy…"

Casey eyed Al. "Yeah?"

"Feel free to unlock the car."

He dug the keys from his pocket, pressed the button, and the locks popped up.

The victim's neighbor lived less than ten minutes away from the murder scene, a short drive up the hill on Lincoln Boulevard through the Presidio, just off Twenty-Fifth Avenue. Al told him their witness said to look for the FOR SALE sign on the house next door belonging to the victim, Trudy. It was easy to spot, swinging from a post in the center of a planter smack dab between the two properties, a two-story beige house with white trim, the other gray with white trim.

Definitely some pricey real estate, Casey thought as he parked. Not quite the tony Sea Cliff neighborhood a few blocks to the west overlooking the Pacific Ocean, but close enough to make anyone envious. Plop them sixty miles due east on the other side of the bay, the price would be cut in half. Another sixty miles east beyond that, and even Casey could afford one on his salary. Here, he'd need the winning lotto ticket just to make the down payment.

A gust of salt-tinged wind hit them as they got out of their car, and Al had to hold the brim of his hat to keep it from blowing off as they walked past the FOR SALE sign toward the house next door. A woman in purple athletic shirt and pants and running shoes stepped out the front door, her smile looking strained, tired. Their witness, Marcie Valentine.

Her eyes were red from crying, and she crumpled a tissue in one hand as she held open the door for them.

Al removed his fedora as he entered then stopped next to a coat-tree. Among the sweaters draped on the wrought-iron hooks was a wide-brimmed black hat trimmed with a purple flower. "Nice hat," he said, smiling, then held up his own, adding, "People should wear them more often."

That was the way Al worked. Find something innocuous, anything to get the witness's mind off the hard stuff, put them at ease. It seemed to work. Marcie eyed the hat then nodded. "I—I was just making coffee. Would you like a cup?"

"Please," Al said, and they followed her through the dining room into the kitchen. Al stepped to the window at the back door, looking out. A grove of cypress and eucalyptus grew just the other side of her backyard fence. "Can you see the bridge from here?"

She glanced over as she poured coffee into three mugs from an automatic drip machine. "From upstairs. Here, bring your cup. I find it particularly calming, and today I need calm."

She led them out of the kitchen door to the brick patio that overlooked a small garden of potted flowers, then on up a narrow staircase ascending to a wrought-iron balcony on the second story. A white iron bistro table and two chairs faced the bay. Casey took in the impressive view through the grove of eucalyptus, their dagger-shaped leaves rattling in the wind, bringing with it the heavy, distinct scent of the trees. There was at least an acre or two of undeveloped tree-filled property just behind the fence of Marcie's backyard, and those of the other houses on the street. A lot of these older neighborhoods in the greater Bay Area had greenbelts behind them, though they were not so common in the middle of San Francisco. This one was probably owned by the city, Casey decided, or it would have been developed ages ago for the multimillion-dollar view. And what a view. To the left, through the trees, was the Pacific Ocean, and to the right, visible through the marine layer, the vermilion Golden Gate Bridge. Casey tried to imagine what it might be like to walk out of his bedroom door and onto this balcony each morning. Perhaps if he'd gone into hedge funds instead of law enforcement, he thought, his eye returning to the fence line and the wide strip of property behind it.

Al nodded. "Nice, eh?"

"I'll say," Casey replied, as he took a seat across from their witness. He opened his portfolio notebook to a blank page, thanked her for taking the time to see them, then asked her what she was doing in the area at the time of the murder.

"Running," she said. "I run every morning along the Presidio and back. Sometimes with my neighbor, Trudy."

"The woman who was killed?"

"Yes."

"Was she with you?"

She shook her head and turned away. When she looked at him once more, her eyes glistened. "Not this morning. I was… late."

"Late?"

She nodded. "She left before me. When I got there, I saw—That couple who had been running in the area found her."

"Did you see anyone else on the run?"

"No. Not that I noticed."

He wrote down her answer then asked, "Any reason you could imagine why someone would want to kill her?"

"Kill her?" She seemed surprised by the question. "Are you saying it's not that same guy...the Landmark killer?"

"We don't know. But what makes you think that?"

"Because it's near the bridge. Even my husband told me I shouldn't jog near there anymore. I just—Oh my God...That's who killed her. Isn't it?"

"We're still investigating."

She set her coffee cup on the table, her hand shaking.

"Just a few questions for now, if that's okay."

"Of course."

"You're a substitute teacher?"

"Yes."

"And your husband." Casey poised his pencil over the paper. "Where does he work?"

"Why do you need to know?"

Al stepped forward, his expression one of empathy, something he did so well. "Empty boxes on the report form, Mrs. Valentine. Have to fill them all out. Sorry."

"He owns his own company. Valentine and Son. He's the son."

"What sort of place is that?" Al asked.

"Construction."

Casey made a notation then asked, "Is he here?"

"Um, no. I think he's at work."

"You think?"

"He wasn't here when I got home." She dabbed at the new tears.

"He hasn't heard yet?"

"I sent him a text." She looked away, and he wondered more at what wasn't said.

Al shifted slightly, and knowing his partner, Casey realized he was probably thinking the same, because Al pointed to the backyard and the view of trees, suddenly changing the subject. "That's quite the grove of eucalyptus and cypress behind your fence."

Her eyes lit up. "The last good place."

Al smiled in return, waiting for her to explain.

"That's what my grandfather always told me. When I was little, we'd sit right here at this same table…" She ran her hand across the glass insert of the tabletop.

"This used to be your grandfather's house?" Al asked.

"I inherited it from him a little over five years ago," she said, a soft smile playing about her mouth. A gust of wind brought with it the faint scent of eucalyptus. She closed her eyes and took a deep breath. "I always think of him when I smell the trees…" When she looked at Casey this time, her expression had surprisingly hardened. "Can you believe the real estate agent who listed Trudy's property contacted the city to cut them down? To capitalize on the unobstructed view? I can't even believe Trudy would ask. She knows how I feel about those trees."

"Why was she selling?" Al asked.

A slight hesitation, then, "Divorce." A few tears sliced down her cheeks, and she seemed to be struggling with her emotions, perhaps tempering her anger over the property dispute as well as the loss of her friend.

Al turned back toward the view, a silent indicator that he was relinquishing the interview. Casey took a sip of his now-cold coffee, curious about Al's interruption. The man did everything by instinct. Maybe one day Casey would handle it all in his head like Al, but for now, he depended on his list, referred to it once more, and continued with his questions, most routine, all answers he expected. "I know this can't be easy," he said at the conclusion, handing her a business card. "But if you think of anything else…"

"I'll call." She started crying again.

Al stepped forward, placed his hand on her shoulder. "We'll let ourselves out if you'd like some time to yourself."

"Thank you," she managed.

Casey followed Al down the patio staircase. The backyard wasn't exactly what one would call spacious, the long narrow lot being mostly occupied by the house. But it had a decent-size brick patio off the kitchen door filled with flower pots, as well as a brick planter box filled with yellow-and-white pansies that ran alongside the fence that separated her property from that of the victim's home next door. The whitewashed gate was latched, and Casey lifted it, pulling the gate open. The sound of screeching tires caught his attention from down the street, and he looked over, saw a royal-blue Toyota pickup turning the corner, then drive up the hill, parking in front of the house. A dark-haired man got out, ran toward the porch, then stopped suddenly when he saw Casey and Al. "Are you the police?"

"Sergeants Kellog and Krug," Casey said. "SFPD."

The man glanced toward the house, then at Casey. "I just heard. I—I can't believe it."

"You are…?"

"Devin Valentine. Marcie's husband. Is she okay?"

"Understandably upset," Casey replied. When the man ran up the steps, Casey asked, "A minute of your time?"

Devin stopped midstep, turned toward them. "Can it wait? My wife hasn't been feeling well lately. I've been worried about her for some time now."

"She was fine when we left her," Casey assured him.

Al smiled sympathetically. "Just a few questions."

He nodded, then sat on the steps, apparently not interested in inviting Casey or Al inside.

While Al took his preferred position off to one side where he could observe unnoticed, Casey sat beside the man, opened his portfolio. "How well did you know Trudy?"

"She and my wife have been friends since we moved here."

"Any reason you can think of that anyone would want to kill her?"

He dropped his head into his hands, staring down at the porch. "No," he said, his voice broken. "No one."

"Where were you this morning?"

"Oh my God. You don't think that I...?"

Al smiled again. "Routine questions, Mr. Valentine."

"Of course. I was here until my wife left for her run. That would've been...seven."

"And you?"

"Me? I left for the office maybe—I don't know—five, ten minutes after. My secretary will know what time I got in. We had a meeting that started at eight. I—I picked up coffee at Starbucks..." He dug into his pocket, pulled out several dollar bills and a receipt that he handed to Casey, his fingers shaking.

Casey took the paper, saw today's date and the time stamp: 07:35. "Mind if I keep this?"

"Feel free."

He tucked it into his portfolio to book into evidence, then asked a few more questions, the location of his office, how long it took to get there from the Starbucks. Assuming the man's answers were truthful, it would put him well out of the area at the time of the murder. When Casey couldn't think of anything else to ask, he finished with, "Any reason at all you can think that someone would want to kill Trudy?"

"You asked that already."

"We did," Al said. "Maybe you've thought of something since then?"

Devin shook his head. "No. Everyone loved her..."

Al nodded. "But her husband was divorcing her?"

THE LAST GOOD PLACE

"Yes."

"Was it a contentious divorce? Any fights, that sort of thing?"

"Nothing physical, but—No. He wouldn't have…"

"Wouldn't have what?" Al asked.

"Killed her. I don't think—I guess you never really know someone, do you?"

"No."

"But what about that Landmark killer that's been in the news?" he asked Al. "I mean, that path where they were jogging. It's practically in the shadow of the Golden Gate, isn't it?"

"I suppose it is."

"Oh, God…"

He seemed genuinely upset. Casey almost felt guilty watching him and was just about to end the interview when Al said, "One more question, Mr. Valentine. You said you only just found out about the murder…?" He let the question hang.

"My wife sent a text to me."

"When was this?"

"I don't know. Twenty minutes ago?" Devin pulled out his phone, unlocked it, then showed the message to both investigators: *"Trudy was killed at the Presidio. You have to come home."*

Al slipped on his glasses to read it. "Thanks," he said. "That should do it."

Casey handed the man his business card. "In case you think of anything else. Anything at all."

The man nodded, stared blankly at the card, as though he wasn't even sure what was in his hand. Then, after a moment he stood, and without another word, he walked inside the house.

Al eyed the closed door. "Well, that was interesting."

"What was?" Casey asked.

"That text was sent right before we got here."

"So?"

"Not sure yet. Just that I gathered some underlying tension on Marcie Valentine's part. I mean, maybe I'm asking the wrong person, since you're not married. But in my house? My wife would've been on the phone the moment she learned her friend was murdered. Heaven forbid I let it go to voice mail."

"He did mention she wasn't feeling well."

"Why wait an hour to tell him?"

"He was at work. Maybe she didn't want to disturb him."

"I think murder is a valid reason to ignore that rule." They walked to the victim's house next door, and Al rang the bell. "Makes me wonder if all is not well in paradise." Which was one of the strangest aspects of their job. They dug into people's lives, learning secrets that would have stayed hidden—if not for someone else's misfortune.

Al rang the bell a second time. When no one answered, Casey telephoned dispatch. "Anyone notify the deceased's husband?"

He heard the clicking of a computer, and a moment later the dispatcher saying, "Patrol made notification in person at his place of employment then brought him to the Hall. He's waiting in the fourth-floor lobby."

"Thanks. Have someone inform him that we're on our way."

FIVE

Marcie heard Devin running up the stairs, then into the bedroom. But she didn't move from the little table on the balcony. Here, at least, she felt safe.

And right now she needed safe.

The balcony door clattered as he threw it open. "Marcie? What are you doing out here?"

She looked up and saw him staring at her, his bloodshot eyes glistening. "I'm fine. Thanks for asking."

"What happened?"

"I don't know. These people found her on the ground." After the rush of emotions from earlier in the day, Marcie felt strangely detached from the entire incident. "I heard someone strangled her."

"Are there any witnesses? Did anyone see what happened?"

"The police chased someone."

"Did you see who it was?"

"It all happened too fast."

Devin pulled out a chair and sat opposite her, his face pale, his hand shaking as he covered his mouth, then turned away. "I can't believe this." He got up, turned to leave. "I think I need a drink."

Marcie followed him into the house, then on down the stairs into the kitchen. He pulled open the cupboard with the glasses, staring blankly inside, apparently forgetting why he'd even come in here.

She wondered if he'd be this upset if she had been killed instead of Trudy.

Of course not. And she could no longer hold back what she knew. "I saw her, you know. Trudy was here this morning."

It seemed several heartbeats before he turned, looked at her. "Why would you say that?"

The last thing she was going to tell him was what she'd done, who she'd hired. She'd have to take care of that later. Somehow. "Because I *know*. All those times she suddenly couldn't go running? She's been over here on *several* occasions. My best friend. Alone with my husband. Or are you going to try to deny it?"

He gave her a weak smile. "I suppose it's pointless to deny it now, after what happened this morning."

She crossed her arms over her chest. She *knew* they were having an affair. "Then go ahead. Tell me," she said, unable to keep the accusation from her voice.

"We were trying to put together a surprise party for you."

It took a moment for his words to sink in. "For me?"

"Who else?"

"My birthday's not for another two months."

"Some things are worth planning for. Trudy had this crazy idea that—" He gave a casual shrug, reached into the cupboard, and pulled out a glass. "Well. It doesn't matter now, does it? Apparently she was a better friend than you thought."

Her stomach twisted with nausea. It couldn't be true, could it? That Trudy had been coming over here for something so innocent?

She leaned against the counter, her legs feeling weak. What was it they always said? Be careful what you wish for? She'd wanted Trudy dead...

Devin filled his glass with water then looked over at her. "How'd you know she was here?"

"I only pretended to leave. That's when I saw Trudy come over, and I didn't leave until after she did."

"But I saw you. I heard you go out the front door."

"I was hiding in the kitchen."

A gamut of emotions crossed his face as the realization of what she said apparently sank in. "Oh my God...What did you tell the cops?"

"I—I just said I left. I didn't tell them I was hiding."

He stared mutely at her for several seconds. Then, setting his glass on the counter, started pacing. "I need to think."

"About what?" she asked, not liking that he seemed so worried.

"Do you know how that's going to look if they find out we didn't tell the truth?"

"Are you saying you lied, too?"

"No. I'm saying I told them that Trudy left *after* you. I sure as hell didn't say she was *here*. They'd start asking all sorts of questions. Just like they will if you tell them you never really *left*." He stopped then looked at her. "My God. She was murdered. What if she didn't tell her husband what we were doing? Planning this surprise for you? Look at what you thought. Imagine what Tony will think. What the *cops* will think. This is a nightmare."

"But they're not thinking *we*...They wouldn't, would they?"

"If they discover we weren't up front? How do you think they'll take it? For God's sake, I told them you left at seven. We could be in trouble. Both of us."

She realized he was right. Lying to the cops was bad enough. Lying during a murder investigation? "What do we do?"

"I have to think about this," he said, pulling her into his arms, holding her close. It had been a long time since he'd held her. And she didn't know if it was her heart, or his, beating so fast.

SIX

The victim's husband, Tony Salvatori, was, as dispatched advised, waiting in the fourth-floor lobby at the Hall of Justice. An officer was standing by when Casey and Al got there, and both investigators took a moment to observe the man before they were seen. To an outsider, peering on the newly bereaved might seem callous, but that was their job. To observe and make split-second decisions on who was genuine, who wasn't. And what Casey saw was that Tony Salvatori certainly *appeared* to have the proper demeanor for a bereaved husband. His eyes were red, clearly he'd been crying—not that that trait absolved anyone of guilt. In this case, he was probably innocent—an easy assumption when they were fairly certain the real suspect was on his way to the morgue, which was where Casey wanted to be. The Landmark Strangler murders had been such big news these past few weeks, one would have to live in a cave not to know how important today's case was.

Mr. Salvatori looked up as they approached, and Casey said, "Mr. Salvatori? I'm Sergeant Casey Kellog. Homicide. And this is my partner, Sergeant Al Krug."

Salvatori stood, his clasp limp, his palms sweaty.

"I'm sorry about your loss," Casey said, once they were in an interview room.

"I can't believe this. I just…Do you know who did this?"

"We're still investigating. I know this is hard for you, but we're going to have to ask a lot of questions. Some of them may seem insensitive, but it's the only way we can solve this."

"Was it that Landmark Killer? Strangler? I keep hearing about him in the news. We were talking about it, my wife and I. I just—I told her not to go jogging there. Not while this guy was on the loose…" He looked away, his eyes shimmering.

The best way Casey knew to distract someone temporarily from their grief was to ask the basics. "How old was Trudy?"

"Um, she just turned thirty-four."

"Did she work?"

"Yes. For Congressman Parnell. She was, uh, finance director for his reelection campaign."

Casey saw Al's eyebrows go up a fraction at that revelation. It was going to be tough enough having the connection to the Strangler, but adding a high-ranking politician to the mix? Talk about being under the microscope. Casey almost wished he hadn't been so eager to take the case. "What time did she leave this morning?"

"Around seven. Maybe a little after…"

Casey consulted his list. They needed to learn everything leading up to the time of the murder and then verify it so that there were no questions. "You're sure about the time your wife left?"

Salvatori nodded. "Trudy was locking the front door as I drove off. I—we were both running a little late, and I remember looking at the dash, wondering if I had enough time to stop for coffee. I decided against it, since I had a board meeting to prepare for."

"So you got to work at…?"

"I don't know. Maybe seven thirty, quarter to eight?"

Al stepped forward, his hat against his chest. "Where is it you work, Mr. Salvatori?"

"Kahler and Pico Finance. Off Market."

"What is that?" Al asked. "A twenty-minute commute?"

"It depends on traffic, but yeah, that'd be about right."

"Is there anyone who can verify your presence?"

"You don't think that I…?"

Al gave him that sympathetic smile he was so good at. "Like we said, Mr. Salvatori. Routine. It's best if we can eliminate everyone we can so we can concentrate on who *really* did this."

Salvatori nodded. "Of course. I, um, I don't think anyone else came in until maybe…seven forty-five? Eight, maybe? I—Oh my God…When was she killed? I should have been there for her."

"Who was it?" Casey asked. "The person who can vouch you were at the office?"

"My secretary. Janis Stansbury." He gave Casey her contact information then added, "If there's nothing else? I really would like to see my wife. She's here, isn't she? At the morgue?"

Casey glanced at Al, who said, "One more question, if you don't mind. Anyone at all you can think of who might want your wife dead?"

The color faded from Tony Salvatori's face. "*Want* her dead? Why would anyone—" He got up, started pacing, then stopped to face Al. "She was jogging near the Golden Gate Bridge! Are you saying it *wasn't* the Landmark Killer?"

"I'm saying we need to look at every angle, Mr. Salvatori. When we catch the person who murdered your wife, and it goes to court, the defense is going to try to pin it on everyone else but their client."

"I don't know. I really can't think right now. Can I go? I—I just need to go."

"Of course," Al said. "I'll walk you down."

"Thanks, but I'd really like to be alone. Please."

He left the interview room, his footsteps echoing down the hallway toward the elevator.

Al leaned against the doorway, watching Casey finish up his notes. "You sure you want the case?"

"Why wouldn't I?"

"Because you might be mistaking it for a career maker."

Casey closed his notebook. "Why would you say that?"

"Working anything with politicians can be career suicide. Especially that one. Parnell won his last campaign because he was all about increasing funding to the police to fight crime. And he's close to a lot of cops here. Come to think of it, I'm pretty sure he and our captain are on a first-name basis, which means you're going to have to be on top of your game."

"I'll take that as fair warning," Casey said as he and Al returned to the office. They were greeted with cheers and jeers from their fellow investigators as they walked in the door.

Zwingler crumpled up a piece of paper and tossed it at Casey. "Heard you killed the suspect by running him into a car. Instead of Casey Kellog, we're gonna have to call you Casey Killer. Way to go, Hotshot!"

The room erupted in laughter just as their boss, Lieutenant Timms, walked in. He looked over at the white board, where someone had written: Wanted, dead or alive. Landmark Strangler. Some joker had crossed out the word alive and circled the word dead. Timms saw it and said, "Erase that. Now. Kellog and Krug? A minute of your time."

The laughter died as Haynes got up, erased the board.

Casey and Al walked into the lieutenant's office.

He sat at his desk, telling Casey to close the door. "What the hell happened out there?" The question was directed at Al, since he was the senior investigator.

"We got there, the suspect fled, and Hotshot here chased him down. Car got in the way."

"Tell me he's at least the killer."

"That part looks pretty good. At least from the witness's point of view. Whether he's the Strangler—"

"Could he be?"

"Even our witnesses believe it's another Strangler murder."

"And what do you believe?" Timms asked.

"That we don't know enough about it yet."

"Either way," Timms said, his chair squeaking as he leaned back, "the damned press will be all over this. Get me a preliminary report A-SAP. I'm going to need to get something together for the captain. By the way. Which one of you is taking the lead on this?"

Casey looked at Al, not daring to say anything. This could be the biggest case of his career, and Al knew it.

"The kid wants it."

Timms nodded. "Let's get to work, then."

"One thing you should know," Al told Timms. "The victim? Works for Congressman Parnell."

Timms gaze hit Casey's. "You sure you want this?"

"Yes."

Al said, "Be careful what you wish for is all I've got to say."

They left the office, and Casey slipped out of his coat, hung it on the hook by the door, then sat at his desk. "Thanks."

"Your career, kid. In the meantime, let's get started on that victimology."

With every database at their disposal, both local and national, they would delve into Trudy Salvatori's life, then work their way backward. By the end of the day, they'd know where she was born, every address she'd lived at or worked at, every phone number ever assigned to her, what sort of credit she maintained, and who her known associates were. In cases where there was no known suspect, the victimology was a powerful tool. One never knew who or what might turn up in the victim's background that would lead them to the killer. An old boyfriend, a disgruntled business partner, a spouse who perhaps took out a large insurance policy.

Not that they expected to find anything like that in this case. They had a known killer. And if he was the Landmark Strangler, it was highly probable that nothing in Trudy's background would connect to the suspect. But it was a formality that needed to be done, and Casey thanked Al for his offer. Of course, the same thing would need to be done on the suspect, now that he was lying dead in their morgue, and Casey picked up the phone and called them. What he needed was an ID on the man. If he was the Landmark Strangler, they were going to have to connect him to every other victim.

"This is Kellog, up in Homicide. Any chance they brought in the deceased from this morning's accident at the Golden Gate Bridge?"

"I've got two victims from there. Hold on...male or female?"

"The male."

"Right. Car accident. At this point, he's a John Doe. Soon as we get him identified, I'll give you a call."

"Thanks."

Al looked up from his computer monitor. "Got an ID?"

"John Doe."

"What's with these crooks? Can't even carry proper ID?"

"My sentiments exactly."

"Well, you don't need that for the preliminary report. Get that to the lieutenant. We can fill in the blanks later."

A lot more than filling in a few blanks. By the time they finished investigating the case, it would consist of several thick black binders, what they called the "murder book." The known Landmark Strangler cases already filled two shelves in the Homicide office. Al was the lead on the first two known cases, Carl West caught the third. If this was the fourth, Casey knew he'd be under a lot of scrutiny, especially with the connection to Congressman Parnell. Which meant he needed to do everything right.

Everyone was already watching him closely, waiting for him to stumble and fall. He knew some of that was fueled by jealousy, especially by those who'd applied for the same position and didn't get it. But there were others, Al included, who felt he was too young to be in Homicide. He hadn't put in his time on the streets. At first Casey ignored the naysayers. There were times, though, when he wondered if maybe he had promoted too soon. Between the press hounding them for not catching this or that suspect, or the brass canceling vacations and days off until whichever killer was caught, Casey worried that he might be burning himself out. He glanced over at Al working at his computer, his brown hair flecked with gray, the lines in his face accentuated by the harsh lighting from the window. The man looked far older than his early fifties, and Casey wondered if it had to do with the added stress of working Homicide all these years. More than a decade, Casey realized, and he wondered if he could do this for that long, look death in the face day after day.

"How's that report coming?" Timms asked from his doorway.

"Almost done," Casey said, checking his notes.

"Got an ID on your suspect yet?"

"Waiting on the morgue."

"Call again. I'd like everything on my desk before you leave tonight. Captain wants to hold a press conference in the morning."

"Press conference?" Al said. "Don't you think we're jumping the gun a bit?"

"Get me an ID."

Casey glanced at the clock. Almost five-thirty. In half an hour, Becca would be meeting him downstairs for drinks. He picked up the phone, called the morgue again.

"This is Kellog up in Homicide," he told the woman who answered. A different clerk from the last one. "I'm looking for that ID on the accident victim at the Golden Gate Bridge parking lot."

"Hold on. Let me check...Hey! Bren. The John Doe from the Golden Gate—" He heard her rustling some papers, then a click as she put him on hold. Less than a minute later, she was back. "Our records show we sent it up to you."

"Well, I don't have it."

"It's sort of a madhouse down here. Maybe it got misfiled. Give me a few to dig it up."

"Thanks," Casey said into the phone, then to Al, "Morgue says they already sent up the ID on our Presidio suspect. How long do you think it'll take them to dig it up? I was meeting someone for drinks."

Haynes looked up from his computer. "I think I may have gotten your ID. Darrell Fife…I was wondering who he was. Here." He tossed over a manila folder with a printout on the suspect.

"Thanks," Casey said. He added the name to his report, finished the last few details, printed it for the lieutenant, then hurried downstairs to meet Becca.

She was waiting by the elevator bank when he got off, and he had to do a double take, since he almost didn't recognize her out of uniform and with her hair down. Brown and wavy, it hit below her shoulders. It suited her.

And so did the black hooded sweater, white T-shirt, and blue jeans tucked into low-heeled boots.

"Sorry," she said. "I'm a bit underdressed for much of anything but the usual haunts."

The last thing he wanted to do was hang out in some cop bar. "I was thinking the Ferry Building. Been there?"

"Can't say I have."

"A little touristy," he replied. "But my mom likes it."

Becca laughed. "Your mom? Hmmm. I'm not even sure how to take that."

"I haven't gone there *with* her. She told me it was a good place to impress a girl on a date."

"Is this a date?"

"I'd like to think so." He held the door open for her, and they walked through the breezeway, past the morgue.

Al caught up to them. "Got my message, did you?" he asked Casey.

"What message?"

"To meet me down here—" Al stopped when he seemed to notice Becca for the first time. "Officer Windsor, right?"

"Becca," she said then smiled.

"Becca. Sorry. I hope you two weren't off to something important."

"Drinks," Casey said, even though he knew that Al knew.

"Oh," Al replied. "I can handle it, then."

"Handle what?"

"Follow-up on our suspect in the Presidio murder. Being that he's also a suspect in the Landmark Strangler cases, the LT wants the report on him done before the press conference tomorrow. No worries. I'll grab Haynes. He was still up there when I left."

Becca touched Casey on the arm. "Rain check. Okay?"

"If I get done early enough, maybe a late dinner instead?"

"Sure. Call." She backed away, her smile lighting up her face. "Then again, maybe you'll get lucky and it really is the Strangler."

She turned, headed into the parking garage.

Al waited until she was out of earshot then handed the print-out to Casey. "She cleans up well."

Casey ignored him, turning his attention to the paper in his hand. "This is a no-bail warrant."

"Exactly. For our so-called suspect, Darrell Fife. Which means that he may have been running because of it, not because he killed Trudy Salvatori. We need to walk a search warrant through, see what we can find at his place."

"I liked this better when we didn't know who he was."

"Like the girl said, maybe you'll get lucky and he really is the Strangler."

Casey looked toward the parking garage and Becca's departing figure. "In this case, I'd rather get lucky with her."

"Welcome to adulthood, kid. You're finally starting to figure it out."

SEVEN

Darrell Fife's last known address was that of his mother, Linda Gregory, and her second husband, Jon, who was the one who answered the door. He stood there, an unlit pipe in his mouth, waiting for them to say something. The moment Casey and Al identified themselves as San Francisco cops, he turned and shouted, "Linda! It's for you."

She came to the door, saw the credential cases they held up with their stars. "Oh my G—" She clamped her hand over her mouth, her eyes pooling with tears. "Something's happened. What?"

Al removed his hat, held it against his chest, then gave her that fatherly look, a mixture of authority laced with kindness. "Mind if we come in, Mrs. Gregory?"

She stood there, staring, then, as though it suddenly occurred to her what he'd asked, moved aside to let them in.

Jon Gregory sighed. "I knew this day would come. Mind if I smoke?"

"Yes," Al said.

He lit his pipe anyway then followed them into the living room.

"Sit," Linda told them as Jon made a beeline to a battered recliner, something that didn't match the delicate sofa and matching blue armchair.

As usual, Al stood off to one side. Casey took a seat on the sofa then opened his portfolio. "Darrell Fife is your son, Mrs. Gregory?"

She nodded. "He lives in the garage. We converted it to a studio apartment for him."

Jon pulled his pipe from his mouth, saying, "Keep him out of the damned house is why. No good—"

"Jon!" She smiled at Casey. "I'm sorry. Please. Continue."

"When's the last time you saw him?"

She looked over at her husband. "He works odd jobs, so we don't always see him regularly."

"Odd jobs my ass," Jon said. "Doubt he's ever worked a day in his life. It's why I can't even park my own truck in my own garage. You did find it, didn't you?"

"Find what?" Casey asked.

"My truck. I called and reported it soon as I saw it missing from the driveway this morning. Green Chevy. Seems it went missing same time as Darrell."

Casey and Al exchanged glances. They'd run every vehicle plate found in that area and would certainly have remembered if one was reported stolen.

Al pulled out his phone. "I'll have someone double-check. You have any paper work on that truck, Mr. Gregory?"

"Sure."

He stood, but Mrs. Gregory said, "What's this about? Has something happened to Darrell? Was *he* in that truck?"

And though it would've been nice to get through all the questions before imparting such bad news, Casey realized they couldn't put it off. "I'm sorry to inform you, Mrs. Gregory. But your son, Darrell, was killed."

She simply stared at Casey, nodding as though she'd expected such news all along. Her husband put his pipe down on a tray on the table then moved to his wife's side, taking her hand in both of his. She leaned into him, the tears finally falling.

Mr. Gregory looked at Casey over the top of her head. "What happened?"

"He was hit by a car."

"An accident?" Mr. Gregory asked.

"In a way. He was running from the police. We have a warrant to search his house."

Jon Gregory nodded. "I see. Well, easy enough. He doesn't live here. He lives in the garage. Converted it over. You're welcome to have at it. Isn't that right, Linny?"

She nodded.

"I know this can't be easy for you, Mrs. Gregory, but we're hoping to learn as much about him as possible. What he did. Who he associated with. That sort of thing."

Mrs. Gregory wiped at her eyes. "We wouldn't let him bring any of his friends over. That was one of the rules. The neighbors got very upset when they'd ride up on their motorcycles. You could hear them all the way up the street. Horrible noise."

Casey nodded, trying to appear as sympathetic as Al always managed to look. "Any of these so-called friends of his come by lately?"

"No," Jon said. "I made it very clear that if I so much as saw one of them at my house, he was gone."

"Except," Lin said. "There was that one man a couple of days ago."

"What man?" Jon asked.

"He brought a phone by for Darrell. I told you about that."

"No. You didn't."

"Well, I thought I did. And he was only here for a minute, so I didn't think it was that big a deal."

"What phone?" Casey asked.

"I assume it was Darrell's. He certainly didn't seem surprised when I gave it to him."

Jon made a scoffing noise. "Probably stolen. Not like he was paying for it."

She got up, crossed the room to a small writing desk, and pulled a tissue from the box sitting on it. "He told me it was for a job. So I thought you'd be happy that he was working."

"Working? The only money he ever made was from selling drugs. And that's when he wasn't using them."

Her tears started anew, and Al stepped forward, saying, "Mrs. Gregory. I don't suppose I could trouble you for some water?"

Al led her into the kitchen, listening as she said, "It was the drugs. We stopped giving him money. That's why we couldn't let him in the house anymore. He—he couldn't help himself..."

"Of course not," Al said.

When they were out of earshot, Mr. Gregory leaned toward Casey. "Frankly, I'm glad he's dead. Got to where I was sleeping with a gun in my nightstand. Not that I'd say so to my wife, you know what I mean," he said, nodding toward the kitchen.

"I can understand," Casey said.

"So why were you chasing him?"

"Believe it or not, because he ran."

He gave a slight nod, puffing on his pipe as he took in the news. "Where'd you say this happened?"

"Out by the Golden Gate Bridge."

"Hmm," he said as the smoke plumed up above him. "Saw that on the news. The woman who worked for Congressman Parnell. Lin's boy, eh?"

"It was. Don't suppose he had any dealings with the congressman?"

"Nope. Why? You think Lin's boy had something to do with that woman's murder? That's why he ran?"

"That's one theory. He also had a no-bail warrant."

"And my stolen truck."

"And that."

"Don't think he'd want to go to jail," he said, chewing on the end of his pipe.

"You think he's a killer?"

Jon glanced into the kitchen, probably making sure his wife was out of earshot. "Threatened me a few days back. Said it wouldn't be the first time he killed someone. About when my truck keys went missing, now that I think about it." He leaned back in his chair, nodding to himself. "So I guess the answer is yeah. As long as there's something in it for him."

"You know that moment," Al said on their drive back to San Francisco, "when you think you have a slam-dunk case. Got your dead suspect, got your witnesses. The only thing left is to write it up, then collect the accolades for a job well done?"

"Yeah."

"Well, this ain't it."

Casey glanced over, then back at the road. "Thank you, Captain Obvious. I would've never figured that one out on my own."

"That's Sergeant Obvious to you," he said as his cell phone rang. "Probably the lieutenant. Chomping at the bit."

"Champing," Casey said.

"See? Only you would know that. There's such a thing as too much book learning."

"Those books are what got me here."

"And the stuff I learned on the mean streets are what got me here before those textbooks were ever written." He pulled out his phone, hitting the speaker function. "Hey, LT. We're just clearing the house."

"I'm sitting here in the captain's office. Tell me you have good news."

"That depends. I don't think anyone's gonna sue us for accidental death of the suspect. Regular dirtbag, according to the stepfather."

"Is he or isn't he the Strangler?" It was the captain's voice. Apparently the lieutenant had them on speakerphone as well.

"Right now? We're still trying to make him as the killer, period. The search was a bust. Clothes and drugs were about it. Not even a computer. So personally I'd hold off on the press conference tomorrow if I were you. At least until we get that settled."

"Too late," the captain said. "The moment those reporters found out there was another strangling and the victim worked

47

for the congressman, the phone's been ringing nonstop. So whatever it is you need to do to figure it out? Get it done. *Tonight.* Come tomorrow morning, I want you and your partner front and center."

A beep signaled the disconnection.

"Great," Al said, dropping the phone into his pocket.

"Why do we need to be front and center?"

"So the press knows who to blame should we fail."

Casey glanced at the clock on the dash. Almost eight. "So much for dinner."

"Drop me off at the BART station. I can ride into the city, and you can catch a bite to eat with Becca."

"That'll go over well with the captain."

"One, we haven't eaten since lunch. We're allowed breaks. Two, there's no rule we have to eat together. The only thing left to do is write up the reports and put out a BOLO on the missing truck. Other than that, I'm not sure what it is he thinks we're going to be able to do tonight."

"Maybe it's already been found. You try to run it?"

"Thinking with your head. We might make a good investigator out of you yet." Al turned on the cab light to read the information that Mr. Gregory had given him on the truck, then called dispatch on the radio. "Ten-twenty-nine on the following…" He read the plate, then added, "Status update only. We do not have the vehicle in sight."

"Copy. Stand by," the dispatcher replied. A moment later, she repeated the plate number, adding, "Ten-twenty-nine comes back ten-eight-five-one on a green Chevy pickup reported stolen from San Bruno this AM."

"Copy. Confirm it's still outstanding?"

"Affirm."

"Ten-four. BOLO on that vehicle in the area of Golden Gate Bridge and Presidio. If found, contact me ASAP." Al turned off the light. "So it's still in the system," he told Casey.

"I know they ran the plates out at the scene this morning. I specifically asked. Nothing came up stolen."

"Maybe I'll drive out there after dinner. Don't know about you, but I'm starved. BART station?"

"Your call."

"Your date."

"BART it is."

Casey phoned Becca the moment he dropped Al off at the Daly City BART station. "Any chance you're free for a quick bite to eat?" he asked her.

"They're letting you have some time off after all?"

"I still have to finish a report later, but apparently we're allowed dinner. I'm about ten minutes away. Where do you want to go?"

"Come on by my place. I cook a mean microwave pizza."

"Pizza it is."

By the time Casey pulled up in front of Becca's house, he was as nervous as a schoolboy about to be alone with his first girl. He didn't move, just sat in the car, trying to even his breathing. This was silly, he thought. It hadn't been *that* long.

Or had it?

Okay, it had.

Get out of the car.

With one last calming breath, he exited, walked up to the porch, wiped his sweaty palms on his jacket, then knocked.

Becca opened the door a moment later, standing aside to let him in. She was dressed in jeans that fit her like a second skin, and a turquoise sweater that hugged all the right places. She wore absolutely no makeup, and her damp hair hung in loose ringlets about her shoulders.

He smiled, trying to think of something clever to say, but all that came out was, "You showered?"

"You keeping track?"

"What? No, I—Can we start over?"

She laughed then took his hand, leading him into the kitchen. "I just got back from the gym when you called." She let go of his hand, then walked over to the refrigerator, opening it and pulling out two amber-colored bottles of Anchor Steam. "Beer?"

He found himself staring at her backside as he slipped off his suit coat.

Get it together, Casey, he told himself as she looked over her shoulder at him, waiting for his answer. "Water, please. Still on duty, technically."

She put one bottle back, set the other on the counter, then filled a glass with ice and water from the refrigerator tap. "Your drink."

Once she popped off the top from her beer, she held up her bottle in a toast. "Cheers."

He clinked his glass to her bottle. "Cheers."

She sipped at her beer then opened the freezer, digging through the contents. "Sorry about the lack of a decent dinner offering."

"I love microwave pizza."

"Really?" She looked back at him, surprised.

"No. But I don't care. I'm not here for the food." He set his water on the counter and crossed the narrow space in two steps. "Or was I wrong?"

She shook her head.

That was all he needed to know, and he pushed the freezer door shut, pulled her close, and ran his fingertips against her cheek. "Fair warning," he said. "It's been a while."

He kissed her, tasting the bitter hops on her tongue. She leaned into him, and he into her, until they ended up against the refrigerator. He knew the moment she was his, the moment she seemed to melt in his arms as though her knees had suddenly grown weak. Their breathing turned ragged, even more so when Casey slipped his hand beneath her sweater, running his fingertips across her smooth skin, upward until he reached the lace of her bra. She tilted her head back, closing her eyes.

Her breath caught as he ran his thumb up and over her breast. "Are you sure it's been a while?" she asked and might have laughed. He couldn't tell. But then she pushed him back, and he wondered what he'd done wrong.

"Bedroom," she said.

That he understood, and she grasped him by the hand, leading the way from the kitchen down the hall, stopping suddenly, drawing him back to the kitchen. She grabbed a white paper bag on the counter then led him down the hall to her bedroom. She pushed him back on the bed, tossed the bag next to his head. "Condoms..."

The realization that she'd planned everything down to the last detail intoxicated him. And then she pulled off her sweater, climbed on top of him, her control absolute as she straddled him wearing only her black lace bra and blue jeans. He couldn't have moved if he'd wanted to. Her kiss resonated through him, every nerve in his body taut. She loosened his tie, worked at his shirt buttons, and finally unbuckled his belt.

And the moment she slipped her hand into the open zipper, the moment he felt the heat of her fingers on him, his cell phone buzzed. He ignored it.

She raised up on one elbow beside him. "You're not getting that?"

"If...it's important...they'll—"

She moved her hand lower then smiled. "They'll what?"

It was a moment before he could even breathe. "...Call... back."

And then, as though fate had been hovering over them, just waiting for the right moment, the phone buzzed again.

He dug the phone from his pocket, hoping like hell it was his mother reminding him that he promised to come to dinner that weekend. Something inane that he could blow off.

Al's number showed up on the screen.

Casey closed his eyes. "Sorry."

She smiled as he answered the phone.

"Sorry, kid," Al said. "Dinner break's over."

"For what?"

"What'd ya think? They found the stolen truck at the Presidio. Pick me up at the office. They're standing by until we get there."

Casey dropped the phone to the bed. He didn't say anything at first, then, "I knew I shouldn't have answered it."

Becca zipped up his pants, then nuzzled at his neck. "Anticipation. Think how much better it'll be."

"I'd rather find out now."

She smiled then reached over him, grabbing her sweater.

He watched as she slid it on over her head, her breasts just visible over the top of her black lace bra, then hidden from view as she pulled the sweater down.

"What?" she asked, apparently noticing his stare.

"You might be wearing a uniform to work, but all I'll be able to think about is that black lace bra."

Her smile was decidedly wicked. "Finish dressing. I'm making you my famous gourmet microwave pizza before you go."

"Guess I was here for the food after all."

The one advantage of working at night was that the city was actually fairly easy to get around without the added commuters. He picked up Al at the Hall, then drove to the Presidio, where access to the bridge vista was still closed off. Casey pulled up, showed his star to the uniformed officer manning the barrier erected across the street. The officer moved it far enough for Casey to drive through then replaced it when they drove past.

"Where to?" Casey asked Al.

"Other side of the freeway."

Casey drove through the deserted main parking lot, then under the freeway to the west side. "Just up a ways," Al said. "It's the parking lot on Cranston Road."

"No wonder we didn't see it. Never made it this far."

"Wouldn't have mattered. They ran every vehicle over here, too. It was cold-plated. Just a lot easier to find considering it was the only vehicle left in the lot. After I called in the BOLO tonight, a smart patrolman did an area check and ran the VIN."

Casey pulled into the lot and parked near the black-and-white, where a patrolman sat writing reports. Al went over to talk to the officer, and Casey popped the trunk to retrieve a flashlight from his gear box.

He turned it on, walked up to the truck, aimed the beam into the passenger side window, then tried to open the passenger door. It was locked. He focused on the center console, saw some papers, coins, and an open soda can in the cup holder. Other than that, nothing to be seen, and he walked around to the driver's side, locked as well. "Nothing."

Al joined him a moment later. "The officer called for a flatbed tow. Said it should be here anytime."

It arrived about twenty minutes later, and the driver popped the locks with his slim-jim. Although the vehicle would be processed by CSIs at the impound lot for evidence in the case, Casey and Al donned latex gloves and did a quick preliminary search. Al was checking the contents of the glove box while Casey was fishing around beneath the driver's seat. He felt something toward the back, reached in, and pulled out the original license plates.

He placed them on the driver's seat, then reached beneath it again, this time finding a cell phone. He held it up. "The delivered phone his mom mentioned?"

"Let's hope. Bag it up for forensics. If we're lucky, we'll find something good on there."

EIGHT

D id you hear something?"

Marcie's limbs felt heavy. It took a moment before her husband's words registered in her brain. She opened her eyes, realized Devin was sitting up in bed beside her, his hand on her shoulder.

"Hear what?"

"I don't know..." He threw off the covers, then walked over to the balcony door, pulling the curtains to look out.

"The cat..." Marcie glanced at the clock, saw it was after midnight, then rolled over, barely able to keep her eyes open.

"I'm going to check."

She heard him padding down the stairs, too tired to care; then she was vaguely aware that he'd returned to bed a minute or two later.

"Everything's locked," he said.

She reached up, tucked the pillow beneath her head, and closed her eyes, recalling nothing more until morning.

Light seeped in through the sheer curtains at the balcony door, and she glanced over at the windows, the eucalyptus bathed in the early sun.

Devin was still asleep next to her, and she quietly rose from bed, grabbed her robe, used the bathroom, then went downstairs to start coffee. The moment she walked into the kitchen, she noticed the back door slightly ajar. Devin had gone to bed before her, and she was certain she'd checked all the doors before heading upstairs.

What was it that had woken her?

Devin had heard something last night. He'd gone down to check...

She walked over, the tile cold beneath her feet, wondering if perhaps he hadn't closed it tightly. Maybe the wind sweeping in from the bay blew it open.

But when she examined the door, it wasn't locked at all. She stepped outside to the back porch. At first everything seemed fine, but then she noticed a bit of dirt on the bricks next to one of the many flowerpots lined up by the door. The spare key...She eyed the pot where it should be, lifted it, saw the key, picked it up, then shoved it in her pocket.

Had someone known it was there, entered, then replaced it on leaving? To what end? Nothing else seemed disturbed in the backyard, and she returned inside, locked the door, then started taking inventory of everything downstairs.

Nothing obvious appeared to be missing. Her purse was hanging from the back of a chair at the dining-room table. All her money and credit cards seemed to be there.

What then?

"Marce?"

Marcie spun around at Devin's voice.

He continued down the stairs, his face etched with worry. "What's wrong?"

"The back door was open."

"Impossible. I checked everything after I heard that noise. It was locked. Maybe I didn't shut it tight and the wind blew it open."

"It wasn't even locked when I checked."

His gaze narrowed slightly as he passed her, making a beeline to the back door. He opened it, looked around. "This is weird. The key—?"

"I have it."

"We're not keeping it outside anymore. Is anything missing?"

"I don't think so." She walked into the living room and turned on the television, more out of habit than anything else, because the last thing she wanted to hear about was a rehash of Trudy's murder. And yet there it was, the camera panning over the running trail where Trudy was killed.

She stood, transfixed, somewhat aware that Devin had come up beside her, also watching as the perfectly coifed newswoman reported.

"...police have not released any further information concerning Darrell Fife, the man killed yesterday in the parking lot of the Golden Gate Bridge after being chased by homicide detectives into the path of an oncoming car. Fife is suspected in the murder of Trudy Salvatori, a campaign worker for the reelection of Congressman Parnell," she said as a photo of Trudy flashed on the screen. "Standing by at Congressman Parnell's campaign headquarters is Channel Two reporter Lacy Hudson. Lacy, any word from the Parnell team about the investigation?"

The picture shifted to the street outside the headquarters, its windows plastered with REELECT PARNELL signs visible behind the perky brunette reporter. "Hi, Sarah. Yes. Congressman Parnell issued a public statement in a press release yesterday afternoon, stating that Trudy Salvatori, the woman killed near the Presidio, was a valued member of his campaign team and a true supporter of the causes Representative Parnell believed in, one of which was working to increase funding to police for the reduction of crime—"

Devin walked over, shut off the television. "I don't like this, Marcie," he said, facing her.

She turned and walked into the kitchen, thinking how surreal it all felt.

He followed her. "The police are looking at Trudy's murder as part of that serial killer case. That Strangler. And then this," he said, pointing to the now-closed kitchen door.

She glanced that direction, then back at him. Devin, who had always been so self-assured, smugly so at times, now seemed worried. "What does that have to do with us?"

"You were out there when Trudy was killed. What if you saw something? Someone? They could come after you."

"That's insane. They caught the guy who did it. He's dead."

"Is he? The police don't even know if the man they chased is the one who killed her. What if whoever that was thinks *you* can identify him? How do you know he doesn't already know who you are?"

She stared in disbelief. "Why would you even say that to me?"

"I'm just trying to figure out what's going on."

She took the pot from the coffee maker to the kitchen sink to rinse it, looking out the window as she had every morning, seeing Tony and Trudy's kitchen through her blinds. Tony was sitting at his table. Alone. "What if Tony found out?" she asked.

"Found out what?"

"That Trudy was coming over here. What if he thought the same thing I did? That you were having an affair? They were getting divorced, after all."

Devin joined her at the window, peering through the blinds. "I don't think he knew Trudy was coming here."

She filled the pot with water. "But what if he did? He and Trudy both knew where that key was."

Devin reached up and closed the blinds. "We're getting an alarm. Today. The kind with cameras. If you're going to be here alone, I want to know you're okay." He glanced at the clock, then started from the room, saying, "I need to get ready for work. But I'll call someone out this morning."

Marcie took the decanter to the coffee maker, poured the cold water into it, then leaned against the counter, staring at the machine as it sputtered to life. When she heard Devin moving around upstairs, she returned to the window, cracking the blinds just enough to see through.

Tony was still there at his kitchen table. Alone. Not doing anything at all.

She reached into her pocket and felt for the key she'd removed from the back porch, if nothing else, to reassure herself that she hadn't lost it.

And almost as if he knew she was watching him, he suddenly turned, glanced her direction.

She stepped back, out of view, surprised by how fast her heart was beating.

NINE

Jenn Barstow stood in front of her editor's desk, waiting for him to look up from his computer screen. He didn't. Just grabbed his coffee, took a sip, then said, "You wanted something?"

Sometimes she felt invisible. Or close to it. "I was wondering if you'd mind if I attended the press conference this afternoon."

He looked up. "Is this about the dead hookers?"

"Yes."

"The answer is no. Dead hookers don't sell papers. Murdered white women do. Besides, your job is local politics."

"Yesterday's victim *worked* for a politician."

"I *have* a crime reporter. Translation? The only way you're getting a byline on a homicide is if that politician did it. Until then, I'd suggest getting back to what you're supposed to be writing about."

She backed from the room—not that he was paying her any further attention—then returned to her cubicle.

Taryn, in the cubicle directly behind hers, swiveled her chair around. "Success?"

Jenn gave her a thumb's down as she dropped into her seat.

"So the alien life-form gets to go?" Taryn said, referring to Marty, their coworker who worked at the crime desk.

Both women glanced down the row of cubicles in that direction to see him eyeing them, the corners of his mouth turning up slightly as though he knew he was the topic of discussion. "Who else?"

"The crime desk should have been yours."

"Lot of good that does me now." Jenn tapped the space bar on her keyboard to wake up her computer. Even though their editor admitted that she was the better writer, in his opinion the male-dominated police world was more suited to a man, and so the newly vacated position was given to Martin.

Jenn didn't necessarily want it permanently. Only long enough to bring some attention to some older cases—one being a murdered prostitute. For her it wasn't the fact the woman was a prostitute, it was the story behind the woman, the choices she made and the choices refused to her.

It was going to be her Pulitzer.

But as Jenn's editor had just pointed out, dead hookers did *not* make for sensationalistic journalism. Kill a white housewife on the streets of San Francisco? Golden. Make one of the recent victims a tourist by twisting the facts as Marty did in his last article? Suddenly the Strangler was the national topic *du jour*. The third victim, a former New Yorker, had recently relocated to the Bay Area and had been living in the area for at least six months. That small detail about her residence was left out of his article, and his unfortunate and incorrect statement about her being a tourist at a landmark was picked up by a nightly news show in Los Angeles, then the *Today* show the following morning. Suddenly no one was safe in the city.

And that was exactly how her editor wanted it. The jump in sales anytime the Strangler was mentioned in a headline was enough to convince him that serial murders of white women were good for business. And when this fourth murder at the Presidio came to light yesterday, he didn't care that the case had not yet been determined to be a Strangler victim. He was, however, smart enough to make sure he wasn't accused of printing

THE LAST GOOD PLACE

unverified facts, and so he had changed his first choice of headline from STRANGLER STRIKES AGAIN to STRANGLER STRIKES AGAIN?

What Jenn couldn't figure out was why no one else seemed to notice or care that the current victims were killed in a manner that closely resembled that of the prostitute she had hoped to write about. So her victim wasn't sitting under a specific landmark. But then, really, were any of these victims?

Or was she being too hopeful? Reading too much into something that wasn't there, because she desperately wanted there to be a connection? Maybe then they'd solve it and absolve her of some of her guilt. Or was it more that she wanted them to solve it and allow her to write the article she'd hoped to write?

"Alien alert," Taryn said, pretending to shuffle papers as Marty approached.

Jenn closed out the windows before he could see what she was looking at. She needn't have bothered, because he made a beeline for the TV, then stood there watching the news coverage of the Presidio murder, the screen filled with yesterday's film bites of the police detectives standing in the midst of an accident scene in the parking lot below the Golden Gate Bridge gift shop. It was the younger detective Jenn focused on.

Apparently Taryn noticed him as well. "There he is, the key to your Pulitzer."

"Shut up, Taryn." She glanced around, hoping no one heard.

"You're going to waste your career and talent if you let this opportunity slip by. You have the connection. Use it."

"No. I already feel guilty enough just cultivating it."

"That doesn't make you evil, just smart."

Then why did it feel so underhanded?

"Just go," Taryn said. "You probably won't even be missed. You sort of blend into the background anyway."

"I do not."

Taryn eyed her. "These god-awful pantsuits you always wear," she said, tugging on the navy sleeve of Jenn's jacket.

"This is a perfectly good *business* suit," Jenn said. "And for your information, I prefer the androgynous look."

"You mean cheap, boxy polyester look? Only things missing are white stitching and a ticket to a Florida retirement community." Marty walked past again, and Taryn smiled at him, waiting until he was out of earshot. "Even *he* has better taste in clothes than you."

Jenn eyed Marty at the other end of the office as he sat at his desk. "He's wearing a brown plaid suit. How is that better?"

Taryn gave an exaggerated sigh, then nodded at the TV where the picture cut to a representative from Congressman Parnell's office making a statement about the victim and how much she had been a valued part of Parnell's staff. "See? Even he's exploiting that murder for all it's worth. Which makes it local politics."

"Which I pointed out, and the boss said no."

"So don't tell him," she said, grabbing both of their coats and dragging her to the door. As they passed the editor's office, she said, "We're going out for coffee."

He didn't even look up, which made Jenn think about that remark that she blended into the background. Taryn was right. But once they got outside, she started to second-guess herself. "I'm not sure this is a good idea."

"You've got two hours to work up the nerve to exploit that connection you went to great pains to cultivate."

"Do you know how many TV cameras are there? What if—" She glanced over at their editor's office.

"Just do what you do best. Be invisible. Wait until it's over then walk up to him. What have you got to lose?"

TEN

"**C**'mon, Kellog. What're you so interested in you can't play some liar's poker?"

Casey looked up from his computer screen to see Ralph Zwingler and Denny Haynes staring at him.

Haynes held up a dollar bill, waving it back and forth.

"Sorry," Casey said. The scores for the written portion of the lieutenant's promotional had come out. Casey wanted to see where he'd placed. And who the competition was. "Got better things to do."

"Like what?" Haynes asked, then got up from his desk. Casey blacked out his computer screen when Haynes leaned over to look.

"Whoa!" Haynes said. "Didn't know you took the lieutenant's test. What's the matter? You don't love us anymore?"

"Still making up my mind on that point," Casey said, trying not to let it show he was disappointed the word had gotten out.

Zwingler scoffed. "Don't you have to be old enough to shave?"

Realizing he needed the subject changed and fast, Casey pulled out a dollar bill. "So what're we playing for?"

"The last cream-filled donut," Haynes said. "Full house. Trip aces."

Casey eyed his bill. "Got me beat."

"Damn," Zwingler said. "Three nines."

And Haynes might have collected his winnings, but Al walked in, grabbed the donut, then took a bite.

Haynes gaped as Al stood there, chewing.

"What?" Al asked.

"I won that donut fair and square," Haynes said, waving his dollar.

"Yeah," Al replied. "Only because your partner doesn't realize you've carried that same dollar bill in your wallet for the past year. Three ones, two nines, two eights, and one zero."

Before Haynes could even make a move, Zwingler reached over, snatched the greenback from Haynes's fingers, examined the serial number, then ripped the bill in two, tossing the pieces onto Haynes's desk. "Good try."

"What'd you do that for?" Haynes asked.

"Somebody's gotta look after your health. You keep winning donuts like that, you're gonna eat yourself into a heart attack."

Lieutenant Timms walked in at that very moment. "Quit your whining, Zwingler," he said. "They call it liar's poker for a reason." Clearly upset about something, he turned his attention to Casey. "I just got word that patrol's on what looks like another strangling out at Ghirardelli Square. So we've either got a copycat case, or your Presidio suspect is *not* who you thought he was."

"We haven't confirmed he's the Strangler yet."

"You think that matters? As if the press on our backs isn't bad enough, Congressman Parnell's office is publicly demanding we put more resources into this investigation. We've got a press conference less than two hours from now. If the captain ends up looking like a fool in front of those cameras, I can guarantee any *future* chance you thought you had of promoting? Gone. So get out there, find what's going on, and get back to me, ASAP."

He turned back into his office, pushing his door closed.

"Uh oh," Zwingler said to Casey. "Looks like someone's gonna have to stay a sergeant a little longer."

"What was Zwingler talking about?" Al asked as he and Casey took the elevator down.

"I took the written for the lieutenant's test. I made it. The oral board's next week."

The elevator opened, and the two men stepped off. "Burn yourself out rising that quick."

"And what? Wait until I get old like you, Uncle Al?"

"Poke at my age all you want." Al glanced sideways at him. "With it comes experience. And mine's telling me you should be asking if you're promoting too fast. You're already the youngest homicide investigator we've ever had. So maybe give yourself a chance to settle in. Learn a few things before moving on."

"My mom's on my case, so I did it for her."

"Your mom? We need to find you a woman with a sharp pair of scissors."

"For what?"

"To cut those apron strings."

"I figured it'd be good practice for when I was ready. And to get her to quit bugging me. It's not like I'm going to pass. Everyone taking it has at least a decade on me."

"Who knows. Maybe you'll solve the Landmark Strangler case and gain few points."

"And what if I don't? What if the Presidio turns out to be a copycat case? It's not like we didn't suggest holding off on the press conference until we had a definitive ID."

Al looked over at him as they walked. "Don't ever underestimate the wrath and the memory of a superior officer who finds himself looking less than competent in front of a bunch of news cameras *and* a US congressman. Like I told you yesterday. There's a reason they want us front and center. If things look good, the captain gets credit. If it doesn't? We're the ones sacrificed. Well, you, being that I am technically eligible to retire any day."

"I certainly feel better."

"Buck up. We still don't know what we have yet."

Eighteen minutes later, Casey turned onto Polk, stopping behind a black-and-white blocking the street from traffic, rear ambers flashing. The officer waved Casey through, and he drove halfway up the block and parked. The crime scene was actually across the street in a parking lot. A uniformed officer stood guard at the outer perimeter, clipboard in hand, and the moment they lifted and stepped beneath the crime-scene tape wrapped around a parking meter and strung across the street, he jotted down their names and the time of their arrival. Casey scanned the list, saw the page was nearly full. "Geez, Al," Casey said. "You see the parade that's been here already?"

Al glanced at the clipboard, then took it from the officer to read the names listed. "What gives?" he asked, handing it back.

"They called out the Robbery detail first," the officer said.

Al and Casey exchanged glances, then walked into the parking lot, where a second officer stood guard at the inner perimeter, closer to the actual crime scene. Two CSIs were traipsing around, one snapping photos, the other taking measurements.

Virgil Edwards, one of the Robbery investigators, stood off to one side, talking on his cell phone while the CSIs worked. He looked up, saw them. "Gotta go," he said into the phone, then disconnected as they walked toward him. "What are you two doing here?"

"Came to examine the body," Al said. "Where is it?"

"You're kidding, right?" When neither Al nor Casey responded, he said, "She's in the hospital."

"Guess we can count out homicide. We were told to come out and determine if this was a Strangler case."

"The murder *du jour*," Edwards said. "What better way to keep your homicide from standing out? Make it look like all the rest. Just not in this case. She says the suspect was after her purse. Had it not been for the fortuitous presence of two upstanding citizens hiding back here to smoke a joint—so as not to be seen in public—who knows what might have transpired?"

"Nice of them."

"The suspect was a bit put off by their presence. Apparently he decided to make a hasty escape."

"So what do you think?" Al asked. "Robbery or attempted murder?"

"Maybe if the victim let go of her purse when he first grabbed it, we wouldn't be having this conversation. He was tugging on the straps, pulling her back, and she wasn't going to let him have it. The facts as I know them."

Robbery, Casey thought. Which meant his Presidio suspect might still be the Strangler.

Al tapped Casey on the shoulder. "Let's go have a look at the crime scene. See what's what." Al and Casey walked through the alley, Edwards following, their gazes glued to the ground, making sure they didn't step on something that might turn out to be evidence.

Edwards pointed. "Happened on the other side of that alcove," he said, indicating a retainer wall, built to hide the trash Dumpsters for some of the businesses.

"So," Al said. "What time did this come in?"

Edwards pulled out his pocket notebook, opening it to read from what looked like chicken scratch. "A little before seven this morning."

"And why would they think it's a Strangler case?"

"EMTs noted she had some red marks on her neck from the struggle. Between that and the proximity to Ghirardelli Square, someone probably figured a Landmark Strangler caper. Or rather, attempted caper."

"Well, that explains how it got out. EMT making a crime diagnosis."

They finished up their preliminary inspection then told Edwards they were heading to the hospital to interview the victim.

Casey glanced back into the shopping center. "Seems like a robbery gone bad."

"That's what I'm thinking. Robbery doesn't seem to be a part of the Strangler's MO. Or rather, none of the victims' relatives have reported missing property, 'cause the victims sure aren't making statements."

"There's always the consideration that the real Landmark Strangler's on a slab in the morgue, because he did a face-plant with a car."

"There's that, too," Al said. At the perimeter, they checked out with the officer keeping the log. He lifted the crime-scene tape while he and Casey slipped beneath it, then stopped when he saw a large group of reporters, several with cameras, near the blockade erected to keep them from the crime scene. "Great. Someone's already blabbed about this being an attempted Strangler case. My money's on the EMT."

The two men kept their distance, ignoring all comments and questions thrown at them. When it was clear they weren't going to engage, the reporters lost interest, turning their attention back to the crime scene.

Once in the car, Al telephoned the op center. "This is Krug. Can you pull all the calls in the vicinity of this robbery starting with three hours before and ending with our arrival…? Thanks. Printout would be great. And if you could let dispatch know we're en route to the hospital to interview the victim…" He shoved his phone into his pocket then buckled his seat belt as Casey started the car.

Their robbery victim, Mina Lavish, was about to be released from Mercy General when Casey and Al arrived. Dressed in black from head to toe, her long dark hair pulled back into a low ponytail, she was seated on the hospital bed, one knee tucked up as she attempted to pull on a stiletto-heeled boot over her stockinged foot. She looked up and sighed as they entered. "More police? It seems all I've done this morning is talk to them."

"My partner," Al said, nodding at Casey, "has a few more questions."

"Hopefully not too many," she said, zipping up her boot. She pulled on the other. "I've been in here all morning. I'm fine. I don't even know why they brought me in."

Casey smiled at her then took a small notebook from his pocket. "Probably just to be safe. Can you tell us again what happened?"

She let out her breath in a sound of exasperation. "Like I told it to the other detectives before you. I was walking to work this morning when some dumb ass decides he wants to steal my purse. No way was I going to let him have it. Do you know how much I paid for this thing? Over five hundred dollars."

Casey eyed the soft leather tote, not sure why anyone would pay that much for a purse. "Where was this?"

"Behind the stores. Near the Dumpsters. Maybe that's where he was hiding. I didn't even see him. All I know is that suddenly I feel someone pulling me back, and I'm thinking, what the hell? And then I realize the guy's trying to steal my purse. Except he must have accidentally grabbed my hair. So he got me instead of the purse. So I grab the strap with both hands. And then you know what he does? He starts choking me. The bastard tries to choke me! I'm like, are you kidding? So I jab my heel into his foot. And then those two boys came out from between the Dumpsters, and off he went."

"Choked you how?"

"Well, I guess from behind."

"Can you show me on my partner?" Casey asked.

"I guess." She walked up behind Al, and with her left hand, she reached out and swept her fingers against Al's back. "Like this. Grabbing my purse strap and ponytail. And then I'm, like, falling back. But I'm holding onto the purse strap with both hands, tugging forward, and that's when he reaches up with his other hand and sort of wraps his whole arm around my neck." She brought her other arm over Al's shoulder then wrapped it around his neck. "Squeezing tight, so I can't get away."

"Choking you?"

"I guess. Like he's trying to hold me so he can rip my purse from me. That's when I went like this..." She lifted one booted foot up, then brought the three-inch stiletto heel down onto the top of Al's foot. "Except I did it a lot harder."

She let go of Al and stepped back.

Al turned toward her. "How were you wearing your purse when this happened?"

"Luckily, crossways. So someone couldn't grab it and run off so easy. Good thing, too. Because if I'd just had it over my shoulder? Bam. Out five hundred bucks."

"Miss Lavish," Al said. "If necessary, would you be able to sit with a sketch artist? Describe the person who attacked you?"

"Sorry. I didn't even see his face."

"What about the pair you said ran out from the Dumpster area?"

"I don't know where they ran off to. But I could sure smell the pot back there."

They thanked her, advised that someone from Robbery would be following up, then left.

Casey unlocked the car, and they both got in. "What are you going to tell the lieutenant?"

"Lacking a body and a suspect, it sure looks like a strongarm robbery. Not that that matters right now. With the congressman inserting himself into our investigation, anything that even suggests Strangler involvement is going to get scrutinized," he said, buckling his seatbelt. "Makes you really look forward to that press conference, doesn't it?"

ELEVEN

After returning from Ghirardelli Square, Casey and Al briefed the lieutenant, who in turn briefed the captain as well as the press information office. About fifteen minutes after, Casey and Al took the elevator down to the lobby, then walked out front, stepping into a sea of cameras all facing their direction. In the six months that Casey had been assigned to Homicide, he'd never worked a high-profile case of this magnitude. The thought of appearing before the press seemed much more exciting last night, when he was riding high on the knowledge that he may very well have caught the Landmark Strangler.

How quickly things changed, he thought as he and Al took their places beside Lieutenant Timms. The podium next to Timms where all the microphones with their various news logos attached stood at the ready. And though the press conference had been set to start precisely at ten, it was now several minutes after, the change necessary because of the unforeseen attack this morning.

Casey eyed the numerous television cameras aimed at them. "We don't have to say anything, do we?" he whispered to Al. Not that they needed to worry about being overheard, since everyone seemed to be talking at once.

Al shook his head. "Our job is to stand here and look pretty. So if anyone asks you a question, *defer* to the lieutenant so he can defer to the captain, who will answer. This type of case, last thing the brass wants is for us to open our mouths."

About five minutes later, the captain walked out, stepped to the podium, and began a speech prepared by the press information office detailing how the department was investigating the Landmark Strangler cases and ensuring the safety of its citizens, beefing up patrol at popular tourist sights, increasing undercover officers, and assigning additional investigators to the task force, finishing with, "I promise you this. We have some very good leads. We *will* catch whoever is responsible."

And then the questions started. Casey expected some negativity from the press, but not the animosity. Several newscasters suggested that maybe it was time to call in the FBI, or perhaps reassign the cases to different investigators. The captain deflected the suggestions with practiced ease, stating, "I have every confidence in the men and women working our Homicide detail. The training they receive is on par with anything on the federal level."

"Is there any truth," one reporter called out, "that the Strangler is targeting tourists?"

"None whatsoever."

"The Presidio murder?" another reporter called out. "Is that a Landmark Strangler case or a copycat?"

"As I detailed earlier, we don't yet have results from the autopsy to make a determination. Next question?"

"Do you think someone was specifically targeting Congressman Parnell's office?"

"We have nothing to suggest anything of the sort."

"What about the man who was killed yesterday when your officers chased him? If he's the Strangler, then who attacked the woman this morning?"

"Again, both cases are under investigation. We don't yet know his relationship—whether he is or isn't a part of that homicide—or if either of these cases is related to any others."

A woman in dark-framed glasses stepped forward, raising her hand as though she were back in school. "Is someone making a comparison of the current Strangler victims to the prostitutes found murdered about seven months ago?"

"As mentioned before, we have all available resources looking into past and present cases. Every investigative resource is being utilized."

And so it went.

Casey was exhausted by the time it ended, and all he'd had to do was stand there. He was impressed with the captain, even proud of his show of support.

That is until they all entered the lobby, and the captain turned to Lieutenant Timms, saying, "Get me some goddamned results." He walked off.

Timms turned to Al and Casey, saying, "Clear your schedule for the rest of the afternoon. We need to make some headway on this."

Casey and Al nodded politely and slowed their pace, figuring it best to let the brass have the elevator to themselves.

"Now what?" Casey asked Al.

"Hope we catch this guy before we end up back on patrol. You might be in tip-top shape, but me? I'm too old to go back on the street." He patted Casey on the shoulder. "See you upstairs in a few. I want to see if the coroner's made any headway on yesterday's case."

Al continued on through the lobby and out the back door.

"Sergeant Kellog?"

Casey turned to see a young woman in dark-framed glasses, her mousy-brown hair pulled back into a ponytail. She wore a navy polyester suit that appeared one or two sizes too large for her slim frame, the shoulder slipping as she held out her hand in greeting, saying, "Jenn Barstow."

"Miss Barstow," he said, shaking her hand. Her grip felt tense and slightly sweaty from nerves as though it took all her effort to approach him. "What can I do for you?"

"I know—I mean, I know you don't know me, but I know—"
Her cheeks flushed and she looked down at the ground, giving
him the impression she was hoping for the earth to open wide
and rescue her. But then, surprising him, she suddenly pinned
her gaze on him, saying, "Can you at least tell me if someone is
looking at those older prostitute murders?"

It was then he realized she was one of the reporters he'd seen
out front. The one who asked the question about the older murders possibly being related to the Strangler. He refused to even
answer her question. "You'll have to contact the press information office."

"What about a drink after work? I just want to—"

"I'm afraid a drink is out of the question." He wasn't about to
fraternize with the press. "If you'll excuse me, I have work to do."

As he started toward the bank of elevators, she called out,
"Wouldn't you like someone on your side?"

That stopped him in his tracks. He turned, faced her, not
sure if he should be amused or insulted. "What?"

"What I meant to say is we're *on* the same side. That we could
help each other."

"I'm not at liberty to discuss *any* aspects of this case or any
other with the press. I'm sorry."

She handed him her business card. "If you change your mind.
Even just for the drink. We don't have to discuss the case at all."

"I'll keep that in mind," he said, using the card to give her a
wave of dismissal. It wasn't that she was unattractive. She was, in
a very bookish way. He just wasn't drawn to that sort of woman.

Of course, as pathetic as his dating life was, maybe he was
being too picky. Everyone he'd taken out was either put off by the
job, or put off by the odd hours he worked due to call outs. Case
in point, last night, trying to take Becca out for a drink—or as it
happened to turn out, frozen pizza. Nine times out of ten, a second date never materialized, and if it did, it was usually followed

on the woman's part with the it's-not-you-it's-me speech, which in his mind was a polite way of saying it really is you.

And it probably was, he thought as Al walked up. He eyed the business card. "The *Union-Examiner*? What'd she want?"

"Asked me out for a drink," Casey replied, as he pressed the Up button on the elevator. "Said I needed someone on my side."

"Probably true, the way they're crucifying us."

"So what'd the coroner say about our Presidio victim?"

"Autopsy's not done, but initial evidence says she was definitely strangled. They were scraping her fingernails as I left. A DNA hit with the dead guy would be nice," he said, pulling his phone from his pocket and looking at the screen, which had lit up from a call. "Krug...Yeah. We're on our way up."

He pocketed the phone as the elevator door opened. "That was Timms," he said as the door slid shut. "We're wanted in the captain's office. Apparently Congressman Parnell is gracing us with his presence."

On their arrival, the captain's secretary informed Casey and Al to go on in; the captain was expecting them.

Even so, Al knocked before opening the door.

The congressman stood near the conference table with the captain and Timms. He was tall, gray-haired, probably about Al's age, and, like every politician Casey had ever seen, he had an impeccable plastic smile that he turned on them when they entered. "You must be the two investigators assigned to Trudy's murder."

The captain said, "These are Sergeants Krug and Kellog, two of my best." Then to Al and Casey, adding, "Congressman Parnell."

Parnell shook their hands. "Nice to meet you both."

"Likewise," Al replied.

And Casey added, "A pleasure."

The captain pulled out a chair at the table. "Sit, please."

When everyone had done so, the congressman looked right at Casey and said, "I know your time is valuable, but I wanted to come here and assure you that my office is ready to help in any way we can. In that respect, I'm hoping you can tell me what's being done. What leads have you found?"

Casey hesitated, certain this was one of those instances when it was best to defer to his superior.

Al, thank goodness, stepped right in. "It's still early in the investigation."

"Of course," Parnell replied. "This man who was killed. You're certain he's the suspect?"

"We can confirm he *is* a suspect," Al replied. "We can't confirm that he killed Trudy Salvatori. The investigation is still in its infancy."

"I see." He took a terse breath. "You have to understand. Trudy was a valued member of our staff. Her death has hit every one of us hard. We just want to know that you're doing everything in your power to make sure that justice is served."

Al replied, "You can be assured we are giving it our full attention."

He nodded, but directed his question to Al again. "And where do you go from here? If he is the actual suspect?"

"I'm not sure what you mean, sir."

"How long will an investigation like this take? How long will the victims' families have to wait for some sense of justice? Or an end to their suffering?"

It was Timms, this time, who stepped in. "We're doing everything in our power and within our means to ensure the investigation moves along in the fastest manner prudent."

"Glad to hear it." He stood. "Again, if there is anything my office can do to help. I hope you won't hesitate to ask."

"Thank you, sir," the captain said, standing as well. Then, turning to Al and Casey, "I'll let you two get back to work."

Clearly dismissed, Casey and Al rose from their seats. The congressman leaned over the table to shake their hands once more. "A pleasure to meet you both. And please. Keep me informed of the investigation's progress. I've arranged with one of my staff members to assist Tony Salvatori with anything he might need, including funeral arrangements. I wish I could do more."

"I'm sure Mr. Salvatori appreciates that," Al said.

He and Casey exited via the secretary's office, the congressman's voice, though lowered, carrying out to them. "I don't want to sound crass, but this couldn't have happened at a worse time. With elections right around the corner, if I mention this in any upcoming speeches, they'll say I'm using it to get ahead. If I don't, then I'm insensitive to the…"

Whatever followed was lost as the captain closed the door.

"Politicians," Al said quietly. "Like murder is *ever* convenient?"

TWELVE

"Listen up," Lieutenant Timms said, thirty minutes later, once the post-press-conference meeting started in the Homicide office. "In case you missed the public stoning by the press downstairs, we're taking a beating. And that doesn't count the scrutiny we're now receiving from Congressman Parnell's office as part of his get-tough-on-crime campaign." He looked right at Al. "Speaking of, what's the status on the Presidio case? Is she or isn't she victim number four?"

"The million-dollar question. Still working on the autopsy. Not that the press is going to believe us right now. With a dead suspect, it would've been nice to close the books on it and get the congressman off our backs."

"What about what this reporter was saying? The murdered prostitutes?"

"Cold Case has them and the others I've pulled. Nothing definitive. Yet."

"Yet," Zwingler said, "being the operative word. Remember the Backstreet Butcher? Ten years nothing, and then bam, starts up again? Little prison stint does wonders to the crime rate."

"Good point," Timms said. "The silver lining about Parnell's attention is that we suddenly have approval to up the resources. I think our best bet here is continue the divide-and-conquer approach. Krug, see if there are any similars in any other tourist locales. New York, DC, whatever," he said, taking a marker and writing the word *similars* over Krug's name. "Since you have the first known Strangler case, I'd like to get a fresh set of eyes. Who do you want on to take the case for a second review?"

He looked around the room, glanced at Casey, then said, "Zwingler and Haynes."

"You two okay with that?" Timms asked.

They nodded, and Timms wrote their names below Al's. "Walk the beat in the area, see if we can't come up with new witnesses, overlooked areas where video surveillance might be found, see if anything can be recovered, etc., etc. West, you had the second case. You okay with it?"

Carl West had been in Homicide almost as long as Krug. "I like to think my partner and I can handle it. But if you want to throw a couple of investigators my way, I'm not going to turn down the extra help."

Timms looked around the room. "Burnett and Johnson?"

"We're in," Burnett said, and Timms wrote their names below West's.

By the time he was done, naming Al as the liaison for the cases, reporting directly to him, the only investigator who didn't seem to have a job related to the Strangler was Casey. "Any questions?" Timms asked.

"Yeah," Zwingler said. "What about days off?"

"You're lucky you'll have time to sleep," Timms answered, holding Zwingler's gaze. "So anyone here who scored Giants tickets to this weekend's games, maybe put up a notice in the break room."

"Seriously?" Zwingler said, then looked around for support. "They're playing the damned Dodgers."

Timms capped his dry-erase marker. "And they're on a losing streak. You really want to see that in person?"

Zwingler gave a tired sigh. "They're for sale. Cheap."

Al laughed. "How about a game of liar's poker?"

Haynes snickered.

Timms tapped the whiteboard with his capped marker. "You want a day off? Identify the Strangler, or there won't be any tourists left in the city to sell the tickets to."

He returned to his office, and Al swiveled his chair around. "You heard the guy. Let's get to work so Zwingler can find a buyer."

"You actually gave away a Strangler case?" Casey asked. "I could have worked it."

"You heard what he said. He wanted *fresh* eyes on it. Besides. You have the Presidio case."

Casey rolled his chair closer, keeping his voice down. "I could have handled that investigation. At least I was there for part of it."

"Look, kid. I know you don't want to hear this right now, but worry about the job at hand. Not what you *think* it takes to ace a promotional interview."

"This isn't about the promotional," Casey said, even though he realized that's what it looked like. "I just want the experience."

"You have enough on your plate. Work on that."

Casey's phone rang, preventing him from arguing the point. "Kellog. Homicide."

"Well...?" His mother's impatient voice on the other end.

He knew exactly what she was inquiring about, and after Al needling him about cutting the apron strings, he pushed his chair farther against the wall, keeping his voice low. "I came out in the top five. The oral board is this coming Wednesday."

"And will you take the position if you pass that?"

"I told you, I'm only doing it for practice."

"You spent *how* many months studying for that thing, and you wouldn't even take the position if they offered it? I think you should take it. It has to be safer than what you're doing now. More administrative, right?"

Time to change the subject. "How's Dad doing?"

"He's fine. He wanted me to remind you about coming to dinner tonight. I told you about that girl I met at church. I think you'd like her."

"Mom—"

"You're almost thirty. Your friend Mark already has two kids *and* a career where no one's trying to kill him."

"No one's trying to kill me, Mom."

"Oh? What about that last case you worked where the guy tried to run you over with the car? Or that one where—"

"I get the point."

"I think you should take the lieutenant's job if you pass."

"I'll think about it."

"And don't forget, dinner's at six. You promised."

"I'll see you tonight. Love you." He disconnected, worried about this dinner she'd planned. The last thing he wanted was to be set up with one of her church friends, and he could well imagine the type of person she'd pick for him.

The very thought was enough to make him consider pleading illness at the last minute—something he would have tried had he thought for an instant he could get away with it.

"Hey, Al. You think you could text me, say around eight, that I have to come into work?"

"For what?"

"My mom's trying to play matchmaker. With someone from church."

"How do you know you won't like her?"

"Trust me. There is no one who attends my mother's church worth taking a second look at. Or I'd remember."

"Eight o'clock," Al said, taking out his phone and setting an alarm.

"Thanks," Casey said, putting his mother's church dinner from his mind, and getting back to the Presidio case, sorting through his notes. Which was when Casey finally noticed the time discrepancy between when the neighbor, Marcie, said she left, and the time that Trudy was killed. "Hey, Al. You know how Marcie said she left at seven?"

"What about it?" he said, his fingers clicking away on his keyboard, his attention focused on his computer screen.

"How is it she got there *after* Trudy was killed, when everyone seems to confirm that Trudy left at least five minutes after Marcie?"

Al stopped typing and looked up at Casey. "You caught that, did you?" Al picked up his notebook, turned a few pages and showed it to Casey. Down at the bottom, next to Marcie's name, he'd circled "7:00" and scrawled, "time discrepancy" right over the top of it.

"You could have said something."

"Could've," Al replied. "But that's part of the learning curve. Wanted to see not only when you noticed, but what you plan to do about it."

"Go talk to her, of course."

"Is that it?"

"Check with her husband and Trudy's husband. Find out if there was a mistake."

"Good start. For textbook thinking. A good investigator's also going to be looking outside the box. And for the record, I hear they're big on that sort of thing in promotional interviews. In case you plan on going to one anytime soon. So what else would you do?"

Casey leaned back in his chair, trying not to look at his calendar, knowing he only had five days until the promotional. "Find out why it would take her longer?"

"How?"

He turned to his computer, but before he even brought up the map, he realized the answer. "Run it myself."

"Now you're thinking."

Casey glanced at the clock. "If I leave now, maybe I'll miss some of the commuter traffic." He stopped when he saw the look on Al's face. "No?"

"Think, College Boy."

When nothing came to him, he said, "What is it I want, then?"

"To see what she saw when she saw it."

A second or two passed, then it struck him. "Leave when she left."

Al nodded. "See you here bright and early."

"You're going to run with me?"

"My job is to mentor your investigative abilities, not break my neck while doing it. I'll arrange to have someone from patrol meet you at the scene."

THIRTEEN

"What the hell, Barstow?"

Jenn kept her gaze fixed on her editor's desk, worried her impulsive action at the Hall of Justice would get her canned. Especially after it was plastered all over the afternoon news. "I'm sorry."

"Sorry? You're supposed to be writing about local politics, not crashing police press conferences to compare current Strangler victims with dead prostitutes."

"I merely asked if the police were looking into those old murders to see if there were any similarities to the *current* Strangler cases."

"What the hell is with your obsession with the dead prostitute cases?"

Last thing she needed was for him to find out *why* she wanted to look into the older cases. "I won't let it happen again."

"Damned right you won't," he said, swiveling around in his chair to grab a draft of an article from the printer. "Unless you want to *end* your career at this paper, quit playing girl detective. Your job is reporting local politics. Do I make myself clear?"

"Very." The word barely cleared her throat, but it didn't matter. His focus was now on the story he'd just pulled from the printer, his red pencil slashing at words that didn't fit.

Marty's article, she realized. The things practically bled red from all the corrections, not that writing skill seemed to matter when it came down to the choice of the crime desk.

Back at her cubicle, she stared at her computer screen, trying not to dwell on the thought that Marty was probably sitting on the biggest story of his career and was too stupid to know it.

The very idea caught her up short. When had she turned into such a mean-spirited person, allowing her own goals to consume her to the point that other lives didn't matter?

"Anyone home?"

Taryn's voice seeped into her brain, and Jenn swiveled her chair around to face her friend. "Sorry. Did you say something?"

"Only wondering if you still worked here or I had to break in a new cubicle buddy."

"Still here. For now."

"And...?"

"You're kidding, right?"

Taryn rolled her chair back until she was parallel to Jenn. "You are *not* going to give up now, are you?"

"My job's on the line, so yeah. I'm giving up."

"You're job's only on the line if you get caught. And the only reason you *got* caught was because you had to open your mouth in front of the cameras."

"I saw a chance and took it."

"How is it you can go your entire career nearly invisible, then take *that* moment to make yourself known? Did you at least *talk* to the investigator?"

"I did. And before you ask, no. I didn't say a thing. I chickened out."

"Why?"

"It just seemed so...wrong."

"Wrong? Look to your right. What do you see?"

She glanced down the row of cubicles and saw Marty's plaid suit coat hanging over the back of his empty chair. "Nothing."

"Now glance to your left."

And there was Marty, standing in the doorway of the editor's office, kissing up to their boss as he usually did. The reason he got the job she'd vied for.

"*That*," Taryn said, "is wrong."

"If anything, what I'm about to do tonight is even more underhanded."

"It's no worse than cultivating that friendship with Parnell's campaign office receptionist, or the supervisor's secretary. You cover politics. It's called networking."

"Networking?"

"All you're doing is laying the groundwork. Besides, something good is going to come out of it. The end justifies the means." She glanced up at the clock. "Time to go. Your appointment's in half an hour."

FOURTEEN

It was close to six that evening when Casey pulled up into the driveway of his parents' house, wondering if he was early. Or maybe got the day wrong. There were no other cars there. Relief swept through him as he opened the front door, not seeing anyone waiting in the living room or even the kitchen, where his mother was busy tossing a salad.

She looked up, saw him, and smiled. "You're here."

"Where is everyone?"

"It's just a small party. Us four." She took the pepper grinder, ground a bit too much over the top of the salad. "Your father will be down in a minute."

"Mom. I told you, I'm not interested in seeing anyone else right now."

"What do you mean anyone *else*? You didn't tell me you were seeing anyone at all."

"An officer at my department."

"Then why haven't you brought her home? I'd like to meet her."

Way too soon in the dating process for that—not that he was about to inform his mother on the finer details. "We only just started going out."

"She's a police officer. Those things never last."

"How would you know?"

"Everyone in my uncle's family was in law enforcement. Hand me that cheese, dear." He passed a bowl of fresh grated parmesan to her, and she sprinkled it into the salad. "How many women have you gone out with since you became a police officer? Even less now that you're in Homicide. Which is why I think—if you insist on staying in *that* profession—you should seriously look at accepting this promotion."

"One, I haven't been offered it. There's still the oral board to get through. Two, I'm not planning on changing professions anytime soon."

"Then all the more reason to let me and my church friends help—" Someone knocked at the front door, and she picked up the salad bowl and placed it in his hands. "She's here. Put this on the table, then answer the door."

"Mom. Do you realize how awkward this is?"

"Don't be ridiculous. A mother is allowed to introduce her son to a proper young lady from her church. Honey!" she called out to his father in the den. "Jennifer's here." And then she pushed Casey toward the dining room. "Go. Don't leave the poor girl standing on the porch!"

Casey silently cursed his mother and her meddlesome ways as he walked into the dining room, set the salad on the table, then trudged to the living room, somewhat secure in the knowledge that Al would be texting him as a failsafe, should this church girl turn out to be anything he needed rescuing from.

Suddenly the image of Becca sitting astride him popped into his head. So un-churchlike, it almost hurt. He might not be Catholic, but he was fairly certain that image warranted a trip to confession.

And now his mother was setting him up with a girl from the church he probably hadn't set foot in for—well, far too long. Even then, he didn't recall seeing any woman who struck him as someone he wanted to ask out.

Not that he'd been looking to date anyone at the time, he thought as he opened the door.

To say that he was surprised by his mother's dinner guest was an understatement. Jennifer, it seemed, was none other than Jenn Barstow, the reporter from the *Union-Examiner*. She wore a pink dress, the top few pearl buttons undone, drawing the eye to a hint of cleavage, then down to the white belt that cinched her narrow waist and from there down to the hemline, which hit just at her knees. There was definitely a sense of demureness about her in her pink and pearls, until one glanced down at her long bare legs to her red stiletto heels.

Not the sort of shoe one would see at church. And definitely a dichotomy when compared to the implied innocence of her dress.

It was this last thought that shook him, and it took quite the effort to draw his gaze back up to her face. "You are *not* what I expected. *Who.* Not *who* I expected."

"Who were you expecting?"

"Jennifer from my mom's church. You look…different."

"Highlights and a new dress." This time her smile was timid, reminding him more of the girl reporter trying to work up the courage to talk to him in the Hall of Justice lobby.

He stood there, hand on the door, trying to reconcile *this* Jennifer with that Jenn.

"Casey?" his mom said, walking up behind him. "Are you going to just keep her standing on the doorstep?"

He waved Jenn into the house. "I believe you and my mother are already acquainted?"

"From church," Jenn said, then held her hand out toward his mom.

"Don't be ridiculous," his mother said, taking the girl into a hug. "And you look lovely. I don't think I've ever seen you without your glasses."

"Highlights," she said, lifting a lock of her hair.

"Well, that, too. But you should think about wearing contacts more often. You have beautiful eyes. Doesn't she, Casey?"

Casey smiled and gave a slight nod of agreement, trying not to glance down at her shoes, all while wondering how he was going to get through dinner and keep police work out of it.

He needn't have worried. She never once brought up his cases. More important, it turned out she was well versed in Giants lore, which brought his father into the conversation. From that moment on, all awkwardness was gone, everyone talking at once, arguing points on the season, who they were playing. She held her own, and it wasn't until the topic changed to mutual interests that Casey realized his mother and father were no longer at the table. But then Jenn laughed at something, and his attention was drawn to her once more, and he made the pleasant discovery that they both liked jazz, rainy days—as long as one didn't have to work in it—and skiing.

He leaned back in his chair, studying her while she spoke, marveling at the change in her. Which made him wonder why she'd been hiding all this time in ill-fitting clothes and glasses that were all wrong for her face.

"So," she said, when the conversation finally lulled. "Why a cop?"

The question caught him off guard. "A cop?"

"Did you always know? Playing cops and robbers as a kid?"

"It wasn't my dream, trust me. Or my parents' either."

"What was your dream?"

"Surfing."

"You're kidding?"

"Nope. I actually had an affinity for it, and living this close to the beach made it easy to surf every day. But realizing my chances of making a living from a hobby that depended on money, waves, and luck? I did the math and realized I needed to settle on a more realistic career."

"Policing is quite the jump from surfing."

"It was supposed to be law. But much to my parents' regret, some of my prelaw classes were in criminal justice. Hooked from day one."

"Score one for the good guys."

"How about you?" he asked. "Why journalism?"

"Writing," she said as his telephone buzzed.

He'd forgotten about Al's prearranged text coming at eight, and when he read it, he quickly blacked out the screen then shoved it back in his pocket. "Work."

And before he could tell her it could wait, she looked at her own watch. "I have an article to finish before deadline."

After she thanked his parents for dinner, Casey walked her out. They stood on the porch, the chill air surrounding them. His parents lived in the outer Sunset district, not too far from the beach and almost always in the fog. Tonight was no exception. "I had a nice time," he said.

"I did, too."

When no other conversation was forthcoming, she fumbled inside her purse for her keys, which caught on something then went flying to the ground.

She reached for them the same time Casey did, but he was quicker. He scooped them up, his gaze catching on her red stilettos and her slender legs disappearing into the folds of her pink dress. When he rose, he wished his parents weren't hovering about just on the other side of the door. In fact, he wished a lot of things at that moment, but he knew none of them were going to happen. "Your keys," he said, holding them out.

She took them, her fingers lingering a moment too long. And then, surprising him, she stood on tiptoe and gave him a peck on the cheek. "Good night."

When she didn't move away, he stepped in closer, leaned down, then kissed her on her mouth.

A mistake. He realized it at once. It wasn't that she resisted. Quite the opposite. She was soft and warm, and he felt her heart beating beneath the fabric of that pink dress. He wanted to run his fingers down the neckline, undo the pearl buttons, one by one...

His breath caught, and he moved away. "I'm sorry. I shouldn't have done that."

"It's okay." She tried to smile. Perhaps it was just the porch light, but her cheeks were almost as red as her shoes. "I should go."

He nodded. She turned and descended the stairs with what he thought was extraordinary care, her pink dress swaying with every step. It took a moment for him to realize why, when she nearly tripped, not once, but twice as she navigated the narrow walkway.

The shoes.

"You don't wear heels much, do you?" he asked.

"Never," she called out.

"If it makes a difference, I like them. A lot."

"Ha! Try wearing them." When she almost fell a third time, she stopped, pulled off the shoes, then walked barefoot to the car.

He laughed. Even more when she waved those red heels at him as she got into her car, then drove off.

"Well?" his mother said, when he returned inside and found her in the kitchen, rinsing plates then putting them in the dishwasher. "What did you think of her?"

"She's nice, Mom. Only she works for the press."

"And what's wrong with that?"

"Little bit of a conflict of interest when it comes to talking about the job. Specifically, mine."

"Says who?"

"Says everyone who ranks above me."

"One more reason—"

"Wouldn't matter if I made captain." He took the plate from her hand and loaded it into the dishwasher while she rinsed the next. "Rules are rules."

"Oh..." Her shoulders fell. "And she was so nice."

"She was." They finished the dishes in silence, and try as he might, on the way to his apartment and long after, all he could think about was her red stiletto heels.

FIFTEEN

"So how was your dinner?" Al asked Casey when he walked into the office just after six the next morning. Al stopped at the coffee stand to pour himself a cup. "Or should I ask did you get my text in the nick of time?"

"Dinner was fine," Casey said, capping the highlighter he'd just used to mark the map route Marcie Valentine had run the morning of the homicide. "And yes. Got the text. Thanks."

"So how bad was she? The church mouse?"

The truth was that Casey spent a good portion of the night thinking about the very chaste kiss he'd shared with her, and it was driving him insane. She was not his type. Too girl-next-door. "Trust me. She was no church mouse. More like the forbidden fruit. Jenn Barstow, the reporter from *Union-Examiner.*"

Al looked up as he poured coffee into his mug. "The *same* Jenn Barstow I saw in the lobby yesterday?"

"Yep."

"Someone spiked your coffee this morning? Or was it your drink last night?"

"You should have seen her. She was—"

He stopped when one of the robbery investigators walked in then made a beeline for the coffee pot.

Al strolled over to Casey's desk. "She was what?"

"Just...different. If she wasn't a reporter, I'd—Well, doesn't quite matter, does it?"

"Probably not." Al eyed the map. "If nothing else, a good run this morning should take your mind off things. You ready, Hotshot?"

"Sure you don't want to come? Getting a bit of a paunch there."

"We'll talk when you've been sitting behind that desk for twenty more years." He glanced up at the clock. Six thirty. "Better lace up those running shoes. Your backup should be waiting for you at seven, sharp."

And just as Al promised, a patrol car was waiting just up the street from Marcie Valentine's house. He parked and walked over as Becca Windsor slid out of the driver's seat. Like him, she was dressed in running gear.

"Becca?"

"You seem surprised."

"Sorry. Al said he was going to arrange with someone from patrol, but—I wasn't expecting you."

"I could call for someone else."

"No. I'm glad you're here. Just...You sure you don't mind?"

"It's a nice break from patrol." She lowered her mirrored sunglasses, eying his electric-blue running shoes. "You do realize those things clash with your black jogging suit?"

He looked down at his shoes. "A bit loud?"

"I think it's a good thing we're wearing sunglasses."

"Yeah. My mom used to accuse me of being color-blind. Definitely color challenged."

"Until today, I would've pegged you as a pretty sharp dresser."

"Only because the store salesclerks take pity on me. Trust me. If I'm wearing any color combinations that work, they get the credit."

He gave her a copy of the map to look over. "Figured we'd leave from here right at seven. Get a feel for the route."

She eyed the map, then folded and tucked it into her sweat-shirt pocket. "I don't suppose you're open to suggestions…?"

"You have a better idea?"

"If I'm not mistaken, the victim and her neighbor left about five minutes apart. We split up. One of us leaves at seven, the other at five after. I know it's only five minutes, but maybe there's something like commuter traffic or a bus route or whatever that we pick up on in that difference."

"Not bad for a patrol officer."

"We have our moments."

And so precisely at seven, Casey took off from in front of Marcie's house. Becca intended to follow five minutes later. Of course, there was a slight disparity in that he was at least a foot taller than Marcie, and so he slowed his pace to what he thought a woman of her stature might run, then tried to concentrate on what was around him, not who was jogging behind him.

Once he managed to find a good pace, it was easier to concentrate. Most of the run was downhill until the street that led to the overflow lot, where a few cars were parked. There it finally leveled off to the trail that led through the trees to Crissy Field in one direction and to the bridge in the other. When he reached the location of the crime scene, he made note of the time.

Becca jogged up about five minutes later, arriving right around the time Trudy's body was discovered by Marcie. "Well?" she asked.

"Unless those women ran a completely different route from each other, I still don't get how Marcie arrived *after* the murder."

"Maybe she ran past and doubled back? Or veered off Lincoln into the Presidio."

"According to the couple who found Trudy's body, Marcie came from the same direction as we did. And arrived a few minutes *after* they discovered the murder. I practically jogtrotted," he said, checking his watch. "And I still got here five minutes before Marcie found Trudy. But here you are, right around that time."

"Marcie took a very different route?"

"Or someone got their times mixed up."

Casey called Al and told him what they'd found.

"Okay," Al said. "So what'd you see?"

"What do you mean, what'd I see? I told you."

"No, College Boy, you told me how long it took. Ask yourself what you saw. Sit down, make notes, then analyze what you found and get back to me."

Casey bristled at being called College Boy, mostly because Al's voice carried, and he was certain that Becca had heard every word. He turned slightly, trying to keep his voice from revealing his feelings. "Anything in particular you think I should put in that report?"

"As a matter of fact, yes. How does it compare with the day of the murder? You're looking for patterns. Anything or anyone you can use to verify or dispute the events as they were told to us. *Capisce?*"

"Capisce."

Al disconnected, and Casey shoved the phone in his pocket, his frustration apparently evident enough for Becca to notice.

"Something wrong?" she asked.

"My partner. Almost makes me wonder if he's got it in for me for not telling him I took the lieutenant's test."

"Homicide's sort of the elite detail. Why would you want to promote out so soon?"

"I was only taking it for experience. But trust me. Homicide's not all it's cracked up to be."

"You haven't been in there all that long. How do you know?"

"I just do."

Becca lowered her sunglasses, looking at him over the rims.

Her eyes looked exceptionally blue today, he realized, then quickly looked away, not wanting to get caught staring. Feeling uncomfortable in the ensuing silence, he said, "Al wants what we found written up in a supplemental. Over coffee?"

She glanced at her watch. "I have maybe an hour. If you're buying."

The location she'd chosen was a small establishment that catered to a more local clientele as opposed to the morning commuters and tourists. They took a seat at a corner table, where they could keep their back to the wall and still have a bit of privacy to talk. Becca ordered a breakfast smoothie, and Casey followed suit.

They drank in silence for several minutes, each of them taking notes on their respective pads, Becca's on the table between them.

Then, out of the blue, Becca said, "You really think Al's on your case?"

"Al? Yeah. I do."

"I don't know. He smiles with his eyes."

"Don't let it fool you. He's about as old school as they get. Every time I try to approach an investigation from a new angle, he calls me College Boy."

"College Boy?"

"His dig at my overeducation. Especially when comparing my degree to his graduating from the school of hard knocks, aka his time on the streets."

"I'm sure he means well."

"He has a funny way of showing it," Casey said then turned back to his notes. He was drawing a blank. Nothing seemed to stand out to him. "I've got zip. What about you?"

Becca shrugged. "I don't know. There was that old guy down the street from Marcie's place. Other than that—"

"What old guy?"

"Corner house. Out getting his newspaper. He waved at me. Well, started to. You know, one of those waves that sort of falters when you realize you don't know someone?"

And that, he realized, was what Al had been talking about. What they saw, not how long it took. "What're the chances he was out there the morning Trudy was killed?"

"You could go talk to him. *We* could go talk to him."

Her smile was infectious.

Before he had a chance to respond, a tonal alert sounded over the radio, then the dispatcher's voice. "All units, two-eleven, strong-arm robbery just occurred in the area of Everything Under the Bridge. Suspect is a WMA, late twenties, dark clothing, no further description."

"That's just up the road," Becca said, grabbing her radio. "You coming?"

"Right behind you."

SIXTEEN

Casey followed Becca to the scene, both vehicles using their emergency lights to get through the thick traffic. He pulled up behind her patrol car and left his rear ambers flashing as a warning to any ruthless parking attendants that he was there on official business.

Not that that always stopped them, he thought as he grabbed his portable from the passenger seat, hearing Becca call in their arrival.

A dark-skinned man in his fifties stepped out of a shop called Everything Under the Bridge, and Casey, his star hanging from a chain around his neck, pulled it from his jacket, saying, "Police."

"In here," the man said, waving them over, holding the glass door open for them.

The place was filled with knickknacks, souvenirs, and postcards printed with iconic San Francisco sights and landmarks.

"She's in the back," the man said. "The storeroom."

Casey heard someone crying. He and Becca rushed back into the crowded space filled with shelves of cardboard boxes, some stacked to the ceiling. A woman in her twenties sat in a chair next to a small table covered with pink and yellow invoices. She looked up as they entered, the left side of her face red and smudged with dirt and looking pale beneath the fluorescent lighting. Her disheveled, shoulder-length brown hair was held back by an elastic band that looked ready to fall with the slightest movement.

Becca looked around the room quickly, undoubtedly ascertaining the safety of the situation, then stood in front of the woman. Like Casey, she'd also worn her star on a chain around her neck and had it tucked beneath her sweat shirt. She held it out for the woman to see. "Are you okay? Do you need an ambulance?"

"No," the woman said, shaking her head. "I'm fine."

"What happened?"

And then she started crying again.

Casey drew the employee from the back to the front of the store, giving Becca a chance to talk to the victim in private, and he heard Becca ask, "What's your name?"

"Cynthia Wyland."

"Cynthia. We're here to help."

The employee glanced toward the storeroom as Casey asked, "What's your name, sir?"

"Joe Patel."

"Mr. Patel. Thanks for calling. What happened?"

"The girl ran up to my back door, pounding on it, screaming. I looked out the peephole and recognized her. She works in one of the shops a few doors down. So I let her in. She said someone attacked her. She thought he was trying to steal her computer or something."

"Did you see anything?"

"Just her. I did hear footsteps, like maybe someone was back there besides her, but I didn't wait around to find out. Just pulled her in and locked the door."

Casey glanced toward the storeroom. "So I can get out that way? Have a look around?"

"Sure."

Casey figured with the delay between the call and their arrival, chances of finding anyone was slim. He took a quick walk through the back alley set between a row of shops on one side, with their unmarked back doors, and a dank-looking warehouse on the other. Several Dumpsters were lined up along one wall, probably shared by the shop owners and the warehouse. Unremarkable in every respect. The only time the alley was bound to see any traffic was on trash day and when shop employees came and went from work via the back doors. In other words, a good place to lie in wait.

Casey continued on through, then around to the front. By this time Roberts, the primary uniformed officer, was there taking a statement from the girl. "What happened next?" Roberts asked.

"He grabbed my hair from behind. My ponytail. And then he put his arm around my neck and tried to drag me toward him." She dabbed at her eyes with a tissue, glancing over at Becca, who smiled in encouragement.

"Go on," Becca said.

"That's when I swung around and hit him with my laptop bag. I—I think the weight of it sort of knocked us both off-balance. When he grabbed it, I took off running."

Officer Roberts looked up from his note pad. "You think he was after the computer?"

"At first, but…"

"But what?"

"When I got away, he ran after me, saying, 'Your bag! Don't you want your bag?' Like I was *ever* going to go back and get it."

Casey heard dispatch on the radio advising that Robbery was en route to handle the call. Roberts replied, "Ten-four." Then, to the victim, "Before the attack. Did he happen to say anything else?"

"Just talking to himself." She looked down at the wadded tissue, turning it over and over in her fingers, then stopped, eyed him, and said, "Something about playing tag? I don't know. I couldn't really hear. He was just…weird."

"When was this?"

"Right after I passed him. I mean, he wasn't even looking at me when I turned into the alley, so I didn't really think about that, you know, he didn't belong there. But when I heard him sort of muttering, I remember getting a weird feeling. And then—Oh my God. My bag. It's got all my information in it. My computer, my address, my schoolbooks. My house keys. He knows where to find me."

"Hey," Becca said, reaching out, touching her arm lightly. "We're going to find this guy, okay?"

"What if you don't?" She broke down again. Nothing Becca or Officer Roberts said seemed to calm her.

Casey could well imagine the vulnerability the young girl must be experiencing. "Miss Wyland," he said, stepping forward, figuring what they needed right now was a good distraction. "Maybe you can show Officer Roberts where this happened?"

She looked at Roberts, who said, "That would really help."

"Okay…"

Casey walked over to the back door, held it open. Roberts and their victim led the way. She directed them to the left a few doors down the alley toward the store where she worked. When they neared her shop, the woman pointed toward the last Dumpster. "That's my bag!" She ran over, and was about to pull it out when Roberts stopped her. The suspect had thrown it up on top and it was now wedged between the Dumpster and the brick wall.

"But my computer—"

"We'll get it in a sec," the officer said. "After a few photos. So where'd you first see this guy?"

Casey and Becca moved away, letting the officer finish his interview. Casey glanced in both directions. What he couldn't figure out was why the suspect tossed the bag before he fled.

He thought about yesterday's 211 at Ghirardelli Square. Shades of the same. "You think this was a robbery?" he asked Becca.

She looked over at him, then in the direction of the Dumpster. "Why wouldn't it be?"

"The bag. Why leave it behind? There were no witnesses. Not at that hour."

"We got here pretty quick," Becca said. "Maybe he tossed it when he heard the sirens."

"That's what I was thinking. But why try to lure her back? That thing *looks* like a laptop bag. If I were a thief, and my victim shoved that thing in my hands, the thing I wanted to begin with—"

"Sexual assault?"

"More probable, wouldn't you think?"

"Especially considering this alley is almost deserted at this hour. Who's going to hear her scream?"

A sobering thought. In a city this size with this many people around, there were so many dark corners where someone could end up hurt and alone. Drag her between a couple of these Dumpsters, who would notice?

After checking with Roberts to see if there was anything further he needed, they cleared the call and were walking out to the main street when Casey's phone rang.

It was Al. "Where are you?"

Casey eyed the sign over the gift shop. A replica of the Golden Gate depicted in red neon lights. "Sidetracked by a report of a robbery at a gift shop called Everything Under the Bridge. We were just down the street. The thing is, I'm just not sure it's a robbery."

He heard the sound of papers shuffling, figured Al was going through a stack of reports, probably only listening with half an ear. "What, then?"

He briefed Al on the incident, ending with, "If it was a robbery, why try to lure her back? Or why toss her computer away? What if it's a failed Strangler case? It might not be a specific landmark, but it's a store filled with souvenirs of them."

"You know what I think? You want to catch the Strangler so bad, the liquor store up the street could be robbed, and you'd try to link it." Casey heard the squeak of Al's chair, as though he'd suddenly leaned back. "Let Robbery handle it. If they link it to the Strangler, I'll make sure you get the gold star you're looking for. In the meantime, you have a *dead* woman, a dead guy who may or may not be her killer, and a lot of witnesses that still need interviewing."

"What if I took the case? I'm already here."

"Negative, College Boy. Not if the body's still breathing. You've got evidence to go through on that Presidio case."

Al disconnected before Casey could argue the point.

"Something wrong?" Becca asked.

"Good ol' Uncle Al, reminding me I should get back to the office."

"Same here. Back on patrol, rather."

They continued on to their respective cars, Casey trying to work up the nerve to ask Becca out again. It shouldn't be that difficult, but he found it far easier to discuss police work with her than anything remotely personal. When they reached her patrol car, she stopped, smiled, waited a beat.

His cue, he realized. But all he could say was, "Thanks for your help."

"Anytime."

And then she was gone.

Casey watched her drive off, wondering how tacky it would be to ask her out via text.

Very, he decided as got into his car and drove back to the Hall.

Al seemed to be watching for him when he returned. "So how'd it go out there? On your run?"

Casey had a feeling he was talking about the girl, not the investigation. None of Al's business, he decided, even if the man was instrumental in having her assigned as Casey's backup. "It's possible we may have found another witness. An old man who lives down the street from the victim was out picking up his paper at the time Officer Windsor ran past. We were on our way to interview him when the two-eleven happened."

"Let's go talk with him now," Al said, walking over to the coatrack to get his hat. "The sooner you get everyone interviewed, the sooner we can close out the case."

When they were in the car, Al said, "So what's really bugging you?"

"What makes you think something's bugging me?"

"Because when I talked to you on the phone earlier, you sounded a bit short."

"I wasn't short. I was frustrated."

"Same thing, isn't it? What were you frustrated over?"

"That you wouldn't even listen to my theory that maybe it wasn't a robbery."

"Sure I listened. I'm just wondering if you forgot how we do things around here. Dead body, *we* take the call. *Live* body, someone else gets it. Hence the terms *homicide* and *robbery*."

"What if it's a failed Strangler case? She said he grabbed her around the neck."

"Alive theirs, dead ours. That's how it works."

"We should be working together on this. We're in the same damned office, so what does it matter if some of these cases cross over?"

"Tell you what. When you make chief, you can change that." He nodded toward the intersection. "Turn right, take the alley. It's faster this time of day."

As usual, afternoon traffic was a gridlock in most areas, which in this case was a good thing, since he could focus his attention on the road, not his partner. Besides, Al seemed content not conversing.

So be it.

When they finally reached the neighborhood where Trudy and Marcie lived, he'd calmed considerably and was able to keep his frustration about the robberies at bay.

"Which house?" Al asked.

"Next to the corner," he said, parking the car at the end of the street.

Al got out, glanced toward Trudy's house at the top of the hill, then back at the house in question near the bottom. It appeared well kept, the paint fairly new, Casey thought as he and Al walked up the stairs to the front porch.

Al knocked and eventually the door was opened by a man who looked to be in his midseventies. Al stepped back to let Casey do the talking.

"Good afternoon," Casey said, holding up his credential case, showing the man his gold star. "We were wondering if you might answer a few questions about your neighbor."

The old man eyed the wallet, then both sergeants, before holding the door open wider. "This about the woman who was killed the other day? The one who lived just up the street?"

"Trudy Salvatori," Casey said.

Al smiled. "You mind if we come in, Mr....?"

"Layton. Vince Layton." He stepped aside, letting them in, then sat in a well-worn leather armchair in front of the television. "Not sure what I can tell you. Didn't really know her at all. Except I'd see her running sometimes in the morning with the neighbor friend."

"Marcie Valentine?" Casey asked, opening his notebook.

"Guess that's her name. They lived right next door. Used to run together a lot. Right past here every morning. Well, most days. Sometimes it was just the one. Marcie, I guess."

"What about the other morning?"

"Saw 'em both. Just not together. That was unusual."

"Do you remember who you saw at what time?"

He glanced out the front window. "Let's see...Trudy. I don't know...Five after seven?"

Casey hid his dismay. If it was Trudy who ran past at five after, then that meant Marcie had told the truth. She had left at seven. "You said they weren't together that morning. What time was it that you saw Marcie?"

"You think Marcie killed her? Little thing like her?"

"We're just trying to re-create their steps that morning."

"Saw her, definitely."

"Any chance you know what time that was?"

The man looked off to the side, then up. "Let's see...Maybe a minute or two after?"

"After seven?" Casey asked.

"Nope. After Trudy ran past."

"*After* Trudy."

"Yep." He nodded. "Definitely after. My arthritis was acting up that morning, and she brought my paper to me."

Casey wrote quickly. "Any chance you can pin it down further?"

"Not really. Normally I see her from this chair," he said, patting the arm of his recliner. "Right through my window at seven every morning when the morning news plays their theme. That dark-haired girl is like clockwork. But that morning...? Nope. I'd already poured my coffee by the time Trudy ran past. Got one of those coffee makers with a timer. The first commercial break on the news show, that's when I get my paper. Got a routine. Listen to the headlines, commercial break, go get my paper. By then my coffee's cool enough to drink."

From the corner of his eye, Casey saw Al's eyebrows go up. Undoubtedly thinking the same thing he was. Marcie Valentine had definitely lied about when she left on her run. More important, it appeared that so had everyone else.

The question was why.

"You're sure about the times when you saw each woman run past?"

THE LAST GOOD PLACE

"Positive," the old man said. "First Trudy, then Marcie. Of course, I'm basing this on my coffee timer. You can look if you want."

Al said, "You don't mind?"

"Not at all."

"I'll check," Al said.

Casey asked the man for his contact information then said, "So, as far as you know, Marcie normally runs at seven, sometimes with, sometimes without her neighbor, Trudy?"

"That's right."

"But the morning Trudy was killed?"

"First Trudy ran by a little after seven, then Marcie a minute or two after. Yep. Unless my timer's not set right. But it is."

Al walked out of the kitchen. "Thank you, Mr. Layton. We appreciate your time."

At the car, Casey asked, "What'd you see?"

"A timer with a 7:00 a.m. setting, and a clock that matches the time on my phone."

"So what do you think accounts for the discrepancy in what everyone's telling us?"

"Not sure. But I'd say it's high time we found out."

"We've talked to Marcie twice. Let's hope three's the charm…"

SEVENTEEN

Marcie sat on the couch, her feet curled beneath her, ignoring the ringing telephone, deciding it best to wait until the answering machine clicked on. She'd had two hang-up calls this morning so far. She started pacing the room, telling herself that after finding the back door open yesterday morning, the calls might be related. Then again, maybe Devin had the alarm and cameras installed just to humor her.

The sound of a car engine out front caught her attention, and she moved to the window, parting the curtain slightly. A white Acura sedan pulled up and parked in front of her house, the glare from the morning sun glinting off the car's windows. The Salvatoris' real estate agent, a slightly overweight, brunette-haired woman, exited the vehicle, her impeccable black dress accentuating curves that Devin would have described as voluptuous. Keys in hand, the woman made a beeline toward the Salvatoris', and Marcie wondered if she'd only just heard about Trudy's murder.

Curious, she walked to the front door, opened it slightly, listening as the woman knocked.

"Bev…" Tony said to the woman.

"My God. I just got back to town. What happened?"

"I—I don't know," he replied. And then the sound of his front door closing.

Marcie stood there a moment, but after hearing nothing more, returned to the couch, eyeing the real estate agent's car through the window. It seemed odd that she would show up after a murder. Close friends or family, sure. In fact, Tony's house had been a revolving door since Trudy's death. But a real estate agent?

Trudy had said something about not liking the woman during one of their runs. But Tony had insisted on this particular agent, Bev Farland, even after Trudy had voiced her disapproval. Marcie had assumed it was more of a personality thing with Trudy, especially after the whole can-we-cut-down-the-trees thing.

This, though...Showing up now? Just odd, she thought.

Unless, of course, Bev Farland was worried that she was about to lose a sale due to the death of her client's wife.

To satisfy her own curiosity, Marcie padded into the kitchen, peering through the blinds straight into the Salvatoris' kitchen. Her patience paid off when after a minute or so, she saw the two walk in. Something akin to guilt swept through her at the spying, and she almost turned away. Then again, considering all that that had happened, this was the least of her transgressions. A moment later she saw Bev reaching out, touching Tony's shoulder, almost caressing it. He stepped back, his expression turning hard.

If only she could read lips—

A sharp knock at her front door startled her. Heart beating, she stepped back from the window, feeling as though someone had caught her in the act.

Act of what? Looking through the window at the neighbor?

Go to the door, answer it. That's all you need to do.

When she put her eye to the peephole, she recognized the two police sergeants from the other morning. Forcing herself to take a breath, appear calm, she unlocked the door and opened it.

"Can I help you?" she asked, wondering if that sounded as idiotic to them as it did to her.

The younger of the two answered. "We're hoping you can answer a few more questions."

She didn't move. "Of course."

"May we come in?" he asked.

The older sergeant smiled as he removed his hat, and for some reason she thought of a wolf in sheep's clothing when she looked at him. Al Krug, she recalled, and decided he was the dangerous one. Just as he had that first morning, he let the younger one do all the talking, something about trying to clarify a few things, while Krug remained in the background, his smile in place, so unassuming...

She moved aside, letting the two in, then closed the door behind them. They stood in the center of her living room, and she thought about inviting them into the kitchen then decided against it. They'd be able to see right into Trudy's house, or rather see that Marcie could see right in, and at the moment she wasn't sure she wanted to deal with the questions that might bring. "Have a seat, please."

Sergeant Krug walked over to the fireplace, his focus on the photos on the mantel, while the other one—what was his name? Casey Kellog—took a seat at one end of the couch, leaving a spot for her at the other.

She smiled benignly as she sat. "What sort of questions?"

Sergeant Kellog opened his notebook, lifted a page filled with notes. "Do you and Trudy tend to run the same route each day?"

"Usually," she said, trying to recall what she had told them that first day. "Why?"

"Just trying to figure out which route Trudy might have taken..."

"Route?"

"When she went running that morning. Would you happen to know?"

"Only what we usually take when we're together. I wasn't with her that morning, so I couldn't say."

The older inspector smiled again, his eyes kind, at least at first glance. She looked away and tried to focus on the younger one, who was pulling a sheet of paper from his notebook. A computer printout of a map. "Is it possible to show us?" he asked, holding the paper toward her. "Which way she went?"

She placed it on her lap. "This way," she said, tracing her finger down her street, around the corner, down Lincoln on toward the Presidio trail.

And suddenly the older man was next to her, his gaze meeting hers, his smile so sincere on the surface as he handed her a pen. "Could you mark it for us? The route you think Trudy ran?"

She nodded, took the pen from him, her hand shaking slightly as she drew the route with the blue ink.

He retreated back to the hearth, smile intact.

Crocodile smile, she decided. Right before he opened his mouth and pulled you down to the bottom of the river.

"...Mrs. Valentine?"

It was a moment before she realized that Sergeant Kellog was waiting for some sort of response from her. Realizing she had no idea what he wanted, she said, "I'm sorry. I—I've been like this all day. Ever since that morning. What was it you wanted to know?"

"If that's the same route you took?"

"The same route?"

"On the map. Did you and Trudy run the same route, or did you take a different one?"

"The same. Wait. I'm sorry. This is the route I took. Since Trudy and I weren't together, I can't answer for her, but it's the one we always took when we were together."

"And the one you took that morning?"

"That's right."

"What time did you leave again?"

She tucked a strand of hair behind her ear then wondered if that would look like a stalling tactic. Just thinking about it made her nervous, and she realized she needed to calm down. She was just a witness. "Seven?" She shrugged. "I didn't really pay attention."

"Your husband thought it was at seven."

"Then it probably was." Marcie smiled. "He usually pays attention to those sorts of things."

He wrote something down in his notebook. "Are you a fast runner?"

"Normal, I guess. Some days faster than others."

"That day?"

"I wasn't in any hurry."

"About how long would you say it takes to get to the point where you found Mrs. Salvatori?"

"Um, forty minutes or so? Why are you asking this?"

"Just trying to re-create your neighbor's last steps." He looked at his notes, checking off something she couldn't see. "Notice anyone in the neighborhood that morning who didn't belong?"

She chewed at her nail. "Not really…"

"Not really? What does that mean?"

And what could she say without admitting that she was lying?

"I mean, just…I think someone might have come into my house the other night." There. She said it. Her heart beat a little faster as she waited for a reaction. When there was none, she added, "Don't you find that odd?"

The younger man looked up from his notebook. "Perhaps you should explain, Mrs. Valentine."

"I'm not sure what to think. I—My husband had an alarm installed." The two men glanced at each other but said nothing, and so she continued. "The night of the murder, he heard a noise, and the next morning, the back door was open. There've been other things, too."

"Like what?"

"Little things. Like someone's going through my purse. And then the calls started today. I can hear someone on the other end. Most of the time they don't say anything."

"Most of the time?"

"Sometimes it's just something to make me think they're watching me. Like I'm being stalked."

He proceeded to ask a number of other questions. Any other time in the past when she saw anyone that didn't belong in the neighborhood? Did Trudy complain about being followed? Did she have any concerns about her coworkers? Husband? Other friends? Anything at all that she could add?

There was not. Marcie couldn't even think straight at that point.

Finally, Sergeant Kellog closed his notebook. "That's about it."

Thank God, she thought, exhausted from the entire interview, feeling nothing but relief when she opened the door and waited for them to leave.

The two investigators stepped out, and she was just closing the door when the older one turned, saying, "There is one thing I've been wondering about." He smiled that crocodile smile. "You say you left at seven?"

"I guess."

"And Trudy's husband said she left about five minutes later?"

"I didn't see her leave her house."

"You haven't talked to him yet?"

"Tony? No. I..." A deep sense of guilt swept over her. She should have gone over when she heard him come home. The thought of facing him, though, was more than she could bear. "No."

"Assuming they're both accurate, that would mean you left before Trudy did."

She waited.

"You see," the older man said. "That's what's stumping me, Mrs. Valentine. If you left *before* your friend, how is it you got there *after* her?"

It was everything she could do to stand there and appear calm, and she didn't dare let go of the doorknob, in case they saw her hand shaking.

They knew. Knew she was lying.

And that meant that everything that came out of her mouth would be suspect. She'd seen enough TV cases to know how they could twist what she'd said, use it against her. Not about to let that happen, she smiled at both men then gave the slightest of shrugs. "I have no idea, sergeant. Maybe someone made a mistake?"

He nodded slightly. "Maybe. But if anything comes to mind, anything at all, give us a call."

"I will." She closed and locked the door, her heart thudding as she hurried to the kitchen and found her cell phone on the counter. She accessed the texts, then erased everything on the screen from the day Trudy was killed.

EIGHTEEN

"What do you make of that?" Al asked, nodding toward the real estate agent's car still parked out front as they crossed the street toward their own vehicle. "Visiting the bereaved to make sure the sale's still going through?"

Casey eyed the magnetic signs on the car advertising BEV FARLAND REAL ESTATE. "Is this where you tell me that we need to interview her because the defense for the Strangler suspect will use it against us if we don't? Well, assuming our dead guy is not the Strangler."

"Your case, College Boy. What do you think?"

Casey didn't need to think about it at all, since it was a common tactic in defense strategies. Besides, his suspect was dead. Which made him wonder what sort of information the real estate agent could offer beyond what they already knew.

The front door opened and a brunette woman stepped out, tissue in one hand, dabbing at tears.

Casey crossed the street as the woman approached her car. "Ms. Farland? San Francisco PD. You have a moment?" he asked, holding his coat open so she could see the star on his belt.

Her face turned bright red as she looked from him to Al and back.

Definitely not the reaction Casey expected. "Sorry if we startled you," he said. "I'm Sergeant Kellog, and this is my partner, Sergeant Krug. We have just a few questions."

She glanced back at Trudy's house, then nodded at Casey. "I wasn't even in town on the day of the murder. I—I don't know what I can tell you. Can we do this another day?"

"It'll just take a few minutes," Casey replied. "Why don't you follow us to the—"

"Here is fine," she said, stepping up onto the sidewalk, then crossing her arms. "I have appointments all day."

She'd closed herself off to him in a matter of seconds.

Not a good start, he thought, opening his notebook as Al tipped his hat to her, his eyes lit with the right mix of fatherly concern and empathy. "Anything you can tell us at all," Al said, making Casey wish he could perfect the technique for himself.

She eyed Al. "About...?"

"The Salvatoris? You seem upset. Were you close to Trudy?"

She sniffed as she lifted the tissue to her nose. "Closer to her husband...I mean, I dealt with him on the real estate transaction. I'm afraid his wife doesn't—*didn't*—like me."

Al nodded, his empathetic expression never wavering. "The sale. Is Mr. Salvatori still planning to go through with it?"

"I don't think he has a choice..."

"I thought, well, with Trudy gone, maybe...?"

She gave a cynical laugh, eyeing Casey as he wrote down what she said. "I don't want to speak ill of the dead, but Trudy spent more money than the two of them made. It was *one* of the reasons they were divorcing."

"*One* of the reasons?" Al said. "What were the other reasons for the divorce, if you don't mind my asking."

She hugged her arms tighter about her, giving a slight shrug as her cheeks reddened. "Tony was...He and I were...involved."

"For how long?" Casey asked, always amazed at how Al was able to elicit information so easily.

"Shortly after they listed their house with me. Almost three months? We'd dated years ago. In college. And then...it just happened. And for what it's worth, Tony broke it off over a week ago.

He felt it was best that if we were—well, to wait until after the divorce."

"Who do you think killed Trudy?"

Her gaze widened. "I thought it was the Strangler guy. That's what they were saying on the news, wasn't it?"

"Just trying to do a thorough investigation," Casey said, closing his notebook and smiling at her. "Thank you for your time."

"That's it?"

"Unless you can think of something else."

She shook her head, walked around to the driver's side, then opened her car door. Just as she slid in, Casey said, "Anyone else know about it? Your affair with Tony?"

"Trudy, possibly. Though I can't imagine if she found out that she'd be all that upset. It wasn't like she wasn't screwing around herself."

"Trudy? With whom?"

"I guess it depends on which day," she replied.

"Most recently?"

"Look. I have no confirmation about this whatsoever, so you won't catch me saying anything publicly. Tony, however, believes his wife was sleeping with her manager."

"Manager?"

"At Congressman Parnell's campaign office."

Casey eyed the real estate agent as she got into her car and drove off. "You get the feeling that we're missing something big? We have a dead suspect. We're pretty sure he's the killer. So why is everyone giving us a different story?"

Al got into the car and buckled his seat belt. "Just because everyone's in bed with everyone else doesn't mean jack. It's more about the ripple effect. Someone's murdered, and we get called in and have to dig through all of it to find out why. One thing leads to another. And sometimes it gets ugly. People don't like it, but that's our job."

"And now we've got someone involving a US congressman."

"Someone in his office, you mean. Whether it's actually Parnell or not matters little. At this point it is unsubstantiated rumor. Therefore my suggestion to you, if you value your career, is keep his name specifically to yourself until that time when it becomes relevant."

"And how do we know when it's relevant?"

"Not just when, but *if*. Trust me. We'll know. That man's got friends in high places at the PD. So for now, we note it and move on. We can ask about an affair, just no name-dropping. No sense committing career suicide based on rumors. Capisce?"

"Where do we go next?"

"Personally? I'd call up Mr. Valentine. Get him down to the Hall and figure out if he can shed some light on why his wife is lying. That, at least, we know isn't a rumor. Damned hard to close out a murder case when everyone else's agendas don't match ours."

Casey called Devin Valentine's cell phone. "Sorry to bother you at work, Mr. Valentine. But we have a few more questions. Can you come to the Hall of Justice?"

"Not at the moment," Devin said over the sound of an engine running, then a high pitched steady beep, the sort that might come from a truck backing up. "I'm on a jobsite with about twenty men waiting on orders. A lot of heavy equipment moving around right now."

"We can drive out there if it helps."

"Yeah, okay. If it doesn't take too long."

"Tell me where."

He gave the address, adding, "Not too far from Fisherman's Wharf."

"I know right where it is. See you in a few."

The location was a ten-story high-rise currently being retrofitted. Both Casey and Al were given hard hats on arrival and told to wait near the guard shack, and someone would be there to take them up, or find out if Valentine was coming down.

The latter, apparently, because he appeared at the guard shack about five minutes later. "Hey, sorry about making you drive all the way out here. Just, when we have people working on those open floors at the top, you can't let your guard down, even for a second."

"We understand," Al said, craning his neck upward. "Nice-looking building."

"It's coming along. Just the penthouse floors left. I tell you. With all the new restrictions placed on building heights blocking water views, finding something like this come on the market? Deal of the century."

"Used to be a bank, wasn't it?"

"At one time. So what are you here for?"

Al deferred to Casey, who opened his notebook, saying, "We just wanted to clarify a few things. On the morning that Trudy was killed, you were at home getting ready for work when your wife went running?"

"Yeah."

"What time did you say that was?"

"Seven. Same time as every morning. Why?"

"Just trying to pinpoint times is all. And you left for work when?"

"Not quite ten minutes later."

Casey noted it. "Any chance you got the time wrong?"

"No. I gave you the Starbucks receipt. That's about a block from here."

"Your wife, I mean. When she left."

"Oh. Definitely not. I looked at the clock. Why?"

"Double-checking times is all. Trudy's husband says his wife left maybe five after seven?"

"That'd be about right. I saw her from the window."

Casey looked up from his notebook. "From your bedroom?"

"The front room, actually. I'd gone downstairs by then and was just getting ready to leave for work myself."

"Got it."

Devin looked at his watch. "Anything else? We're short. It gets expensive if I'm down here instead of up there."

Al gave a slight nod, and Casey asked, "Your wife mentioned that you're having an alarm installed. Something about intruders?"

Devin rubbed at the back of his neck then gave an exasperated sigh. "I told you my wife had a nervous breakdown?"

"We weren't aware, no."

"Yeah. Well, I'm sure it's because of the murder, but it's starting up again. The meds that used to keep her calm..." He shook his head. "Things missing. The forgetfulness. Jumping at every sound. Thinking that someone is following her or plotting something that isn't even remotely true. Which is why I had one of my guys come out and install some security cameras—if nothing else, to show that *nothing* is going on."

"She said something about hang-up calls?"

"Honestly? I've never been home when she's gotten one, so I can't say. What I can tell you is that for my wife, it's been a nightmare. She lost her teaching job because she was so paranoid. I'm just trying to get the bills paid the best I can, or I'd be there with her."

"She also mentioned something about a noise the other night?"

"That I did hear. But I checked. There was nothing there."

"Anyone call the police on any of this?"

"For what? How do you know what's real and what isn't? My suggestion? Call her doctor. Maybe *you* can convince him that whatever he's got her on, it's not working. I've tried."

"Was Trudy having an affair, Mr. Valentine?"

The question clearly caught him by surprise, and his face turned red as he looked from Casey to Al, then back. "What the hell does that have to do with anything?"

"Funny thing," Casey said. "We were talking to the real estate agent, and she mentioned an affair."

Devin shook his head. "This is ridiculous. Even if Trudy and I were having an affair, I would never have killed her. I—" He looked away, ran his fingers through his hair. "You don't think my wife killed—? Oh my God..." Devin turned, took a couple of agitated steps, then faced Al once more. "Are you saying the person who killed Trudy is *not* that guy who got run over by a car? That's what the news was saying. That he might even be this Strangler person you're looking for."

Al, his voice laced with concern, said, "We're simply conducting a thorough investigation. We have to look at every lead. Which brings me to my next question. What do you think would happen if she found out? About you and Trudy?"

"I have no idea. Marcie was furious at Trudy for simply suggesting that she have those damned eucalyptus trees behind our houses taken out. I can't imagine what she'd do if she thought Trudy and I were—I love my wife. But the last six months, between her breakdown and the doctor bills, we hit our insurance limit. I was a mess. I just needed someone to talk to, and—Trudy was there for me. That's it. But my wife...She's already messed up as it is. This would ruin her."

"Yo! Val!" The shout came from the man who had given Casey and Al the hard hats. "They need you in the penthouse!"

He looked at his watch. "I really have to go, so if there's nothing else?"

"Actually," Al said, "one more question. Why do you think it was that your wife arrived *after* the homicide occurred, but she left *before* Trudy did?"

Devin's brow furrowed as though he'd never thought of the possibility before now. "I have no idea. I—I suppose Marcie could have taken a different route? A longer one?"

"That's probably it," Al said. He smiled. "Thanks again for your time. And good luck with the project," he added, nodding toward the upper floors of the building.

They returned the hard hats to the man at the guard shack then walked to the car. Once they were out of earshot, Casey said, "So nothing about an affair with anyone from Parnell's campaign."

"Yeah. Seems he took it rather personal."

"You think Devin did it? To keep his wife from finding out?"

"Not sure how, unless he magically appeared in two places. In the meantime, let's rule out your dead suspect before you start hooking up spurned spouses."

On their way back to the Hall, they grabbed a quick late lunch then stopped off at the morgue to see if there were any results on the pending autopsies.

Investigator Melton happened to be eating lunch at his desk when they got there. A sandwich in one hand and a pen in the other, he was doodling on a pad while he ate, coloring in the details of a muscled man in a dark-blue cape and a black mask and the letters DI emblazoned on the front of his superhero costume.

"DI?" Casey asked.

"Death Investigator. Solves crime in a single leap of logic."

Al eyed the drawing as Melton finished his sandwich. "Let me know when he comes to town. We could use his help."

"Funny," Melton said, setting his pen down. The bulletin board next to his desk was covered with similar illustrations. An accomplished artist, Melton moonlighted as a coroner's investigator, while working on his true passion, being an illustrator. "And if you're here for the autopsy reports, get in line."

"Come on," Al replied. "There's gotta be something you can feed us?"

"How about the same line the pathologist told me? Budget cuts. One body at a time. Why do you think I'm eating at my desk? Someone has to man the phones while the clerks get lunch."

"You have to have something by now," Al told him. "The captain's ready to boot us back to patrol if we don't solve this."

"She got to one. I think yours," he said to Casey. "The victim, not the suspect."

"And?" Casey asked.

"Definitely choked, but the bruising doesn't match up to your serial Strangler cases."

"How?" Casey asked.

"I'll show you."

He woke up his computer, accessing photos from a case file. "This is the second Strangler victim, the one that led us to believe we were actually dealing with a serial killer. See this?" He pointed to the photo of the victim's neck.

Casey leaned in for a better view. "What about it?"

"No bruising at all in the front. That crisscross pattern beneath her jaw and the side of her neck is bruising from the suspect's watch or buttons on his sleeve, we think. Something hard enough to bruise her. Similar to markings we found on the other Strangler victims. Like he had her in a carotid hold and kept it tight until she died. Knew what he was doing."

The carotid restraint being the suspected cause of death was a detail they'd held from the press. And would continue to do so until the suspect was caught.

"Not so with your Presidio victim. Come on back and I'll show you." They followed him through the offices into the morgue, its antiseptic smell evident the moment he opened the door. He led them to one of the refrigerated drawers, which he pulled open. "This is your Presidio victim. Probably see it better in the photos beforehand, but see all this bruising around her neck?"

In fact, the bruising continued all the way around.

"You can actually see where his fingertips pressed in. Definitely more violent," Melton said. "And definitely different than the suspected Strangler cases."

"Is there any way we can actually pin her murder on my dead suspect?"

"As a matter of fact, yes. Mind you, it's only preliminary. Nothing confirmed officially. But she fought back. He had her around the neck, and she scratched at the back of his hands."

Al looked skeptical. "How can you tell, when he ate the pavement after that car hit him? Gotta be covered in road rash."

"Except in this case she had a pretty good chunk of his skin beneath her fingernail. Fits like a missing jigsaw piece to the corresponding hole she gouged from the back of his hand." He opened a file folder, showed a photo of the skin recovered from beneath her fingernail, the doctor holding it out with tweezers next to the shallow wound on his hand. "Like I said, just a matter of formality waiting for a DNA match. But even the doc says he's your guy. Or rather, they had close contact within a very short period before their respective deaths."

"Thanks," Casey said, somewhat disappointed he wasn't going to be the one who solved the case of the decade.

"Tough break, kid," Al told him as they walked back up to Homicide. "Would've been nice if it was the Strangler. Wrap it all up in a neat package. But it's not. Which means you have to look at the whole motive thing."

"What motive? The guy committed a copycat murder by choking a girl near a landmark. Happens all the time in serial killer cases, or they wouldn't have a name for it."

Al dropped his hat on the coatrack hook. "If you say so."

"Why? You think it's something different?"

"I'm not the one writing it up," he said as Casey's phone rang. "I'm just saying, cover all your bases."

Casey answered on the next ring. "Kellog. Homicide."

"Hi." A woman's voice. "This is Jenn Barstow...from the *Union-Examiner*. I was wondering if you had a moment. I was hoping to talk to you about those old cases."

"Jenn—Miss Barstow," he corrected, worried that anyone listening in might misconstrue their relationship. "Can I call you back? I'm in the middle of a big investigation right now."

"Sure."

He disconnected, then got to work on the Presidio report, completely forgetting about returning Jenn Barstow's call. It was well after six by the time he and Al left for the day.

Al grabbed his hat and coat on the way out the door. "How's that report coming?"

"The way I see it," Casey said, buttoning up his jacket. "With that piece of skin matching up to the suspect's hand? We know who our killer is. Pretty sure I can get this wrapped up in a day or two."

"Positive thinking, eh, College Boy? Let me know how that turns out for you."

NINETEEN

Jenn Barstow's feet ached from the high-heeled shoes as she tried walking across the restroom floor at their office building the next morning. "Why can't I wear flats?" she asked. "These shoes suck. Even more than the red ones the other night."

Taryn eyed her with approval. "It's all about the way you look."

"Like a call girl?"

"Trust me. You look nothing like a call girl. And if you did, at least it'd be a high-priced call girl," Taryn said as she put all the newly purchased makeup into a zippered bag, then set it on the counter. "The point is, you succeeded the other night. I can't believe you actually kissed him."

"It was more a peck on the cheek."

"Whatever it was, it was pure genius. He kissed you back. Which means there is *no* way he'll ignore you now."

"Ignore me? He didn't even call me back yesterday."

"Because it was over the phone. Trust me. You show up in person? He's going to listen. Cops like talking to pretty girls. Especially girls they've kissed."

Jenn eyed her reflection in the bathroom mirror. The added blond highlights gave her hair a slight shimmer, bringing out the blue in her eyes. The hair she liked. The makeup...not so much. She wasn't used to eyeliner, thick mascara, and blush. "The lipstick has to go," she said, reaching for a tissue.

Taryn slapped her hand away. "Don't touch."

"A girl shouldn't have to be all made-up to get someone to listen to her."

"In a perfect world, true. But when it comes to getting someone's attention to those cases, do you want to leave it to chance? Or do you want to use every tool in your arsenal?"

"Tools? Hardly."

"You have no idea what you're sporting, do you?" Taryn shook her head, grabbed the makeup bag, then started pushing Jenn from the bathroom into the newsroom. "Watch what happens. Go tell the boss where you're going."

"Are you kidding?"

"Not *what* you're doing there. Just *where*. Give it a try."

They stopped in front of his office. "Larry?" Jenn said. "I have to head to the Hall of Justice. I might be gone an hour or two."

Their editor looked up. "Don't you have—" His gaze widened slightly, and it was a moment before he finished. "Take all the time you need."

"Thanks," she said, hiding her surprise. After the way he'd gotten on her about crashing the press conference, she fully expected him to order her to stay clear of the PD.

She started to turn away when Marty walked up, saw her, and nearly dropped his coffee mug. "What the—"

Momentarily stunned, she was glad when Taryn grabbed her arm, leading her back to her desk.

"Was that Jenn?" he asked the editor. "Sizzle, sizzle..."

"Get back to work, Marty."

"See?" Taryn whispered.

And Jenn might have believed it herself. Except the heels definitely sucked. By the time she arrived at the Hall, then walked the two blocks from the parking garage, she felt like a kid wearing her mother's shoes. Somehow she managed to keep her upright bearing long enough to inquire if she could speak to

Sergeant Kellog about a homicide. The officer at the desk smiled at her. "I'll check for you. Name?"

"Jenn Barstow." She decided to leave off her affiliation with the press, which never seemed to go over well.

He called upstairs, and she was glad when he simply asked, "Kellog in…? Yeah. Got it. Thanks." He hung up, gave a slight shrug. "Sorry, miss. Not in. But they said they're expecting him back anytime. Would you like to leave a message?"

"No, thanks."

The elevator bank, she decided, was her best bet of catching him, and she found a spot just inside where she could watch the doors that led to the parking garage as well. She checked the time, wondering how long she should wait. At least her editor wasn't expecting her back anytime soon, and she figured she could give it at least thirty minutes before the shock of her appearance wore off and her editor realized she was someplace she was told not to be.

About twenty minutes later, just when she was certain her feet were going to fall off from the damned shoes, she saw Casey and his partner in the breezeway near the morgue. They pushed through the glass doors then walked straight to the elevator.

She hurried over as the elevator door opened. "Sergeant Kellog?"

Casey's partner stepped onto the elevator, and she thought for a moment he was going to follow. But when he saw her, he stopped. The elevator door closed behind him. "Jenn…"

"Hi."

His gaze swept downward, then back up. "You look nice."

A warmth flushed through her cheeks at his tone. Hoping he didn't notice, she gave him her best business smile. "Thanks. I was hoping you had a few minutes."

"I wish I could. But you're the press."

"Please."

He took a deep breath, as though weighing his decisions. "Five minutes. You mind if we talk outside?" He held out his hand, indicating the area between the lobby and the morgue. "Fewer people around to interrupt."

"Sure."

He held the door for her, and the moment she stepped out, she crossed her arms, trying to ward off the chill, wishing she'd had the sense to wear something a bit warmer than a dress without a coat.

"So, Miss Barstow…"

"Jenn."

"Jenn."

"I know you're busy." She gave an apologetic smile. "And I'm being presumptuous to even assume that no one has looked into any similarities. But with the recent attention to these newer cases, I was hoping you—or someone in your office—would look into that case I mentioned the other day at the press conference. The murder of that prostitute? She was strangled like the other victims."

"Do you mind if I ask why the interest? Are we talking journalistic or otherwise?"

This was it, she realized. She had to tread carefully. Make the right impression. "I—I knew one of the victims. Bella Orlando."

"How?"

"My sister."

"The prostitute?"

She wasn't sure if she imagined the slight step back on his part, but she knew she couldn't let him walk away. Not now when she was so close. "A few nights before she was killed, she told me something. I should have listened. I mean, I did, but—"

Although his tone was polite, his posture shifted to a stance that told her his attention was waning.

"The last time I saw her, she—she'd been attacked by someone. It scared her. I was scared for her. I thought maybe she'd go to rehab after that, but—" It was a moment before Jenn could get past her thoughts. "It was the last time I saw her before she was killed."

"And what was it that happened?"

"She said that someone tried to drag her into the alley by her hair. She might not have gotten away if not for two, um, men who happened to be there. She said that one of them pulled a knife and scared the guy off."

His brows raised. "By her *hair*? Was there a police report?"

"No." Jenn shivered as the wind bit into the thin fabric of her blouse. "I tried to get her to call. She said it wouldn't matter anyway. Who was going to believe her? She was, um, high, and well…" Jenn shrugged, not sure what else she could say. "I just want someone to look into it. She was strangled, and it was around the same time and—and that's it."

He studied her face a moment, then pulled out a small notebook from his breast pocket of his suit. "I know you gave me your card, but let me get your info again."

She recited her desk and cell phone numbers, which he wrote down.

"You realize that case was before my time in Homicide? I can't promise anything," he said, walking her back into the lobby. "But I'll see what I can find."

"Thanks."

He left her at the elevator, and she continued on and out the front doors, calling Taryn on her cell phone. "You were right. He talked to me."

"See? It was the clothes. So what happened?"

"Besides that I froze my ass off?"

"And looked good doing it, right?"

"He said he'd check into it. Then he took my phone number."

"So it all works out in the end."

"Unless of course he discovers I may have been…less than truthful about a few things," Jenn said as she walked out to the street. She flagged a taxi. No way was she walking the two blocks to the parking garage in these damned heels. "Like befriending his mother to get to him and—Well, it's not important. If I'm lucky, he won't find out. Besides. I can't get in that much trouble, can I?"

TWENTY

Sergeant Haynes followed Casey onto the elevator, then up to the fourth floor.

"So who was the woman I saw you talking to outside?" Haynes asked as they walked into the Homicide office a few minutes later.

"No one," he said, dropping a file folder onto his desk, then glancing into the lieutenant's office to check if he was there, maybe even listening. Last thing Casey wanted was for anyone to know he was talking to the press—even if he wasn't really giving her information. The lieutenant was in, and the door was open.

"Definitely a head-turner," Haynes said.

"Aren't you married?" Casey asked, more to shut him up than anything else.

"A guy can look."

Casey ignored him and strode across the room to the Cold Case office, needing to have a look at those cases Jenn Barstow had mentioned. If, in fact, they were related, it could be the break they were looking for.

He knocked on the open door, and one of the investigators, Pat Correa, glanced over.

"I have a favor," he asked her.

"Shoot."

"You know anything about an old hooker murder? Strangulation. Happened in the Tenderloin a few months before the first Landmark case. Victim was a Bella Orlando."

She pondered the question. "Now that you mention it, I remember a couple of prostitute murders. Why?"

"Some reporter thinks they're related to the Strangler. Told her I'd check into it."

"You're welcome to look. Bottom shelf. That's where Timms asked us to put any unsolved strangulations."

He glanced over at the bookshelf against the wall, the industrial-brown metal scratched and gouged from years of use. There were ten black binders on the bottom row. "All of them?"

"Only two. The others are definitely not hookers. But they are strangulations."

"Has Al gone through these?" Casey asked.

"All I know is that we pulled every cold case strangulation, wrote up a report, and submitted it to him. You can have a copy of that, too." She accessed something on her computer, hit the print button, and a moment later, the printer whirred to life, spitting out several pages.

He took the report and the two murder books to his desk. Al was not in the office, which gave him enough freedom to take his time without worrying that he'd crossed some line by assisting a reporter who wasn't even assigned to the crime desk at her paper.

The victims, he saw at a glance, showed "prostitute" as the occupation. The first one had been killed almost a year ago, and Jenn Barstow's sister around seven months ago. Other than that, not much to go on, except that they were strangled. Not a landmark in sight.

Which meant what?

Autopsies, he thought. That should tell him something.

"Earth to College Boy?"

Casey looked up to see Al staring at him. "Yeah?"

"I asked if you'd finished the who's-screwing-who report from your contact with the real estate agent."

"On the printer," Casey said, eyeing the summary of the cold case strangulations that Correa had printed for him. He picked it up. "Hey, Al. Remember the reporter from the lobby?"

"Church mouse?"

"The one," he replied. "She's the woman who stopped me at the elevator."

Al whistled. "You're right. She has changed. So what was she doing here?"

"Asking about the prostitute murders again."

"I don't care how good-looking that reporter is. The last thing you need is a reputation of talking to the press out of turn."

"The victim in this case was her sister."

Al looked down at the binder, then back at him. "That's sort of big. Why would she keep something like that to herself?"

"Does it matter? What does is that I took a look at the cases, and I think I found something in the autopsies. You remember Melton telling us that maybe the real Strangler was using a carotid hold? Well, that might have been the case with her sister. Like the guy was holding something against her neck. A piece of pipe. Asphyxiation with an instrument."

"What about the other hooker?"

Casey opened the second binder to the crime scene photos. "It doesn't fit the Strangler MO. One, she was killed inside a motel room, and witnesses heard arguing for several minutes beforehand. Two, broken hyoid bone. A lot more violent in comparison to the others cases, even the Presidio victim."

"So what do you plan to do about the one you can't rule out?"

Casey leaned back in his chair, trying to determine if Al was serious. The man's expression never wavered. "Look into it. The FBI profiler suggested the Strangler probably killed before. Hookers are easy prey. Of course, there's this whole landmark thing. There isn't one cited in the case."

Al slapped the topmost binder. "Can't hurt to look."

"Exactly." He took the copies of the cover sheets and the witness lists from the murder of Jenn Barstow's sister and slid them into his portfolio notebook. Grabbing his keys, he started for the door.

"Where you off to?" Al asked.

"You just said it can't hurt to look. Thought I'd drive out there."

"Take a backup. I don't care how long ago it happened."

"You busy?"

"Very."

Casey looked around the room, nearly empty except for Haynes and Zwingler. Deciding he didn't want to field any more questions about the reporter from Haynes, he asked Zwingler, who said, "You're gonna owe me for this."

"We'll start a tab." He gave him a rundown of the homicide on the elevator ride down and on the drive over.

"I remember this case," Zwingler said. "Not a lot to go on. You have any idea what you're looking for?"

"Not a clue. Figured we could do a little knock and talk with some of the witnesses. Maybe we can turn up something that was missed the first time around."

"Sounds good." Zwingler looked over the pages of involved parties that Casey had printed. "Got a few witnesses who live in the area—assuming they're still there. The security guard who found her, Francis Dunmore." He laughed. "Who the hell names their kid Francis anymore?"

"Hit him up first?"

"Nah. He doesn't live in the city, and the company's all the way across town. That leaves Gladys White and Samir Singh."

"Probably a waste of time coming out here anyway," Casey said, recalling what he'd read in the report. "Singh's store was closed at the time, and he said he didn't hear anything."

"They all say that. Funny what some of them remember at times with the right encouragement."

Casey found parking about a block away on the next street over. "So," Zwingler said while they walked, "what made you pick this case from all the cold cases sitting in there?"

"That reporter from the press conference. She's apparently been following the cases," he said.

"The nerd girl?"

"Not so nerdy anymore."

"She's the one we saw you talking to in front of the morgue?"

"We?"

"Maybe you were so wrapped up in the conversation you didn't see us watching you from the lobby. You want my advice? Getting in bed with the press, literally *or* figuratively? Not a good idea."

"Who said anything about sleeping with her?"

"About half the guys who saw you talking to her. Besides, I've seen it a million times. You're single. She's single. Why else would she have gotten all gussied up?"

"Not going to happen," he said as he and Zwingler walked to an L-shaped alley that ran alongside and behind a small market and other businesses. The alley was unremarkable. Dumpsters up against the walls, broken glass on the ground, and an assortment of cigarette butts and used condoms. He thought about Zwingler's comment earlier. What was he even looking for after all this time? Something everyone else had overlooked that pointed to the killer?

Yeah, wouldn't that be nice. Waltz in, solve the serial killer case of the decade in one day.

"Where was she killed?" Zwingler asked.

"Here, behind the market, beside the Dumpster."

"Good place for it," Zwingler said. "Protected from view from either direction unless someone's looking out that back window of the market. And at that hour? Not likely."

They left the alley and walked out to the street in front of the market. Three boys, probably late teens, stood on the corner across the street. One looked up, saw Casey and Zwingler, said something to the other two—undoubtedly pegging them for cops—and they all took off in different directions.

"So much for that drug deal," Zwingler said. He eyed the witness list. "Let's go see what Gladys has to say."

TWENTY-ONE

Gladys White's apartment was located on the second floor directly opposite the market and the massage parlor. Judging from her age at the time, mideighties, Casey hoped she'd still be living there and not in some nursing home—assuming she was still alive.

But alive she was, and very much in charge of her faculties. When she opened the door, her deeply lined face lit up when Casey told her why they were there.

"Come in, come in," she said, holding the door wider. "About time someone started investigating that case. Poor girl."

"You remember what happened?" Casey asked.

"There isn't really much to remember at all," she said, tottering over to a battered floral armchair in front of the window. She sat with some difficulty, her hands shaking as she gripped the chair's arms. "I was sitting right here when I heard someone screaming." She nodded toward the window. "There. Across the street. I saw the woman running from the alley, crying." Gladys looked up at Casey, her smile more apologetic. "I'm afraid by the time I got out of my chair and made it to the phone, I heard sirens. So you see, Sergeant, I don't know much about the murder at all."

"You were up that late?"

"No, I was sleeping. Easier for me to breathe sitting up. I woke when I heard the screaming."

"I don't suppose you ever saw anyone hanging about that didn't belong?"

"In this neighborhood?" Her laughter turned into a cough. It was a moment before she could continue. "Darned bronchitis... Where was I? A better question is who I knew. As my late husband used to say, this window is my life."

Zwingler stepped in. "Who *did* you know?"

She looked out the window, then closed her eyes.

A minute or more passed by, and Casey, worried she'd fallen asleep, said, "Gladys?"

She held up one gnarled finger but didn't open her eyes. Finally she tapped her temple as she looked at him. "Works a little slower than it used to..." She pointed to the window. "No one I knew. But I saw a girl, the one who screamed."

"A girl?" There was nothing about any other witnesses. "You're sure?"

"I used to see her every now and then. An Asian girl. Fairly young."

"How young?"

"Heavens. Teens? Twenties? She was crying and ran from the alley into Mr. Singh's shop across the street."

"I don't suppose you knew her name?"

"No. I saw a taxi come later that day, and she got in it. Never saw her again after that. I expect Mr. Singh knows who she was, since he was the one talking to her. I don't see him out and about as often as I used to." She sighed as she leaned back in her chair and looked out the window. "It was nice when he hired the security guard. We felt a lot safer, but, well, the girl was murdered anyway, and I think times are hard now."

When she had nothing further to add, Casey and Zwingler thanked her and let themselves out.

Zwingler looked up at her apartment, then over toward the store across the street. "She'd certainly have a good enough view of the store."

"Except Samir Singh said the store was closed and he didn't see anything."

"So he lied about this girl? Gotta wonder what for."

They crossed the street, then entered the shop, where Casey detected a faint scent of curry and spices. A man of Indian descent, late fifties, early sixties, stood behind the counter watching the two sergeants warily as they approached. Casey held up his identification and star. "Mr. Singh? I'm Sergeant Kellog, SFPD, and my partner, Sergeant Zwingler."

The man gave a slight nod to acknowledge them but said nothing.

"We're here looking into the murder of the woman behind your store a while back."

"The prostitute? Yes. I remember the officers coming by to ask about it. The store was closed at the time. I didn't see what happened."

"I realize that. I'm hoping you might remember something that might have been overlooked at the time."

"Or," Zwingler said, "maybe heard anything about it afterward that might help."

The man shook his head. "No. Unfortunately not. I'm sorry…"

"One of the witnesses seems to remember you talking to someone—a young Asian girl—right after the murder."

Singh shook his head. "Bad things happen all the time around here. That's why I had to hire a security guard, just so my customers would feel safe shopping. It didn't work. And after the murder, even he quit."

"You understand you are not a suspect in this? All we're asking for is who it was you were talking to. She might have seen something."

"I don't know who you're talking about."

Why would he lie about this? Casey was at a dead end, and he referred to his notes, trying to come up with something, anything. He looked over at Zwingler, who gave a slight shrug, and all Casey could think of was what Al would do.

Of course, he thought, closing his notebook. He looked at Mr. Singh, attempting to smile with his eyes with what he hoped was something akin to Al's fatherly concern. "Surely you remember something else?"

Singh merely stared, and Zwingler leaned toward Casey, searching his face. "You don't look so well. You okay?"

Casey turned, coughing into his hand. "Sorry. Something caught in my throat," he replied, then saw the CLOSED sign on the door. What the hell, he thought, and walked over, peering out the window. "Lot of violence in this neighborhood?"

"All the time," Singh said.

"Like those three punks dealing drugs when we pulled up. You saw them, didn't you, Zwingler?"

"Scattered like rats when they saw us."

Casey nodded out toward the street. "They're back. What do you think would happen if they thought Mr. Singh was giving us information about them?"

"Expect they wouldn't be too happy," Zwingler said.

"My thoughts exactly." Casey turned the CLOSED sign so it was facing out to the street. Then he looked at Singh. "I have no problem calling narcotics out here right now." He held up his radio. "Then informing them that we received info from you."

"I haven't told you anything."

"You think that matters? I only hope the punks out front don't think so." Casey keyed his radio, which caused Zwingler's to crackle with static.

"Wait," Singh said. "I did see a girl."

"And what did she see?"

"The dumb guy."

"The dumb guy?"

Singh nodded. "Or dumb door guy. She was crying, and her English is not very good. But she made this motion." He crossed his arms over his neck. "She told me he used a stick. Over and over. The dumb guy. Like the wizard."

"Did this girl have a name?"

"I only knew her as Ping. I don't think that was her real name."

"And some reason why you didn't mention it at the time?"

"I wanted to. But she begged me. She said they would kill her if she talked to any police. I believed her."

"Who would kill her?"

"The snakeheads."

Casey and Zwingler exchanged glances, and Zwingler said, "Snakeheads?"

Singh nodded. "The Chinese gang that runs the massage parlor."

"This girl. She worked at the massage parlor down the street?"

"Yes."

"She still there?"

"No. A taxi came that very day and took her away. I haven't seen her since."

When it was clear Mr. Singh had nothing more to add, they left, then walked down to the massage parlor.

It was located a half block down the street from the market and adjacent to the same alley where the murdered prostitute had been found. A green sign reading MASSAGE hung from the building, a once-white facade that was now gray with filth. Rusted iron bars covered all the first-floor windows as well as the front door, where a camera looked down into the entry. Any clientele walking into that particular establishment were undoubtedly paying for something more than a back massage.

"Nice place," Zwingler said as Casey knocked on the door.

An Asian woman, her dark hair flecked with gray strands, answered, saw their IDs, then shook her head. "No English. No English." She closed the door before he could get a word in edgewise and didn't answer when he knocked a second time.

"That was a bust," Casey said.

"You weren't expecting she'd still be here, were you? They probably moved her the moment the police ended up on their doorstep."

"One could hope," he said, even though Zwingler was probably right. Most of these girls were victims of human trafficking, smuggled into the country for the express purpose of prostitution, then shuffled from one so-called massage parlor to another, not only to keep the girls from attaching to customers who might help them, but to keep the police at bay.

"Maybe vice will have something on her."

But they both knew that would be fruitless, and as he and Zwingler walked back to the car, he wondered if any of those unfortunate women ever escaped that life.

"You find anything worthwhile?" Al asked when they returned to the office.

"Depends," Zwingler said, "on your definition. We got a suspect name."

"How's that not worthwhile?"

"Let me count the ways," Zwingler replied. "It's not the most *viable* name we've ever run across. It's officially hearsay. The woman who saw the suspect and provided the name is nowhere to be found. That, and it was reported to us after the fact with a little coercion."

Al raised his brows. "What sort of coercion?"

"College Boy threatened to sick narcotics on the witness."

"*Our* College Boy?"

"Yeah. I think he's been corrupted."

Al glanced over at Casey, asking, "So what was the name?"

"Dumb Guy or Dumb Door."

And Zwingler said, "Don't forget the thing about the stick and the wizard."

"That, too," Casey said. "But a lot was lost in translation. According to our witness, the girl spoke very little English, and she's no longer available to interview."

Al walked over, read the name on Casey's report. "Dumb Door...stick...Wizard? What's a stick got to do with it?"

"Not sure. But Singh said she crossed her arms, then placed them over her neck. I'm assuming she was describing how the girl was strangled."

"So maybe the guy was holding a stick in his hand, or he used it in a carotid restraint?"

"It fits."

The lieutenant walked in, and Al told him what Casey had found.

"What's your gut instinct?" Timms asked Casey. "You think it's related?"

"I don't think we can discount it."

"Anything else that can be followed up? Bring us more leads?"

"Possibly," Casey said. "The victim was in rehab just prior to the murder and made some statement about having been attacked before. Maybe she reported it there."

"Follow up on it."

"I figured you'd want me to finish up the Presidio murder."

"Isn't your suspect dead? Or did that change between now and then?"

"It hasn't. But what about Congressman Parnell and his insistence that we put forth all our efforts?"

"Last I heard, he wasn't heading this unit. If we have our choice between a dead suspect and a live killer, we'll take the latter. Follow up on your rehab lead. The Presidio murder will be here when you get back."

TWENTY-TWO

Unfortunately, it wasn't simply a matter of driving back out to the Tenderloin and the clinic to ask questions. Because of privacy laws in the medical field, Casey needed a warrant for their victim's information.

"Why," Casey asked Al after returning from the district attorney's office, "is it even necessary to get a warrant for a dead patient? It's not like they're going to care anymore."

"Because some dimwit somewhere figured that privacy of health information trumps the need for the cops to know. My guess? Some politician trying to avoid revealing some relative has a dreaded disease or that insanity runs in the family, thereby ruining his political career. One more hoop for us to jump through to catch a killer. Whatever. You get it?"

Casey patted his coat pocket.

"Let's go then."

The rehab clinic was located a few blocks from where Bella Orlando was murdered. In this neighborhood, they'd be pegged as cops the moment they left the car. It was one of the few exceptions Casey made to his rule of not violating parking laws, and he parked in the red zone in front of a corner liquor store. The clinic was a few doors down, tucked between a hotel that offered daily rates and a night club that advertised LIVE GIRLS. Men and women, their gaunt faces smudged with dirt, sat on the gray sidewalk on both sides of the street, their backs against the walls, some holding backpacks, others with large black plastic bags that probably contained their worldly possessions. Those closest to

Casey watched as he and Al strode down the street, one even holding up a cup, asking for money.

Casey hesitated until Al said, "Negative, Boy Scout. You can give to the homeless shelter. At least you know where the money's going to."

They reached the clinic, and Casey pulled open the door, then held it for Al, both stepping into a small reception area. A few clients sat in the chairs in reception, one woman bouncing her foot up and down as she waited. She stopped abruptly when she saw them walk in. A counter separated the space from the office, where an auburn-haired woman sat at a desk, absorbed in reading something on the screen of her cell phone. She glanced up and saw them. "Can I help you?"

Casey showed his star and credentials. "We need to check into the records of a past patient."

"Sorry. But we don't give out that info. HIPAAs, you know."

"We have a warrant." He pulled it from his pocket and handed it to her.

She unfolded it, scanned the contents, then stood. "Can you wait a sec? I need to show this to the manager."

"Sure thing."

She returned shortly. "This way," she said.

They heard a buzz coming from the door. Casey opened it, and the secretary pointed down a narrow hallway. "Third door on the right. Dr. Arbuckle is who you want to talk to."

The floor dipped in some spots, the boards beneath the drab brown carpet squeaking as Casey and Al walked to the indicated room. A sign on the door read DR. ARBUCKLE.

Inside, a gray-haired woman sat behind a desk, working at her computer. She closed a thick file that she'd apparently been reading. "Officers?"

Casey introduced himself and Al then added, "We're hoping you can provide us with some information on a past patient. Bella Orlando."

"The name's not familiar. What's this regarding?"

"She was murdered about six, seven months ago."

"Of course. That occurred right before I started working here. I cover the weekends only, though. Sit, please. I'll look up her file."

She typed something on her keyboard, checked the monitor. "Not a lot here. Heroin addict with a history of prostitution, trying to kick...Second time in, left before treatment was over. No reason given."

Al leaned forward, smiling. "Anyone working here back then who might recall the woman? Or any of her visitors or stories? Why she left?"

She stared at the computer screen. "Um...Yes. Her therapist. I'll get her for you." She picked up the phone and made a call. "Char? Can you come on down? Two police detectives are here to talk about Bella Orlando."

A few minutes later, a stout, middle-aged woman entered, glancing at Casey and Al before turning her attention to the doctor. "I've got a session starting in just a few minutes."

Al stood. "This shouldn't take long. Please have a seat."

She settled into Al's vacated chair. "I'm not sure what I can offer. She wasn't here all that long."

Al nodded at Casey to take over the questioning. He opened his notebook, poised his pen over paper. "What do you remember about her?"

"With as many patients as I've worked with over the years, I think the only reason she stands out at all is because she was murdered after she left here."

Al smiled. "Anything at all will help."

"I remember she was nice. She really wanted to get out of that life, but..." The woman gave a slight shrug. "I think if she could have left the city and somehow gotten away from that pimp of hers, the methadone might have worked. In a city like this, it's hard when you have no available support system. Medicaid can only take you so far."

"She ever talk about it?" Casey asked. "Anything that ever happened to her out there? Anyone in particular?"

"No one that stands out. It was always about what she was going to do once she was clean. Write a book about her life and her sucky childhood. There were some definite abandonment issues in her past. I do remember her saying that working the streets was nothing like *Pretty Woman*, where Prince Charming comes to sweep you off your feet. It was usually dirty men trolling for a quick trick. Other than that…? I couldn't tell you."

"What about someone attacking her? Before she came in for treatment the last time?"

"Not that I recall. But we would've noted any injuries in her records."

Casey glanced at Dr. Arbuckle. "Is there anything there?"

"Nothing stands out," she said. "At least there were no visible injuries documented."

"Anything else?" he asked the therapist.

"Honestly? Not that I can remember."

The doctor glanced at the clock. "Thank you, Char. You should probably get to that session."

She stood and started from the room.

"Thanks," Casey said. Then, to the doctor, "Her sister mentioned that she'd talked about someone who attacked her right before she entered rehab that last time."

Char stopped in the doorway. "What sister?"

"Jenn Barstow," Casey said. "She's a reporter at the *Union-Examiner.*"

Char shook her head. "Reporter, maybe. Sister? No. That's the one thing I *definitely* remember about Bella. No family."

"What makes you think they're not related?"

"She blamed the foster system for *everything* that happened to her. Shuffled about until she ended up in a home with foster parents who only required her attendance when the social worker came by for monthly visits. That's how she landed on the streets. Needed some way to support herself."

Al asked, "You're sure about this? Her not having a sister?"

"Definitely. We have a lot of former foster children here. It'd be nice to think that every person who applies to take children in is picture perfect. And some are, which is when the system works. When it fails, it's an epic failure. Not surprisingly, a lot of them end up on drugs."

Casey glanced at Al, whose face remained impassive. The man was too much of a professional to let anything show—something Casey was grateful for at the moment—but he knew what was coming the moment they were out of earshot, and so he thanked the doctor and gave her his card. "If you turn up anyone else who can offer us some background on Bella, I'd appreciate a call."

"Of course."

Outside, Casey braced himself for Al's reaction.

Al, however, decided to wait until they were in the car. "What the hell?"

"How was I supposed to know?"

"By checking the facts. That was shoddy police work. Do you have any idea what could happen if this reporter ends up on the stand and it comes out that she lied?"

"People lie to us all the time. How is this any different?"

"Because we're talking about a potential witness in a murder case that's being splashed across the national news on a daily basis thanks to some other dimwit reporter from the same paper, who turned it into a tourist thing. And even if this homicide you're looking into isn't part of the Strangler cases, how do you know you're not being manipulated by some reporter who's suddenly decided to write a book or something?"

"She seemed sincere."

"You might want to rethink that lieutenant's test, kid. For someone with two college degrees, you amaze me with how much you don't know. She lied to you. Just be glad you found out now and not on the witness stand."

Casey bristled at the dig over rethinking the lieutenant's exam. He was as ready for that as he'd ever be. More important, though, he knew that Al was probably right about Jenn Barstow lying to him. What he needed to know was why, and the moment they got back to the office, he called and left a message, asking her to come down for a few more questions. And though it didn't do him any good to direct his anger at her, the longer he waited for a return call, he kept imagining what would happen if it turned out she *had* been manipulating him. What if she *was* writing a book, and he ended up in it?

To hell with waiting for her call, he thought. He was driving straight to her office and—

"Sergeant Kellog?"

Casey glanced up to see the secretary for Homicide standing beside his desk.

"This came for you while you were gone."

She handed him a manila envelope for interdepartment correspondence.

"Thanks."

"Everything okay?" she asked, still watching him.

"Fine. Just…a lot of paper work to get through."

She nodded then left, as he unwound the string that secured the envelope. Inside was a CD with a sticky note attached, reading: "Thought you might want to see this. A copy of the security video from Ghirardelli 211."

It wasn't signed. But there was only one person who knew he wanted to see it.

Becca.

The thought made him smile, and he inserted the CD into his computer and sat back to watch. His thoughts kept turning back toward Becca while he fast-forwarded through the surveillance video. The perfect time to text her. Ask if she'd sent over the CD. Then ask her out.

A proper date, not between calls. As incompatible as homicide and social life were, it made him wonder how anyone in here found a spouse. But then he looked around, realized how much older everyone there was. They were probably married before they ever got in.

Which didn't bode well for him.

Al walked in about a half hour later. "You hear back from that reporter?"

"Not yet. But I left a message for her to stop by. She has no idea why. Better that way," he said, trying not to get worked up about it again.

"What's that from?" Al asked, eying the surveillance video playing on Casey's computer.

"From Ghirardelli. I think Becca might've made a copy for me."

"The guys from Robbery said there weren't any clear shots of the guy."

"There's not," Casey confirmed. "If this is the suspect, he seems somewhat aware of the cameras." Casey watched as the white male, possibly in his twenties, ran through the open-air mall and out to the street after the shop clerk had escaped and called for help. Unfortunately the suspect wore a baseball cap, which kept his face from being picked up by the cameras that were mounted above him. He wore a thick jacket and dark pants and black shoes with glossy toes. "Look at his shoes. What do you think? Military?"

"His hair's a bit long."

"Maybe he's AWOL."

"Something to check out. No attack on tape, I heard."

"No. Before and after. But it's damned close to the attack by that gift store, and that definitely fits my theory that this wasn't a robbery. He tried to lure her back."

"You're *still* trying to link this to the Strangler?"

"They could be failed sexual assaults. You can't dispute how eerily similar both attacks were. Early morning, where the victim was walking alone then attacked from behind. More important, if they are related, they're two *failed* attempts. If I'm right, this guy's going to strike again. But look at this…"

He rewound the video to where the suspect had been standing in the entryway to the courtyard prior to the attack. "See his hand? He's resting it on the banister."

"Sure is. Wonder if the CSIs dusted there?"

Casey's phone rang, and he picked it up. "Kellog. Homicide." The secretary. "There's a Miss Barstow in the lobby."

"Be right there." He looked at Al. "She's here."

TWENTY-THREE

"Go get her, College Boy. I'll make sure Robbery gets the info on checking for prints."

Perhaps Casey shouldn't have shut the office door quite so hard. But the more he thought about being lied to, the madder he got. He slowed his pace as he neared the lobby, forced himself to act calm on the outside, pretend he hadn't allowed a pretty face to manipulate him.

Jenn Barstow sat in the lobby chair, looking at something on her phone screen. She'd changed into flat shoes and pulled her hair back into a ponytail, and was once again wearing her dark-framed glasses. Like the female version of Clark Kent, he thought. Hiding her true self. Except it didn't matter what she wore. He couldn't erase the image of how she looked this morning in her formfitting skirt and high heels. How had he never noticed the woman behind the glasses before now?

When she saw him, she smiled.

He smiled back, even though it took some effort. "This way," he said, leading her down the hall to a regular interview room. It was not one of the so-called soft interview rooms, the ones that looked more like a comfy corner in a high-end doctor's office, color-coordinated with upholstered chairs and framed prints on the wall.

This was the room where they interrogated suspects. It was hard, cold, and very much how he was feeling at the moment.

Apparently she noticed, because she stopped in the doorway, eyeing the scarred table and industrial-looking metal chairs. "What's this about?" she asked.

"Just a few questions. Please. Have a seat."

She pulled out a chair, sat, then folded her hands in her lap.

He sat opposite her, tossing his notebook on the tabletop. "We found the methadone clinic where Bella Orlando was a patient right before the murder."

Jenn's brows rose slightly.

"And we interviewed the therapist she'd been seeing at the time."

"Did you learn anything?"

"As a matter of fact, yes. Apparently Ms. Orlando never had a sister."

"Oh."

"Oh?"

"What do you want me to say?"

"Why you lied, for starters."

"I didn't lie. Not really."

"Not really?"

She shrugged. "You wouldn't understand."

"Try me." When she didn't respond, he said, "Maybe you don't get the severity of what we're dealing with. We're talking homicide."

"I get it. Completely."

"Then why would you, a member of the *press*, no less, lie to an officer of the law in the middle of a murder investigation? Does this have something to do with why you changed the way you looked?" He thought of the dinner at his mother's, and a sinking feeling gathered in his gut, that maybe she used his mother to get to him. "What are you trying to pull here?"

"Would you have listened to me otherwise? Because my experience these last few months is that no, you wouldn't."

"What's that supposed to mean?"

"That every time I've tried to get the police to reopen that case, they've ignored me."

"Maybe because they had nothing to work with."

"Or maybe because no one cares about dead prostitutes."

"As I told you, I wasn't working Homicide back then. But I'm sure that's not the case."

"That's exactly the case. Those women weren't pretty to look at, and they didn't matter to anyone. Just like no one listened to me until *after* I changed my appearance. I was invisible before then. But suddenly, a prettier version of me shows up, and then you sit up and take notice. Admit it."

He couldn't believe she was actually accusing him of this. "You think we pick and choose what cases to work based on someone's appearance?"

"Appearances, occupations, yes. Otherwise those older murders would've been solved by now."

"First of all," Casey said, doing his best to rein in his temper, "you have no idea what has or hasn't been done to try to solve those older cases. Sometimes, things just don't turn out the way we hope. Second, you're still overlooking that you have lied to us in the middle of a murder investigation. And while you may not think it's important, I do."

"You're right. I don't think it's important," she said, standing. Angry. "And I really don't want to sit here and talk about this anymore. So if you have no further questions, or something to arrest me for, I'm leaving." She stalked to the door, pulled it open.

"Do you have any idea what your lie can do to our case?"

She turned, looked at him. "I'm sure you'll inform me."

"Should we be fortunate enough to identify and arrest the person responsible, we'll have to testify in court about the investigation. Someone may call you to the stand. And they may even ask why you lied to us. The defense, for your information, loves that sort of thing. Anything to throw a shadow on the suspect's guilt. They'll rip you apart for lying. And then they'll suggest to the jury that you've lied about everything else."

For a moment he thought she might respond. Instead, she left.

He got up, followed her out. "Why would you risk your career as a reporter by lying to me?"

"Does it matter?"

He walked faster, caught up with her at the elevator, and saw that she was crying.

She removed her glasses, wiped at her tears, jabbed the Down button, her hand shaking.

The door opened, and she started to step on.

He grabbed her arm, stopping her. "What aren't you telling me?"

"Just leave me alone," she said, trying to pull away.

"Why?" he asked, and as the elevator door started to shut, he shoved his foot in to keep it from closing. "Why the hell would you lie to me about something like this?"

"Because…" She looked away, wouldn't face him. "It's…"

Whatever she said was too faint for him to hear. "It's what?"

"My *fault*, damn it! *I'm* the reason she's dead."

TWENTY-FOUR

"What do you mean it's your fault?" Casey asked, his foot still against the elevator door.

Jenn wiped the tears from her eyes as the elevator next to them opened and two officers stepped off.

They looked from her to Casey, and he felt like a cad, certain they were judging him for making her cry. "Miss Barstow...Jenn," he said softly. "Can we please go back to the interview room?"

She allowed him to lead her back.

"Tell me what happened," he said. "From the beginning."

She sucked in a breath, nodding. "Have you ever wanted something so bad that you were willing to go to any length to achieve it?"

His police career came to mind, not that he was about to admit any such thing to her. "Go on..."

"I wanted to be this star reporter. For as far back as I remember. It was my ticket out. I—" She cleared her throat. "I was also in the system as a foster child. Just after my sixteenth birthday, Bella was taken in by my foster parents. I caught her stealing from them. I—I told on her, and, well, they ended up reporting her, and she was placed in another home."

"And you think this is why she's dead? You were a kid."

"No. Maybe..." She shrugged. "I went on to college, and she went on to...Well, you know what she went on to. And then I ran into her years later, after I'd graduated and started working at the *Union-Examiner*. The guilt overwhelmed me, but I ignored it. Here she was working the streets. And then...my editor wanted more human-interest stories. As I said, star reporter, and I wanted to do this big piece that would highlight the downfall of the foster care system. What happens when some of the kids fall through the cracks. They nixed it. Been done. That's when I came up with the bright idea of shadowing a prostitute. Because it was right after the first murder, they loved it. And—" She looked away, brushed at her eyes. "I just thought she'd be okay with everything."

"Hold on a sec." He got up, left the room, then returned with a box of tissues. "Here." He slid the box across the table toward her.

"Thanks." She grabbed one, dabbed at her face.

"You were saying?"

"Um, that they accepted my story proposal. So I approached her. She wanted nothing to do with me at first. She really did blame me. But I made promises. I'd get her out of there. Help her move away...She really did want that. She—she met with me several times. She let me follow her, as long as I parked far enough away, and I..." Jenn closed her eyes, took a breath, then looked at him once more. "She caught me."

"Caught you?"

"Filming her. On my phone. She got mad. That wasn't part of the deal, she said. She wanted me to erase everything. I tried to tell her that no one was going to see it. It was more for my reference than anything else. But she made me erase the files, then searched my phone to make sure there was nothing else on it."

"How long were you filming her for?"

"Pretty much the entire time. Half of it is useless, glare from headlights, but what I did capture? The way she looked when she shot up. The people she associated with. It was..." Jenn's face seemed to crumple, and it was several seconds before she continued. "She accused me of using her to get ahead. And I'm ashamed to say that was the truth. I sat there in my car, filming her, thinking of Pulitzer Prizes and promotions and…Here's how selfish I am. Even after she was murdered I thought about using what I did have. Thank God, the guilt got to me. I couldn't do the story after—"

"Wait," he said, not sure if he heard her right. "Use what?"

"The story. I couldn't do it. That's why when these Strangler cases came up, I realized I had to make sure she wasn't forgotten. I can't stop thinking about her." She twisted the tissue in her hand. "She was so mad after she caught me, she wouldn't let me shadow her again. And—"

"Not that," he said. "You said something about using what you *did* have."

"No. There's no way I could use it. Not and live with myself."

Casey leaned forward. "*What* files do you still have?"

"Just a few clips I downloaded to my laptop each night. But there's no way I'm doing the story. Not anymore."

"You still have those?"

She nodded. "They're at my office on my laptop."

"I need to see them."

"Now?"

"I'd be glad to follow you. But yes. Now."

Casey left Jenn in the interview room, telling her he'd be just a few minutes while he returned to the office to get his radio and brief Al. He had no idea if what she had was even relevant to the case. But there was no way of knowing that until he actually looked at the files she'd saved. Which was why he intended to personally escort Miss Barstow to her office, then pick up the flash drive himself, just to make sure nothing happened to it between here and there.

Unfortunately, the moment he walked into Homicide, Al said, "Glad you're done. Jon Gregory wants to show us something he found belonging to his stepson."

Casey glanced at the clock, not even sure where the day had gone. It was a little after five. "When?"

"Should be here any time. So how'd it go with the reporter?"

"Not quite the lie we thought. Apparently she and the victim were foster sisters way back when."

"Which has what to do with anything?"

"She feels partly responsible for the murder."

"Because…?"

"It's complicated and not as important as the fact she *might* have video of the victim out near the crime scene a few days before the murder."

"*That* would be worth seeing," Al said as his phone rang. "Krug," he said, answering it. "We'll be right out." Then, to Casey, "Mr. Gregory's here."

"What about Jenn? Miss Barstow?" he corrected as they walked down the hall to the lobby.

"She can wait a couple of minutes. Shouldn't take long. Short of a signed confession, can't imagine what, if anything, Mr. Gregory could show us that'll change anything."

The man in question was seated in the lobby, a brown paper sack in his lap.

"Mr. Gregory," Al said. "Thanks for coming in."

"Um, should we talk here? Or is there someplace we should go?" He stood, lifting the lunch bag. "You're gonna want to see this."

Al eyed the sack, then held his hand out. "This way," he said, then led him to an empty interview room. "We can talk in here."

The adjoining room, its door cracked open, was occupied by Jenn Barstow, and Casey felt a slight sense of guilt for leaving her there without informing her that he'd be a few minutes more. Deciding he should at least let her know, he was about to step out when Mr. Gregory dumped the contents of the sack onto the table, and any thoughts about who was next door vanished with what he saw.

A bundled stack of one-hundred dollar bills.

"I'm sorry," Casey finally said, drawing his gaze from the money to Mr. Gregory, thinking of the implications as he calculated how much was in that bundle. "*Where* did you say this was from?"

"Under the bed. *My* bed. In this," he said, holding up the paper sack. "The reason you didn't find it in Darrell's room when you searched was that he gave it to my wife to hold. He asked her to keep it safe for him until he got back from his job. Only he never got back."

"When was this? That he gave it to her?"

"The night before that woman was murdered out at the Presidio."

Al used his phone to snap a picture of the money. "Is there some reason she didn't tell us at the time?"

"Well," Mr. Gregory said. "Technically she *did* tell us the night you came over. Something about a guy dropping off a phone. For some job."

"But not the money."

"Well, no. But who pays someone ten thousand dollars for a job?" The man looked at the bundled bills. "I think she was a bit scared is all. We watch enough TV to know what this looks like."

Casey eyed the mustard yellow strap binding the money. One hundred hundreds...Ten-thousand dollars. There was no doubt in his mind what it looked like. That was hit money if he ever saw it.

TWENTY-FIVE

"A hit?" Lieutenant Timms was just leaving for the day. "What makes you so sure?"

"This," Al said, showing him the photo he'd snapped on his phone. "Ten K."

"Ten thousand? You book the money?"

"We didn't even touch it. Had a CSI come up and deal with it. Figured we'd want to process it and the bag for prints, then verify the serial numbers in the morning. See what pops up."

The secretary knocked as she poked her head in the door. "Casey? Miss Barstow is still waiting for you. What would you like me to tell her?"

"Damn. I forgot all about her."

"Barstow?" Timms said.

"The reporter asking about the old prostitution murders. She may have some video evidence on one of the victims."

"Let's get Zwingler on it," he told the secretary. "Kellog's tied up for now."

When she left, Timms said, "Run this by me again…"

"The facts as we know them," Casey said. "Trudy out running. Strangled at the park, we believe by Darrell Fife, now DOA at the morgue, in what appears to be a copycat murder. Waiting on DNA, but the doc feels it's our guy."

"But," Al said, "looking less like a psycho copycat and more like a *planned* copycat. Which, when you think about it, supports the hit theory. What was it Edwards told us? The murder *du jour*.

What better way to make sure your homicide gets lost in the shuffle? Make it look like all the others."

"Suspects?"

"None that stand out," Casey said. "We have her husband, Tony Salvatori, who had fling with his real estate agent. Then the neighbor, Marcie Valentine, whose husband Devin seemed to bristle at the mention of an alleged affair. Only he thought we were talking about one between him and Trudy." Casey looked over at Al, figuring this was now the time to mention the information about the allegations made by the Salvatoris' real estate agent. Al nodded, and Casey said, "What we were asking about was an affair between our victim, Trudy, and someone in Congressman Parnell's campaign office. The office manager, apparently."

"Which," Al added, "certainly moves a lot of people up a notch as suspects—at least if they had issues with the affair and being discovered. This is about as far from some random copycat murder as you can get."

"Where did you hear about the affairs?" Timms asked Al.

"The real estate agent. The one with her and Tony. And that Trudy was sleeping around and Tony knew it."

Timms's telephone rang, but he muted it and let it go to voice mail. "Does the husband have any insurance policies on her?"

"We'll be checking. As for Devin, the kid here just sort of threw the affair question out there, and he reacted. But he denied having one. So there you go."

"This alleged affair with the office manager. Tell me we haven't gone charging into Parnell's offices demanding to know who's sleeping with who."

"Not yet," Casey said. "But he did say to call if we needed anything."

Al scoffed. "Which would be nice if it meant anything more than a politician simply moving his lips. And that offer was made before we realized someone placed a hit on the victim."

"If," Timms said, "you even *look* in that direction, you better make sure we have good reason."

"Murder's a pretty good reason," Casey replied. "Why would he object?"

"Politics 101, College Boy. It's election time," Al said. "You turn over the wrong rock in the congressman's camp, he'll crush you with it."

"Unless someone in his camp is guilty of murder. Look at what we're dealing with here. A rumor of an affair had to start somewhere."

"Unless," Al said, "she was screwing Parnell himself, hard to imagine anyone there would pay to off her. What would some volunteer worker have to lose?"

"Don't forget," Casey said. "Trudy also handled the books for Parnell's campaign office. What if she discovered something? Some impropriety with the accounting?"

"Parnell?" Al replied. "Skimming his own funds? I'd like to think someone who's been in office as long as he has isn't that stupid. I voted for him, after all."

"Casey's right," Timms said. "Doesn't have to be the congressman. Maybe it's someone else. Money's money, and people have killed for a lot less."

"Maybe," Al said, "it's someone who has access to the books. Skim enough and she notices, maybe approaches the guy, and bam, she's on a hit list."

"All good theories," Timms said. "Except that we have nothing to base them on. Get Jon Gregory's wife in here. Let's see if we can't ID the person who gave her the money to give to her son. If someone placed a hit on Trudy Salvatori, we need to find out who and why. And that includes anyone from Parnell's camp, should they end up on the suspect list." Timms turned a stern eye on Casey. "Parnell and the captain are personal friends, and I, for one, don't want to be transferred to midnights. So cover all your bases." He glanced out the window, his gaze fixed on the gray buildings for a moment before turning back toward Al and Casey. "I'll brief the captain. You get started on the affidavits for the search warrants. First thing in the morning, I want those things served."

TWENTY-SIX

Casey was printing out the search warrants for phone and bank records on the Salvatoris, the Valentines, and Parnell's campaign office when Zwingler and Haynes walked in the next morning. Zwingler saw him, unlocked his desk, and held up the video evidence that Jenn Barstow had given him. "Here ya go, kid," Zwingler said, tossing the flash drive onto Casey's desk.

"Thanks."

"So aren't you going to pop it in? Take a look?"

"Don't suppose you could have a look at it? Need to finish up these warrants so they're ready to go. New lead in the Presidio case."

"What's the lead?"

Casey pulled out the photo the CSI had printed of the money found in Fife's mother's house.

"Whoa," Zwingler said. "Glad it's you and not me."

Haynes took the photo from Casey. "Maybe you can check with the bank, see if they remember giving anyone ten K recently. Can't be all that many people walking in, asking for that kind of money."

"Already thought of that," Casey said. "Just that there's an awful lot of banks out there."

"Start with the branch used by your suspects. You might get lucky."

Zwingler gave a sarcastic laugh. "Who's that stupid they're going to use their own branch to withdraw hit money?"

"It happens," Haynes said. "There's a lot of dumb crooks out there."

Casey took back the photo. "Someone went to a lot of trouble to make this look like a Strangler case. Can't imagine they'd slip up on something simple like that."

"Never know," Haynes replied.

"Bad news," Al said, hanging up his phone. "Jon Gregory can't get ahold of his wife. This whole Strangler accusation of her son's got her freaked out—his words. Apparently she left a note saying she and her sister were going to some spa in Calistoga and won't be back until late tonight."

"No idea what spa?"

"Not a clue. He'll call the moment she gets back."

"Guess all we can do for now is hit the banks."

Casey and Al served the first search warrant at Devin and Marcie Valentine's bank, since it was the closest. When the branch manager, a man in his early thirties, was waiting for the records to come off the printer, Casey showed him the photo of the bundled hundreds. "Any chance you know if this came from your bank?" Casey asked.

"Was our stamp on it?"

"Your stamp?"

"We stamp every band that leaves our bank with the branch number. The employee who counted it initials it. That way if there are any errors, we know where to look." He opened a drawer, pulled out a stamp, then pressed it against the manila folder in which he'd placed the printouts of the Valentines' records. The branch number in purple ink was clearly visible along with a line where the employee would presumably place his or her initials. "Just one of our rules. Of course, those currency bands can be purchased anywhere. Internet, Walmart. It may not have even come from a bank."

Casey and Al thanked him then left with records in hand.

Al immediately started scanning the paperwork when he got into the car.

Casey, however, eyed the stamp on the folder. "Was there any writing on the band around those hundreds?"

"What?" Al said, looking up.

"On the currency band."

"I only looked at the one side. Didn't want to smear any possible prints. But the CSI who handled it must have snapped a dozen pictures before she processed it. Give her a call and see if she can't text a photo of the other side to you."

Casey did that. Then he started the car and drove to the next bank, a ten-minute drive from their location. He parked in front at the street, and Al placed the OFFICIAL SFPD BUSINESS placard on the dash.

"Anything show up in the Valentine documents?" he asked Al.

"Nothing that screams 'look at me.' A thousand withdrawal here and there. Definitely nothing that adds up to ten K. Of course, were you really expecting to find anything in the Valentines' records?"

"No reason to. Yet. Maybe we'll have better luck with the Salvatoris' bank."

Al carried the manila folder containing the search warrants and the Valentines' bank records into the building. Casey followed him in, checking his phone for a response from the CSI who had photographed the money in its wrapper. "Got it," he said, showing the photo to Al.

The mustard yellow wrapper had a BT 2462 written in blue ink and below that AB. All of it appeared to be in the same hand. Just no official stamp.

"Better than nothing," Al said.

And like at the first bank, they served the warrant to the manager, this man older, about Al's age, early fifties. He printed out the requested records for the Salvatoris. Once that was done,

Casey showed him the photo on his phone of the money and what was written on the band.

"Not ours," the man said. "We always use a stamp. But BT could be Bay Trust. There's a branch right across the street."

Casey and Al glanced out the window to the Bay Trust Mutual office. It was, in fact, the bank used by Parnell's campaign office. And next on their stop.

"Keep this low key," Al told Casey as they entered the Bay Trust branch office. "We don't show the paper work to anyone but the manager, and we sure as hell don't mention Parnell's name aloud. They can read it on the documents."

A lot of good it did them, because the moment they handed over the warrant, the manager, a young man in his early thirties named Bob Kingston, said, "As in *Congressman* Parnell?"

"Not him personally," Casey said, aware that several tellers and their customers looked up on hearing the man's voice. "His campaign accounts. I believe that Trudy Salvatori would have had signing authority on the checks."

"Right. This way, please."

He took them to his desk which was set toward the back, facing all the tellers on the floor. "The congressman wasn't involved, was he?"

Al said, "This is all routine. We're just trying to re-create Ms. Salvatori's last days. Did she handle the banking at this branch?"

"I don't recognize her name or the congressman's," he said, typing into his computer. "I mean, as customers. It looks like... Yes. They did most of their banking online. I don't show either using *this* specific branch."

Casey leaned over, trying to see what the manager was referencing. "Do you have any idea when's the last time she came into this branch?"

"She didn't. At least I don't show a record of it. She, or rather someone from the campaign office, did conduct a few transactions at the branch closer to their office. Looks like a few checks were made out to cash."

"For how much?"

"Couple hundred here and there. Petty cash fund, maybe?"

"Anything bigger?" Casey asked.

"No. Nothing that I can see in the last few months. Big deposits, of course. I expect those are contributions, but withdrawals?"

He printed out the corresponding documents and handed them over.

Al thanked him then to Casey said, "Show him the photo."

Casey took his phone and brought up the picture the CSI had sent, showing it to Mr. Kingston. "Any chance this money came from your bank?"

Bob's gaze narrowed. "Can you enlarge the writing on the currency band?"

Casey ran his fingers across the photo so that the writing filled most of the screen.

Bob nodded. "It had to come from this office. That's our branch number."

"Any idea who might have written that on the band?"

"That's got to be the teller's initials. AB..." He glanced out to the floor. "Possibly April Brennan?"

"Mind if we talk to her?"

"I'll get her for you."

He walked over, said something quiet into the teller's ear. He stood by while she finished her transaction then put a CLOSED sign in her window. She followed him over to his desk, where he introduced her to Casey and Al, finishing with, "They have a few questions about some money you may have handled."

She seemed a bit nervous but smiled at them, saying, "Okay."

Casey showed her the photo on his phone. "Is this your signature?"

The bank teller looked at the photograph of the mustard yellow band around the stack of hundred-dollar bills. "My initials. Yes."

"Any chance you recall banding this money?"

The young woman stared at the photo for several seconds. "Is something wrong? I counted it very carefully."

Al leaned forward slightly so that she could see his face as he turned that fatherly smile on to her. "You're not in any trouble, April. Anything at all you can tell us about that money and who-ever you gave it to will help."

She smiled back, nodded, then returned her gaze to the band. "A woman came in. She had ten thousand dollars in cash in her purse. A lot of tens, mostly twenties. She said she found it in her grandmother's closet after she died. Her grandmother, uh, didn't believe in banks, is what the woman told me."

"You're sure that was *this* stack?"

"Definitely. It's the first time I ever counted that much money. Like I said, all tens and twenties." She glanced at the manager, then back at Al. "She wanted it changed to hundreds, so I counted the money from her purse, then turned it into the manager to exchange it for a bundle of hundreds. I'm new. So I wanted to make sure everything was right."

"And when was it you put your initials on the band?"

"After I removed the hundreds, counted them out to verify, then rebanded them."

"Did she count them at all?"

"Not here. She watched me count it, of course. Then she put the stack in her purse and left."

The manager said, "We can pull the security video for you to see if that will help. It'll only take a few minutes."

"I'd appreciate it," Casey told him. As he left, Casey said to the teller, "It'd help if you recall anything else about her."

She glanced toward her window as though trying to recall that day. "I remember she was dressed all in black and wore a big hat and sunglasses. She told me her eyes were swollen from crying. But I recognized her anyway."

"You recognized her?"

"She cashes checks in here all the time. Give me a sec and I'll think of her name. She was always so nice. Chatting about this or that…Why do I think her last name starts with an F? On the tip of my tongue."

The manager returned. "I have the video if you'd like to come back and see."

The three followed him to a back office where he accessed a computer, bringing up the day in question, fast-forwarding until the teller stopped him. "Right there," she said, pointing to the screen. "That's her walking in the door."

And as described, they saw a woman wearing a black hat, the wide brim shadowing most of her face. It was only when she turned slightly that Casey saw she also wore sunglasses, the sort favored by movie stars who wanted to hide from public view. She was dressed completely in black and carried a black tote over her shoulder. Casey watched as she waited in line, then strode up to the teller window, placing money on the counter from her tote.

"Foulke!" the teller said, her face lighting up. "Her last name."

Al, his gaze still on the video, said, "Any chance you recall a first name?"

She eyed the screen, then closed her eyes. "Marge?"

"She have an account here?" Casey asked.

"I don't think so. She came in quite often, though. To cash checks. Nothing too big. One or two hundred dollars. But they were all from the same account."

"Belonging to…?"

"Congressman Parnell."

Al nodded at the monitor. "Can you back up that video to when she walks up to the teller window?"

The manager did as asked.

"Recognize that hat?" Al asked, pointing. "The purple flower?"

The moment he mentioned it, Casey remembered where he'd seen it. "The coatrack in Marcie's house."

"No," the teller said. "Not Marcie. *Margie.* That was her name. Margie Foulke."

TWENTY-SEVEN

Marcie's first instinct after receiving the call from Sergeant Kellog was to telephone Devin to let him know. But ever since Trudy's murder and the installation of their alarm system, he treated her like she was this fragile thing that might break.

In some ways he was right. If it weren't for the pills he was giving her at night, she wouldn't be able to sleep. How could she? Every time she closed her eyes, she saw Trudy's lifeless eyes staring up at her.

The guilt weighed on her.

Gnawed at her gut.

She'd thought Trudy was sleeping with Devin. How could she not with all the time those two seemed to have spent together?

Planning a birthday getaway, Devin had said. And she opened the drawer in the kitchen, found the pamphlet for the bed and breakfast in Napa. She'd ruined everything with her petty jealousy of Trudy.

Everything.

And now the police wanted to talk to her. Again.

That gnawing feeling intensified, and she sucked in a breath, told herself it was nothing. What was the term they used? Just routine? And really, if it was something serious, wouldn't they ask her to come down to the Hall of Justice? Not come here?

That was the thing she clung to. The belief that if they thought she was guilty of something, they wouldn't be talking to her in her own house.

She glanced up at the camera on top of the refrigerator aimed toward the back door. Ever since that one night, there had been no more incidents. Granted she never returned the spare key to the flower pot on the back porch. That whole thing, finding the door open, had been freaky.

The knock at the front startled her, even though she'd been expecting it. She returned the pamphlet to the drawer, closed it, then walked into the living room.

At the second sharp knock, she hurried over and opened the door to the two detectives who had been there before. She told herself to smile but somehow couldn't make it happen. "Come in," she said.

They filed past her into the living room. The older one removed his hat, saying, "Thank you, Mrs. Valentine. We appreciate your time." His gaze caught on the coat-tree. "Is that yours?"

"What?"

"The hat. I noticed that on our first visit. It's yours?"

She eyed it, trying to figure out why he'd be interested. "Yes."

"I like hats. You wear it often?"

"Not really. I just like the way it looks there." She saw him pull out his phone, accessing something on the screen. "Is there something I can do for you?"

He smiled at her, then turned to his partner, Sergeant Kellog, who opened up a dark-blue portfolio containing a manila folder thick with papers. "Mrs. Valentine," Sergeant Kellog said, "can you give me your cell phone number? We don't seem to have that number listed anywhere."

"Of course." She gave it to them. After all, she'd erased the texts.

The front door burst open, and Devin strode in. "What's going on?" he asked.

Sergeant Kellog stood. "Just a few more questions while we try to finish up our investigation."

"Then you can come back when our attorney is present," he said. "My wife is under enough stress without you interrogating her in our own living room."

"Why would I need an attorney?" she asked, worried that the very mention of one made her look guilty. "I haven't done anything wrong."

Devin pulled out his cell phone. "I'm calling him now," he said.

She turned to the two detectives. "What other questions are we talking about?"

Sergeant Kellog deferred to his partner, who said, "Do you have an account at Bay Trust Mutual?"

"No."

"Do you know anyone named Margie Foulke?"

Devin looked up from his phone at the name.

She tried to remain calm. It meant nothing. "You mean *Marcie* Foulke? It's my maiden name. What does this have to do with anything?"

"Because," the detective said. "Someone wearing *that* hat with *that* flower"—he said, nodding toward the coatrack—"cashed checks under the name Margie Foulke."

Devin pinned his gaze on her. "Not another word, Marce," and then into the phone, he said, "Adam? Devin Valentine. The police are here questioning my wife..." He turned his back to them, walking out to the porch, where he lowered his voice. "I don't know...Some stupid hat hanging in our house. Black with a blue flower."

"Purple," Marcie corrected.

"*Purple* flower," he said, sounding annoyed. "They think my wife was wearing it in a bank where some *checks* were cashed..."

Marcie leaned forward so that she could see out the door. His back was to them, and she saw his shoulders tensing as he nodded. "Okay. Got it." He turned, walked into the house, faced the two detectives. "You need to leave. At once. If you want to question us further, you can do it through our attorney, Adam Murphy."

"Actually," the older one said, "we're questioning your wife. The decision is hers."

Marcie glanced at her husband. He said nothing. He didn't have to. She could see it in his face. "I'm sorry," she said to them. "You'll have to leave."

Devin stood aside, waiting for the two detectives to file past him and out the door. The older one smiled again. "We'll be in touch."

Devin slammed the door, then faced Marcie. "What are you thinking, talking to them?"

"What was I supposed to do?"

"Call me. Lucky for you, one of the neighbors did. What if you said something that—" He suddenly remembered that their attorney was still on the phone, and he put it to his ear. "Sorry, Adam…. Yeah. They're gone." He listened a moment, then, "We will. Talk to you later."

He shoved the phone in his pocket then walked over to Marcie. "No more talking to the cops without Adam by your side. Promise?"

"Promise."

She glanced out the window, saw the two detectives standing by their car. But instead of getting in and driving off, they walked over to Tony's door. "Why are they going over there?"

"Doesn't matter. Tony's not home," Devin said, pulling the curtain aside. And sure enough, a moment later the cops returned to their car then drove off. He faced Marcie. "What did you tell them?"

"I didn't need to tell them anything. They wanted my cell phone number."

He walked to the front door and opened it.

"Where are you going?" she asked.

"Out. This is too much for me to deal with. I just need some alone time."

She heard his car drive off. Then she sat there, chewing her nails to shreds, the whole time her gaze locked on that hat...

TWENTY-EIGHT

The office was abuzz with activity when Casey and Al returned
with the bank documents as well as the photo Al took on
his phone of Marcie's hat. But before they even had a chance to
sit down and analyze the significance of what they'd learned,
Zwingler called them over to his desk. "You have to see this. The
video I picked up yesterday from your reporter friend."

Casey hesitated. There were definite issues with what they'd
discovered at the bank, possibly turning the Presidio investigation around. Casey wanted to be there when Al briefed Lieutenant
Timms on what they'd found. But his curiosity about what might
be on Jenn Barstow's flash drive got the better of him. "How long
are the videos?"

"Not more than a couple minutes each."

Al slapped Casey on the back. "You go ahead. I'll get started
with Timms."

"Be right there," he told Al.

Casey rolled his chair over to Zwingler's desk and sat while
Zwingler inserted the flash drive into his computer. "Check out
the date," Zwingler said, tapping his monitor.

There were four files containing video clips, each marked by
the date about a week before the murder, and he opened the first.
It appeared to have been filmed from inside someone's vehicle,
but between the poor resolution, the glare of headlights, and the
sound of passing traffic, little could be heard of what was going
on outside. Just shaky video images of Bella Orlando walking

the street. Every now and then a vehicle would stop, and Bella walked up to talk to the driver. Most times the vehicle left. On one occasion, Bella got into the car. But instead of driving off, the vehicle backed up then pulled into the alley, driving to the far end.

Zwingler tapped his screen again. "Isn't that where she was killed?"

Casey leaned in for a closer look. "Looks like it."

But if he was expecting anything unusual to happen there, nothing did. Not that they could see into the truck, since the headlights were on. After a few minutes, Bella got out, pocketing money or drugs, then sauntered back down the alley to the street where she waited for the next customer.

The second clip was much the same as the first. The third, however, was shot just before dusk, giving them a better view of the vehicles and the men driving them. A pickup truck slowed, the driver rolling down his passenger window, leaning toward Bella, apparently conversing with her. But suddenly Bella started yelling at someone off camera—at least it appeared that way, since she was too far for them to hear—and they only had Jenn's voice, narrating, "Uh oh. I think she got caught," as Bella stormed toward the source of her displeasure. A uniformed security guard walked into view, pointing with his side-handled baton, as though telling her to leave, and Jenn saying, "Yep. Caught," as the driver of the pickup truck sped off, probably unnerved by the guard's presence and the verbal altercation. It ended with Bella running the opposite direction and the guard following her.

It didn't seem like anything that could be used.

The fourth clip was filmed on the same date as the third and started with a shot of the same alley with Jenn's voice narrating. "I hope she's okay. I'm worried in case that guard called the police on her—" She stopped when Bella stumbled into view from a recessed doorway in the alley. The prostitute hesitated then walked across the street toward Jenn Barstow's car, which is when the picture abruptly shifted, the view swinging toward the steering wheel, then downward, everything going black, as though Jenn had dropped the phone out of view, not even having time to shut off the video as a muffled voice said, "Hey. Let me in."

The sound of automatic locks popping, a door opening then closing, the locks again, and Jenn saying, "What were you thinking out there?"

A hoarse laugh. "Ruin your big ex-*pose*-ay?"

"Forget the article. He could have you arrested."

They heard a sharp intake of breath and then several loud thuds as though someone was hitting the car or its windows. Then a man's voice yelling, "You bitch! Look what you did to me!" More pounding.

Bella's voice saying, "Go to hell."

"Oh my God," Jenn said. A rustling noise as she pulled her phone from wherever it was hidden. Then brightness, the picture flashing across her purse, then to Bella in the passenger seat. And finally a shot of a man at the window, a stream of blood pouring down his temple.

He slammed his hand against the glass. "Bitch! I'll kill you! Look what you did to me!"

And the video stopped.

"You see that?" Zwingler said, his voice excited.

"What do you think? She whacked the guy with something?"

"Not that. Take a closer look at the guy in the window. Hold on." He backed it up to that point. "Right there."

It was a moment before Casey saw past the bloody hand against the glass, concentrating less on the man's reaction and more on his identifying features. And that was when he realized what it was he'd missed the first time around in the corner of the screen. There one second, gone the next.

A white patch on the dark sleeve of the guy's jacket. Not the whole thing, but enough to be sure.

"The security guard," Casey said.

"What are the chances he's the same one listed as a witness in her murder? That Francis Dunmore."

Casey leaned back in his chair, his thoughts spinning as his gaze settled on the far side of the room where Robbery was housed. "Hey. Edwards. You ever get a CSI to check that banister for prints out at Ghirardelli?"

Virgil Edwards looked up from his computer. "Yeah. Good catch, by the way. We found one. But it was a partial. Decent, but unless you're pulling a suspect out of your hat, there it sits. Useless."

"Actually, I might have one for you."

"You're kidding?"

"A long shot, but worth looking at."

Edwards slid his chair back, stood, then walked over.

"Play the last video, Zwingler," Casey said.

He did as asked, and Edwards watched it through to the end. "What makes you think it's related?"

"That video from Ghirardelli shows a guy in dark slacks and dark shoes. What if it's the bottom half of a security uniform? Who better to blend into the background than a security guard?"

"Hey, Bishop," Edwards called out. "Bring over that Ghirardelli CD."

Mark Bishop gave it to Zwingler. "About three minutes in."

Zwingler popped it into the drive, opened the file, and found the segment.

"Pause it," Edwards said. Then to Bishop, he asked, "That look like a security guard's bottom half to you?"

Bishop leaned in closer for a better look. "Or a bus driver."

"Son of a…Zwing, show Bishop the video of the guy banging on the window."

Zwingler switched to that picture.

"Damn," Bishop said. Then to Casey, "You got a name for this guy?"

"Possibly Francis Dunmore, the security guard named as a witness in the murder of Bella Orlando. That'd be the girl sitting in the passenger seat."

Bishop jotted the name down on a piece of paper. "If he's working security anywhere, there's gotta be prints on file. I'll run him, see if we can get those prints, and do a comparison on that partial."

He and Edwards returned to their desks, and a moment later Al walked in from the lieutenant's office. "Find something interesting?" he asked.

"Maybe."

"Hey, Kellog!" Bishop called out from across the room. "What's the name of the security company Dunmore was working for at the time? I ran him, and he's not showing up as a licensed guard in California."

"A2Z," Casey said. "The two being a numeral."

"Thanks."

Al said, "What's that about?"

Casey told him about the security guard in Jenn's video.

"Huh. Wouldn't that be the catch of the decade." He set a thick manila folder on Casey's desk. "More good news. Texts from Trudy's phone are in."

"What about Marcie's?"

"Different phone company, unfortunately. But they're pretty quick." He opened the folder, tapping on the top page. "This, College Boy, is about as close as you can get to a smoking gun. Trudy's affair was not with the office manager. It was with Congressman Parnell."

"Can't imagine his constituents would be too thrilled if that were to get out."

"Can't imagine he would be, either. The lieutenant wants us to get out there and serve that search warant on Parnell's office ASAP."

TWENTY-NINE

As much as Casey wanted to find out the results on Bishop's comparison of Dunmore's prints to that found at the Ghirardelli assault, his priority was the Presidio murder. Between the teller's recollection of checks being drawn on Parnell's account and the phone records showing what could only be described as highly suggestive texts between the congressman and Trudy Salvatori, the course of their investigation had changed. If anyone had reason to silence Trudy Salvatori about the affair, it would be the man up for reelection.

Congressman Parnell.

Twenty-five minutes later, they arrived at the campaign office, on the ground floor in one of the high rises in the Financial District. FOR LEASE signs plastered in the windows were now covered over with REELECT PARNELL signs. Casey pulled open the glass door then held it for Al. Inside, a pretty brunette woman in her twenties sat at a desk facing the front door. "May I help you?" She smiled.

Casey glanced around the near-empty space. She was the only person present, although there were several desks besides hers in the room, but also a couple of closed doors at the back, possibly private offices. "We need to speak to whoever's in charge."

"That would be the campaign director, Roy Webber. May I tell him what this is regarding?"

"I'm Sergeant Kellog. My partner, Sergeant Krug. We're here about Trudy Salvatori."

Her pert smile faded.

Al's expression turned sympathetic. "How well did you know her?"

"Trudy?" Her glance strayed to one of the empty desks, where someone had left a bouquet of yellow roses. "I know she worked hard on the campaign. Always the last one to leave. But other than that?" She sighed deeply. Then, as though remembering her job, she picked up the phone, keyed in a number, and said, "There are two police detectives here to see you."

A moment later, a dark-haired man in his forties stepped out of an enclosed office from the back then crossed the room toward them.

Politician in training, Casey thought. Perfect hair, perfect teeth, perfect tie, and perfect suit. And perfectly bland smile as Casey identified himself and Al to the man.

"Please. If you'll step into my office."

He led them back to his office, closing the door behind them. "This must be about Trudy. Have you made progress in the case?"

"Little by little," Casey said. Then taking a lesson from Al's playbook, he asked, "What can you tell us about Trudy? How well did you know her?"

"Oh. Well, she was a good worker. Devoted to the campaign cause."

"Did she come in often?"

"During the week, yes. Usually late mornings. She handled the finances."

"Finance director?"

"A fancy title for the person who issued checks, paid out petty cash, that sort of thing. But she also helped with fund-raising. Putting together dinners, gatherings. She worked tirelessly for the cause."

"Did you ever associate with her outside the campaign?"

"No. Other than in here, I didn't know her at all."

"Mr. Webber, I hope you don't misconstrue this next question, but do you know any reason at all why someone would have killed Trudy? Something that might have had to do with this office?"

"*This* office?"

"Yes."

"No. Of course not. Everyone here loved Trudy."

"There haven't been any problems here? Nothing odd happening the days or weeks leading up to Trudy's death?"

"I—I don't understand," he said, his gaze shifting from Casey to Al and back. "I mean, no. Nothing. But wasn't she killed by that man at the Presidio? Are you saying someone else killed her?"

"We're just trying to be thorough," Casey said. He pulled out his notebook, turning to the page of notes from his bank interview. "Any chance you ever heard the name Margie Foulke?"

"No. It doesn't sound familiar at all."

"Marcie Foulke?" When he shook his head, Casey said, "She cashed several checks written on the campaign account."

"A vendor possibly? We write a lot of checks. Carlotta would be better able to tell you."

"Who's Carlotta?"

"The treasurer."

"Perfect. Can you take us to her?"

"Now's not a good time. We're extremely busy."

Casey and Al glanced outside the office onto the main floor, where the receptionist was reading from a paperback novel, and Al said, "Doesn't look busy."

"Trust me. We are. Perhaps we can reschedule to a later time."

"Who else works here?" Al asked.

"Ann," he said, nodding out the door toward the receptionist. "And Carlotta Tremayne. The treasurer."

"Then Carlotta would be the one who can help us go through the campaign financial records. Along with phone records and last but not least, a search of Trudy Salvatori's desk."

"Actually," Webber said, walking over to a file box on a shelf against the wall, "everything from Trudy's desk is right here." He patted the top. "I emptied it out after…Well, it's all here. You're welcome to it."

"Thank you," Casey said, thinking this was going better than planned.

But then Webber said, "As for the rest of it…With Trudy gone, we've had to double up the workload. And the volunteers are due any time. Perhaps you could come back later in the week?"

Al looked at his watch. "Let me check my schedule. Gee, sorry. That's not going to work. Give him the papers, Kellog."

Casey pulled the warrant from his portfolio notebook. "The court orders, allowing us to search."

Roy Webber took the papers, looking them over. He reached up, pulled at his tie as though it was suddenly choking him. "Search what, specifically?"

"As Sergeant Krug said, phone and bank records. I'm assuming there are some sort of check registers or accounting books?"

"There are. What, exactly, are you looking for?"

"Evidence."

"Of what?"

Al didn't usually lose patience, but clearly that wasn't the case here. "You did catch the part where we mentioned we're running a murder investigation?"

"And I'm running a campaign office. Do you realize what that'll look like to have you camped inside here?"

Al's phone rang. He pulled it from his pocket and looked at the screen. "Take care of this, will you?" he said to Casey, then stepped from the office, saying, "Krug…Yeah. Hold on. Let me get to a place I can talk…"

The moment Al left, the manager crossed his arms, his expression hardening. "I'm sorry. I just can't allow you to run about unchecked here on the premises. You have to understand how it will look."

And Casey thought, What would Al do?

Unfortunately this wasn't the sort of neighborhood where drug dealers hung out on street corners and one could threaten to send in narcotics. Political offices and the people who ran them were a lot more sophisticated.

And then it hit him. He offered what he hoped was a benign smile, the sort Al would give. "I understand," he said. "We do try to be low key in these high-profile cases, so hopefully the press won't pay much attention to us camping out front, waiting for you to close up shop. Then we'll come back in after hours—well, after posting uniformed officers inside and out to make sure evidence isn't tampered with or destroyed."

The man looked down at the warrants. "Can you wait here one moment?"

"Sure."

He opened his door, then crossed the outer office in several long strides, knocking sharply on a closed door before disappearing inside.

Al returned just then. "What'd I miss?"

Casey told him.

"Seriously? You threatened them with the press?"

"How's that any different than the drug dealers on the corner?"

"Because the people in those cases weren't personal friends with the captain who has the chief's ear who can sign the transfer orders moving us from investigations to some godforsaken beat working midnights."

"What would you have done?"

"Called for uniformed officers to stand by while we searched. Only I would've left out any mention of the *press*. That never goes well in these situations."

"Maybe he won't notice."

"The guy's paid to notice that stuff. Let's just hope he doesn't mention it to the congressman."

And no sooner were the words spoken than who should come walking in with the office manager but Congressman Parnell. "Sergeants Krug and Kellog, isn't it? What's this about notifying the press?"

Al said, "A bit of a misunderstanding, sir. What my partner was trying to say was that we were hoping to be discreet in all our dealings, so as not to cause your office any further—"

"Cut the bullshit," Parnell said. "Tell me what you're searching for, and I can save the trouble of hours of ripping my campaign offices apart. That way we can resume business, and you can get back to finding the real killer. Who is *not* someone in this office, I assure you."

"We're going to need the accounting books, financial records, et cetera. And phone records. It's all in the search warrant we gave your office manager."

"This way," he said, then led them to the adjoining office, knocking on a closed door, then opening it. "Carlotta, sorry for the interruption. These investigators need to see the books."

The gray-haired accountant looked at them over the rims of her gold-framed glasses. "Any particular dates?"

Casey said, "From the time this office opened and Trudy worked for you."

"Trudy?" She appeared shocked, and her gaze flew to Parnell's.

"It's okay. Just give them what they need."

"Of course. I'm just—That poor, poor girl..." She took a breath, then swiveled in her chair toward a shelf behind her where she pulled out two large green clothbound books. "These are the check registers Trudy kept. She would, um, give them to me after each day, and I would enter the expenses into the computer. Deposits and withdrawals I enter right into the database the moment I receive receipts, checks, or expenses from petty cash. I—you'll just have to excuse me," she said, her eyes pooling with tears. She grabbed a tissue from a box on her desk. "I'm normally very organized, but—you must think I'm heartless. Feeling sorry for myself when it was Trudy who was killed. She was such a sweet woman. Always so helpful..."

Congressman Parnell put his hand on her shoulder. "We're all affected by it. Carlotta, though, worked very closely with Trudy."

"I did. And now I need to replace her...I—I'm left trying to piece together her accounts and records. I don't even know where to look..."

The tears started anew, and Casey realized he needed to distract her in order to get her back on track. "I'm sorry. What exactly is the difference between your job and what Trudy did?"

Congressman Parnell answered. "Trudy handled the day-to-day monetary issues. Petty cash, checks written to vendors, that sort of thing. Carlotta did the heavy banking. Expenditures and contributions that she reported daily to the FEC."

"Daily?" Al said. "That's gotta be time-consuming with that much money going in and out."

Carlotta nodded as she dabbed the tissue at her eyes. "It is and there is," she replied. "But it's a rule, so that your opponents will know what you're spending. Transparency."

"Got it," Al replied. "Which means you'd know if there was anything untoward going on with the money?"

"Well, yes. That's my job, after all."

"And you'd notice if someone, say, had skimmed off ten thousand dollars?"

"I think I'd notice that right away."

"Anyone write a check for ten K?"

"I don't believe so. I'd remember an amount like that."

"Ten thousand?" Parnell said. "What does this have to do with Trudy's murder?"

"Mr. Parnell," Al said. "Is there anyone in this office who might have wanted to kill Trudy Salvatori?"

"*This* office? I was under the distinct impression her killer is lying in your morgue."

"And we believe he is, too. Only he may not have been acting alone."

"*Everything* here is transparent, *including* my accounting books. So what does Trudy's murder have to do with my campaign accounts?"

"We believe," Al said, "that someone paid Darrell Fife money to kill Trudy Salvatori. Possibly someone from this office."

It was a moment before the congressman spoke. His gaze swung from Casey and Al to Carlotta, whose hand went up to cover her mouth. "This is baseless," he told her. "I know it is." And then to Casey and Al, he said, "What would make you think it came from *my* office?"

"Someone from the bank recognized a woman who we believe gave the killer, Darrell Fife, money that may been drawn from your accounts."

Roy Webber pushed farther into the office. "That's insane. No one from this office dealt with that man."

"We've connected the money given to Fife to this office. She cashed checks drawn on the congressman's campaign account."

A vein pulsed in Parnell's temple, but he appeared outwardly calm. "That's impossible."

"Sir," Roy Webber said. "We need to speak privately. Now."

It was a moment before Parnell moved, his gaze locked onto Al's. "If you'll excuse us," he finally said. He followed his office manager from the room, leaving them alone with Carlotta, whose gaze lingered on the empty doorway

She finally turned her attention to Casey and Al. "No one here would do anything like that."

"Ma'am," Casey said, hoping to get what they needed before more interruptions. "Is there any way you can look up two things for us before you turn over the records? Any checks drawn for ten thousand dollars."

"Of course."

She booted up her computer, typed in the amount she was looking for. The search results showed no matches. "Nothing for ten thousand."

Al said, "Maybe a couple of five-thousand-dollar checks?"

Again, nothing.

Casey opened his notebook and read the name given to him by a teller. "Any chance you know anything about a Margie Foulke? Or a Marcie Foulke?"

"The name's familiar..." She entered that into the search bar, hit ENTER. A list of checks written popped up onto the screen. "She's a vendor. And it's Margie. With a G."

Casey scanned the totals. They all seemed to be for small amounts. Mostly in the one- or two-hundred-dollar range. "What'd she vend?"

Carlotta accessed a different screen. "Looks like mostly Internet ads."

Al leaned over for a closer look at the numerous entries. "That all the checks written to her?"

"It is."

"Any chance you can print that out for us?"

She did as asked, then picked up several sheets of paper from the printer, handing them to Al, who handed them to Casey. "What else do you need?"

Casey gave her a flash drive he'd brought for that purpose. "All the records, actually. And any written ledgers used for check-writing and accounting purposes."

She inserted the flash drive into her computer, and he watched as she copied the files onto it right about the time the congressman returned.

"Gentleman," Parnell said, "I hope you won't misconstrue this as my not cooperating with your investigation in any way, but I've just spoken with my attorney on the phone, and he's advised me and anyone from this office to end any discourse until he's present."

Casey glanced at the folder of text messages that Al was holding, wondering when the best time to bring that up might be.

Al, however, didn't seem perturbed by the interruption. "No problem," he said. "We'll finish gathering the records, do a search of Trudy's desk contents and anywhere else she might have worked, then get out of your hair. As long as you agree to have everyone come down to the Hall for an interview. Today."

"Everyone?" Parnell asked.

"Everyone. Including you. Feel free to bring your attorney."

THIRTY

Jenn was finishing her political roundup report when the phone rang. Already behind, she considered letting it go to voice mail but answered it at the last second. "Barstow."

"It's Ann. Check your texts." The line went dead.

Jenn dropped the phone into the cradle, pulled out her cell, and stared at the blank screen, wondering, Ann Who? "That's weird."

Taryn rolled her chair back until she was even next to Jenn. "What's weird?"

Suddenly Jenn's phone screen lit up. She scanned the message, realized exactly which Ann it was, then read it again just to make sure she hadn't imagined the whole thing.

Taryn eyed her. "You gonna share?"

"The receptionist at Parnell's campaign office," she whispered. "The police just served a search warrant for bank and phone records on the Salvatori murder."

"You're kidding..."

Jenn handed her the phone.

Taryn read it. "Would she be willing to talk?"

"She'd so get fired if anyone found out."

"Fired? Once this gets out, it's not like she's even going to have a job. Parnell's election is over."

This had to be related to what she'd overheard in that interview room while waiting for Casey yesterday. Just a few short seconds of conversation before he and Sergeant Krug closed the door to the adjoining room to speak with that witness. Ten thousand dollars hidden by the suspect's mother. Which is why she wasn't at all surprised when over thirty minutes later, she was still sitting in that room listening as people came and went next door, hearing the flash of a camera as a uniformed tech took photos.

She could well understand why Casey had forgotten she was there. Or why he'd sent another sergeant to accompany her to pick up the videos of Bella she'd saved to her laptop.

What she hadn't dared do was mention to anyone here in the office what she'd overheard. Found money was one thing, but it did little good without linking it to someone in particular.

Linking it to a congressman running for reelection? Gold.

Jenn stood, glanced over at their editor's office. "Wish me luck..."

She knocked on his open door. "Remember when you told me the only way I was getting a byline was if a local politician committed the murder?"

"What about it?" he asked, barely sparing her a glance. Apparently she was back to being invisible.

"I have it on good authority that the police just served a search warrant for Congressman Parnell's bank records in relationship to the murder of his campaign worker."

Larry looked up, his full attention on her now. "How did you come by that information?"

"Someone from his office. I can't ask her to confirm it. Sort of a deal we struck when I asked her to pass on any interesting news my way."

He leaned back in his chair, his gaze never leaving her. "You think it's legit?"

"I think the guy's in the middle of a huge reelection campaign, and for the police to even be *looking* that direction brings up all kinds of possibilities we never imagined."

ROBIN BURCELL

He chewed on the end of his pen, his gaze locked on her as though contemplating his decision. "Go. Find out what you can. I'd like to know what his reaction is. And take a photographer."

She nodded then returned to her desk. "I'm in," she told Taryn.

"Finally!"

Finally.

THIRTY-ONE

In the end, Casey and Al walked away with several file boxes filled with financial records, a flash drive of the computer copies of same, Trudy's belongings from her emptied desk, and assurances from Parnell and his office manager that his staff would be en route to the police department once his attorney arrived.

At the Hall, they started sifting through the records, and Casey wondered if they'd ever make sense of anything. At the bottom of the box he found the first printout, given to him by Carlotta when they'd asked her to separate all of the checks written to the vendor Margie Foulke. He placed the dozen or so papers on his desk, looking at the check amounts, most no more than a few hundred dollars, definitely nothing that stood out. But there were an awful lot of them, and he pulled out his calculator and started adding them up. No sooner had he entered the last one, looked at the total, when Bishop and Edwards walked into the office. "Kellog," Bishop said. "You heard, right?"

"Heard what?"

"Your security guard. The one from your video who's apparently *not* a security guard anymore. His print matched up to the Ghirardelli robbery."

Casey saw the figure and did a double take. "Son of a..." He looked up, saw Al watching him. "I think I found the hit money."

"Where?"

"The checks written to our vendor. Margie Foulke. Guess how much they add up to?"

"Ten K?"

"Exactly."

Bishop walked up to Casey, bent down so that he looked Casey right in the face. "Did you even hear a word I said? Your security guard. The print matched. You did it."

"Did what?"

"Possibly caught the Landmark Strangler."

"The Strangler?" Casey started from his chair. He wanted in on the arrest. "Are you going to pick him up on it?"

Al put his hand on Casey's shoulder, keeping him in his seat. "Easy, College Boy. Let him talk."

Bishop said, "Wish we could. He walked through an open-air mall and touched a banister. Hardly enough to hook him on murder. In other words, it gives us nothing, just like you've got nothing."

"I'm a bit confused. Then why all the excitement?"

"You're kidding, right?"

Casey waited for Bishop to finish.

"Two alleged robbery attempts and your security guard's fingerprint shows up? One, he's no longer a security guard, and that video shows him wearing what looks like a uniform beneath that windbreaker. What better way to blend into the background than be the guy who's supposed to be watching out for you, right? Two, you're the one who said those robberies didn't look like robberies. So let's say he *is* the Strangler and those are failed attempts. Then he's gonna strike again. And we've got nothing to hold him on but a video showing him in a moment of anger threatening a past victim."

"The print," Casey pointed out.

"A mall. Anyone has a right to be there. Doesn't mean he attacked the girls."

"What about a photo lineup?"

"Already ran one by them. They can't ID him. We're sitting on him now. We're gonna put him to bed at night and get him up in the morning. He so much as sneezes, we're gonna know about it."

Lieutenant Timms's office door opened, and he and the captain walked in. When the captain's gaze landed on Casey, a sinking feeling settled into his gut. He recalled Al's warning about threatening Parnell's office with the attention from the press and knew this was it.

"Sergeant Kellog," the captain said. "I understand congratulations are in order."

Casey was certain he'd misheard. "Sir?"

"The possible break on the Strangler case. Sergeant Bishop informs me it was your lead on an older case that brought everything together."

"Teamwork, sir. And it's far from solved."

"Even so, I just want you to know your efforts haven't gone unnoticed."

"Thank you."

Timms gave a slight nod toward Casey before following the captain from the room.

"Wow," Casey said to Bishop. "That was the last thing I expected. Thanks."

"You deserve the credit," Bishop said. "Let's hope it's a solid lead."

Al gave a slight laugh. "Especially if the other case goes south."

"You got that right," Casey said as his phone rang. He picked it up to answer, thinking if Parnell complained about the way he handled the search warrant request in his office, he was toast. "Kellog. Homicide."

The department secretary. "Congressman Parnell and his attorney are here."

"Be right there." Casey told Al, "Guess who's here."

"That was fast. I was figuring they'd try to delay for a few days at least." He picked up the file folder containing the text messages. "Let's go do this."

Parnell's attorney, a gray-haired man in his early sixties, introduced himself as Jared Monroe, not that he needed to. Casey had seen Monroe on other high-profile cases. As expected from a lawyer of his caliber, he was a sharp dresser, his charcoal suit and blue silk tie probably costing more than what Casey made in a month. Maybe two months. He wasn't even about to factor in the cost of the tasseled loafers.

Casey and then Al shook hands with him.

"Gentlemen," Mr. Monroe said after they were seated on their respective sides of the table in an interview room. "I understand you believe that Congressman Parnell's office is somehow connected to the death of Trudy Salvatori, a fact we can assure you isn't true. That being said, perhaps if you described to us what it is you found, or why you feel Mr. Parnell's campaign financial records are of importance, we can clear his name and be of some assistance to your investigation."

Casey glanced at Al, who gave a slight nod. "Mr. Parnell, thank you for coming down." Casey opened his portfolio. "What sort of relationship did you have with Trudi Salvatori?"

"Coworkers. Friends. We've known each other a few years from working on my campaign in the past, so I suppose you could say we were closer than most."

"How close?"

"Friendly. Joking."

"Did you see her outside of work?"

"No. Not unless it was at some campaign function. A fund-raiser dinner. That sort of thing."

Al rested his hand on the manila folder, giving Casey his cue. "Did you share text messages with her?"

Parnell hesitated, then, "Yes."

"Do you recall any of them?" Casey asked.

Again that hesitation. "We flirted."

His attorney asked, "Where are we going with this?"

Al opened the folder, turned it so that it was facing Parnell and his attorney. "Mr. Parnell. Do you recognize these texts?"

His attorney reached over, pulled the folder closer, then picked up the top page. He was too much of a professional to show any outward expression. Congressman Parnell, on the other hand, said, "These are just harmless flirtations."

"Are they?" Al asked. "I'm sure your constituents would feel the same way come voting time. Or maybe not."

Jared Monroe dropped the sheet into the folder, slammed it actually. "What is it you're implying about my client?"

"That he was involved in an affair with Trudy Salvatori."

"That's preposterous," Monroe said.

"Is it, Mr. Parnell?" Al asked.

"It's okay," Parnell said to his attorney. "We weren't sleeping together. Not anymore."

"Not anymore?" Al asked.

"My first election campaign, we, uh—It just happened. And we promised each other no more. And nothing happened. Those texts are just that. Harmless flirtations."

He seemed believable, Casey thought. But that's probably what made him a good politician. Making people think he was sincere and caring. "What would happen to your campaign if this got out?"

Monroe started to speak, but Parnell waved him off. "I'm running a strong campaign. For the most part, what happened between Trudy and me was a long time ago."

Just like a politician, Casey thought. Double speak. "For the most part?"

"We may have...gone out a time or two recently. But that doesn't mean I killed her."

"Did anyone in your office know about the affair?"

"No one did."

"Did Trudy ever threaten to tell anyone?"

"What? No. Never."

"Mr. Parnell. Do you know a woman named Margie Foulke?"

"The name's not familiar at all."

"She's a vendor on your books. For Internet ads."

"I don't handle any of that. Trudy did. Why?"

Monroe said, "What are you getting at?"

Casey kept his gaze focused on the congressman's face. "As I explained to you at your office, I believe someone paid Darrell Fife to kill Trudy Salvatori."

He opened his mouth to speak, but then shut it as his attorney put up his hand and said, "A contract killing? The idea that something like that could come out of Congressman Parnell's office is preposterous."

"And yet," Casey said, "we found the money in Darrell Fife's home. Money that was picked up from Bay Trust Mutual by Margie Foulke, a woman who has cashed numerous checks drawn on the congressman's campaign accounts."

Parnell shook his head. "That's impossible."

"It's time to shut up," Monroe said.

"No. Because I didn't kill her. And I didn't pay anyone to kill her. My God. This is a nightmare."

Casey asked, "Are you *certain* that no one knew about your affair?"

He nodded. "Positive. We were very careful. And there's no one on my staff now who was around back then."

Jared Monroe placed his hand on Parnell's shoulder then looked right at Casey. "Are you charging my client with anything?"

"No, sir. We're conducting a murder investigation."

"What makes you think this money came from Mr. Parnell's accounts?"

"This." Casey pulled the accounting sheets that Carlotta had printed out. "These are checks written to Margie Foulke for Internet ads. They add up to exactly ten thousand dollars."

"A coincidence."

"Except this same woman was seen exchanging smaller bills for a packet of one-hundred-dollar bills that amounted to exactly ten thousand dollars, the same amount we believe was paid to Darrell Fife." He pulled out a photograph of the bundled money. "This is the money found in Darrell Fife's belongings. These are the banker's initials and the date she gave the money to Margie Foulke. She not only identified her by name, but recalled that she's the same woman who cashed checks drawn on the congressman's campaign account."

"Then she was mistaken," Monroe said.

"We also have a video showing her accepting the same ten-thousand-dollar bundle from the bank teller."

"We'd like to see it."

Casey glanced at Al, who said, "Give me about two minutes. I'll get it and a computer we can view it on."

It was more like five minutes, and Casey grew uncomfortable every time Parnell's attorney glanced at his watch, certain he was going to drag the congressman out of there, thereby ending their interrogation. But he didn't, and Al finally returned with a laptop and the CD from the bank. He popped it in, then fast-forwarded through the video until the moment when the woman in dark glasses entered the bank. He paused the picture, then turned the computer screen so that it faced Parnell and his attorney. "The woman just walking into the door," Al said, hitting PLAY. "Do you recognize her?"

Parnell nodded. "Yes. Of course."

"So you do know Margie Foulke? Or possibly as Marcie Foulke?"

"Who? I—I told you, I have no idea who that is."

Al stood then leaned over, pointing at the computer screen. "*That* is Margie Foulke."

"That," Parnell said, "is Trudy Salvatori."

THIRTY-TWO

Casey stared at the woman in dark glasses and the hat on the video, certain he'd misunderstood what Congressman Parnell said. Or that Congressman Parnell had misunderstood what they were asking about the woman. "You're sure?" Casey asked, just to clarify. "That's Trudy Salvatori?"

"Of course I am," Parnell said. "She worked in my campaign office and, well—I'd recognize her anywhere. Why? What does Trudy have to do with this Margie Foulke you keep asking about?"

"That," Casey said, "is a very good question."

Al directed his fatherly smile toward Parnell's lawyer. "So you understand, Mr. Monroe, why we have questions about Congressman Parnell's dealings with Trudy? This video is rather incriminating. She's picking up the ten thousand dollars we found on the killer."

"Incriminating for whom?" Monroe said, pushing back his chair and standing. "Trudy Salvatori? Are you accusing her of paying for her own hit? Unless you're charging my client with anything, we're done here."

"What the hell?" Al asked after they left. "How did we not see that?"

Casey eyed the picture of the woman in the bank video. "One, she's wearing a dark glasses and a distinctive hat that belongs to her neighbor. Two, she looks nothing like the dead version of her."

"Three, our whole murder investigation just took a nose-dive." Al closed the laptop then gathered his file folders. "Good thing our suspect is dead. We'd be kicking him out of jail right about now."

"Maybe we're thinking too deep on this one," Casey said as they walked back to Homicide. "Let's say that is her getting that money—"

"A safe bet at this point."

"What we don't know is why. She had the means and motive to skim money from the campaign accounts to pay off a blackmailer. Prior experience, familiarity, and access to the money. Create a fake name, write out a lot of low-level checks. Who's going to suspect her? Maybe it was simple greed. Someone caught her in the act."

"And what?" Al said. "Paid someone to kill her with the money she skimmed? That makes no sense whatsoever."

"Unless they decided to keep the money for themselves."

"Then why give all ten K to Darrell Fife?"

A good question, Casey thought. "Maybe while she was busy skimming money, she caught an even bigger embezzler, and he paid to have her killed?"

"With the money she withdrew herself?"

"What if someone was blackmailing her about her affair with Parnell? She—and even Parnell—would have a very good reason not to want that info out."

"Again," Al said, "why did the money *she* embezzled and carefully exchanged into hundreds end up in the hands of the person who killed her? I seriously doubt she would pay someone for her own murder."

"Okay, I haven't worked out that part yet. Maybe she was dying and wanted her husband—"

Al stopped at the door to their office. "Seriously? You have how many degrees, and that's what you come up with?"

"Just throwing it out there."

"Might throw you out there, you come up with more crap like that." Al opened the door to Homicide, saw the office filled with investigators, standing room only, with the lieutenant at the front addressing them. "Clearly there have been developments," Al whispered as he and Casey slipped in then walked toward the back, standing against the wall, since Timms was in midspeech.

Timms looked up from the sheet, saw them. "Good. You're here. Someone pass back a couple of op plans for Krug and Kellog. Note the cover sheet says 'Ghirardelli 211' on it. There is nothing on here that states it's anything beyond the robbery report taken from our victim at Ghirardelli Square. The last thing we need is for the press to get wind of this, have it plastered on the morning news, and thereby ruin any chance we have of seeing what this guy is up to."

Edwards stepped forward. "Page three. Decoys. On the list, Cooper, Brendan, Jones, and Parker," he said, naming female sergeants from Property and Vice. "They'll be splitting shifts. Two in the morning, two in the evening. This should get us some round-the-clock coverage if we see him getting out to case his next victim, and if we need to switch them out. We don't want to use the same one each time, should he start noticing that all the female joggers look alike."

Casey read the names, then glanced at each woman in turn. He raised his hand. "I know this might be a bit late, but I think we might have a problem with the decoys."

"So how would you handle it, Hotshot?" Edwards asked. His expression was almost daring.

"Your decoys need ponytails."

"Not all the victims had ponytails."

"One had her hair in a bun, but they all had long hair. And the Ghirardelli victim specifically said he grabbed hold of her hair and pulled her back."

Al was looking at the line of victim photos on the op plan, nodding. "I think he's right. Grab her ponytail from behind and he's got control of her."

"Except," Edwards said, "it didn't work on the two robbery victims."

"Possibly," Casey said, "because he was thrown off balance by about twenty-five pounds of college books and her laptop. And Ghirardelli girl wasn't going to give up her purse. Make her a jogger. No backpack. No purse. Just don't forget the ponytail."

"Okay. We do it your way. Who do you have in mind?"

"Didn't get that far." Casey glanced at the women in the room, but those with long hair were too old to fit their needed decoy range. "Patrol?"

Al said, "What about that officer you went jogging with on the Presidio case?"

"Windsor?"

"Yeah. Her."

Casey hesitated, ignoring the teasing looks from Haynes and Zwingler at the mention of her name. It wasn't that he didn't think Becca could do the job. More if he was going to date her, he really didn't want to throw her out as serial killer bait. Not that it would have been okay before. No one should have to be a decoy for something like that.

"Good idea," Timms said. "I'll see who else we can get from vice."

"Fine. But I'd like to work on the surveillance part of it."

Haynes crumpled his burrito wrapper into a ball. "Pretty sure he won't strike if you're hanging all over her, Kellog," he said, tossing the thing at Casey's shoulder.

It bounced off, and Casey leaned over, picked it up, and lobbed it into the trash. "You throw like a girl, Haynes. Maybe you oughta volunteer?"

"Too ugly," Haynes said. "Now you…"

"Knock it off," Timms said, "or I'll put wigs on all of you and throw you out there. Kellog, if I'm not mistaken, you and Krug have another case to finish up, but thanks for the offer. Zwingler, Haynes, you two can kiss and make up in the surveillance van for the first shift. Bishop and Edwards, you'll take point first shift." He looked down at the sheet, read off the names for the remaining teams, then finished with, "Any more questions before we meet back here tomorrow at oh-dark-thirty?"

No one had any, and the meeting came to a close. Al and Casey returned to their desks once the room emptied and their seats were vacated.

Casey glanced at the clock, saw Becca was still on patrol, and texted her: Meet for drinks tonight? Need to talk to you about a surveillance tomorrow.

Her response was almost instantaneous, as though she'd been watching the phone.

"Kellog, Krug," Timms said from his doorway. "Let's get an update."

Casey was texting the location for drinks as he followed Al into the lieutenant's office.

Timms sat on the edge of his desk. "So where are we?"

Al laughed. "Damned good question. I'm not even sure we know."

"Kellog?" Timms asked.

Casey looked up from his phone. "Sorry. What was the question?"

"Your investigation?"

"Right. Parnell had an affair with Trudy Salvatori, who we believe set up a fake identity and an account from which she embezzled ten thousand dollars by cashing checks drawn on the campaign fund."

"The *victim*? You're saying Trudy Salvatori embezzled the money used to kill her?"

"Assuming Congressman Parnell's ID is accurate. Not much of her face is visible."

"Let's see if we can't get a secondary ID. I'm still trying to wrap my head around that."

"Yeah," Casey said. "So are we."

"And what did Congressman Parnell have to say about it?"

"The affair was no longer going on," Casey replied. "The texts between them were harmless flirtations. He denied killing her or paying anyone to kill her. And then his attorney decided to end the interview. But on the bright side—"

Al cleared his throat. "Not sure we have a bright side."

"A suspect?" Timms asked. "Do we even have one yet?"

"Well," Casey said, then looked at Al, hoping he'd at least come up with a name.

"We got nothing," Al said. "Who expected such a cluster?"

"What's next?" Timms asked Casey.

"We're still waiting to hear back from Darrell Fife's mother as to the source of this alleged hit money—which seems questionable now. I mean, it's not like Trudy Salvatori would have paid for her own hit."

"On reflection," Al said, "stranger things have happened."

"Find Fife's mom," Timms said. "I want to know where that money came from."

Al stood. "I'll give Mr. Gregory another call."

"Kellog," Timms said as Casey started out the door. Casey turned toward him. "If it weren't for this case, I'd have you front and center on the Landmark Strangler op tomorrow. You deserve to be there."

"Thanks. No worries."

Al was already on the phone when Casey got back to his desk.

"Appreciate it," Al said. "See you tomorrow morning." He hung up. "That was Jon Gregory. His wife should be back tonight. He'll bring her first thing in the morning."

"Can't wait to hear what she has to say."

Al looked up at the clock. "Aren't you meeting Becca for drinks?"

Casey saw the time, realized he was twenty minutes late, and grabbed his keys. "See you in the morning." He rushed out the door, texting Becca, hoping that she was still there.

THIRTY-THREE

The bar was crowded when Casey walked in, and he recognized a number of officers from his days on patrol, several nodding to him as he walked past, as well as a few senior officers refusing to acknowledge him at all. Jesse Turner, a member of the latter group, had tested the same time as Casey for Homicide. When Casey made it, Jesse and the others were vocal in their opinion as to why he shouldn't have been promoted over them. They had a good decade on him in age *and* time on the streets, and their belief was that he hadn't yet paid his dues.

In a way, they were right. Technically he hadn't paid. Not the way they had, working year after year in a beat car. He'd done the minimum time required. It didn't matter that he'd worked hard in those few short years, that he'd set his mind to a goal and stuck with it. All they saw was that he'd caught some lucky breaks with big cases and used that to his advantage.

And maybe he had. But there were sacrifices to promoting so young. Here he was, almost thirty, with no family of his own outside of his parents, not even a girlfriend to speak of. Hard to believe he'd only dated about three women after promoting to Homicide, none of them sticking around past the first callout that got in the way of weekend getaways. Which made the idea of dating Becca even more attractive, he realized, seeing her at the far end of the bar.

Becca understood the job, the callouts, the uncertainty of what they did on a day-to-day basis.

He took the seat next to her, saw she was drinking beer, Samuel Adams, and ordered the same. When it arrived, he lifted it in a toast. "To the end of shift."

"Hear, hear!" She tapped the side of her bottle to his, her smile lighting up her face.

He liked that smile. A lot. And he was just about to tell her so, except someone came up behind him, grasped his shoulder, then leaned in, saying, "You want to know why that Landmark Strangler's still out there? Because they promoted dumb-ass rookies like you."

Casey recognized the alcohol-laden voice. Jesse Turner.

He set down his beer bottle then swiveled the barstool to face the man.

Turner's bloodshot eyes narrowed, his temple pulsing. "You got something to say, Kellog?"

Casey, having the advantage of not being drunk, kept his expression neutral, even when Turner's friends got up and took a stand behind the man. "As a matter of fact, yes." Casey glanced over at Becca. "You want to go somewhere else?"

"Sure."

He and Becca stood.

When Turner didn't move, Becca stepped between them. "You mind?"

"As a matter of fact, I do," Turner said, eyeing Casey over the top of her head.

"And what?" she responded. "You gonna pound me, too? Back off, Turner. There's no glory in hitting a girl."

He looked down at her. "Maybe you should wait outside."

Casey knew what Becca was doing. But he didn't want or need protecting. "Look, Turner. They should've promoted you to Homicide. You and I both know that. But are you telling me that if the roles were reversed, you would've stepped aside, let me have the position? Or would you have taken it if it was offered to you?"

That caught Turner's attention as he attempted to process Casey's question. "Of course I'd take it."

Casey smiled. "See?" Then, digging a couple of twenties out of his pocket, he held it up toward the bartender who had moved closer, just in case things started to spiral out of control. "A round for Turner and his friends."

The bartender nodded, took the money, and said, "What'll it be, Turner?"

Turner, looking slightly confused, glanced at Casey, then the bartender. "Uh, same."

"Have a seat. I'll bring it to your table."

And then, just as quickly as it started, it was over. The four men, including Turner, took their seats at their booth, and Casey and Becca slipped past them unscathed.

"Impressive," Becca said, once they were outside. The wind gusted, and she brushed her hair from her face. "The way you turned it around, telling him what he wanted to hear."

"Not really. When you think about the number of years he's worked, he did deserve it more than me. Makes me think that maybe I should accept the promotion if I pass that lieutenant's test. Turner gets Homicide, and I move on. One less reason for them to hate me."

"Somehow I doubt it. Guys like them are never going to be happy."

She wrapped her arms about herself in the chill air as they both started walking toward the parking garage. "So where do you want to go?" she asked.

"Maybe somewhere quieter. Something I need to talk to you about anyway."

She glanced up at him as they walked. "The surveillance you mentioned?"

"They wanted me to ask you if you'd step in as a decoy in our Strangler op tomorrow. I didn't want to take advantage..."

"How is that taking advantage?"

"I don't know."

"The look on your face tells me otherwise. So what is it?"

He glanced over at her, a bit embarrassed not only because he had taken the matter so seriously, but because she could see right through him. "I didn't want you to feel obligated."

"Over what?"

"The other night..."

She laughed then swatted his arm as they walked. "Frozen pizza? I'm pretty sure I won't feel obligated because of it."

He shrugged, trying to ignore that he was slightly disappointed by her response. The question was why. Because she didn't think the fact they'd almost slept together was that big of a deal? Or because he wanted this to be something more than a casual work relationship? "Nice to hear," he said, trying to brush the whole thing off like it didn't matter much.

The longer they continued down the street, the more their silence seemed an overwhelming obstacle. At one point, he glanced over, saw her looking intently at the ground as she walked, her hands shoved in her pockets, and he wondered if he'd ruined everything by his awkward disclosure.

When they reached the parking garage, he was sure of it, because she kept her hands in her pocket, her gaze averted. "So about tomorrow...Tell them I'm in."

"Okay. It's going to start early. About five."

She finally looked at him. "Which means maybe we better call it a night? Catch our rest now while we can?"

"You don't want to grab a bite to eat?"

"I'm not sure it's a good idea."

Disappointment washed over him at the realization that he'd somehow blown his chances with her. He smiled, hoping she couldn't tell how he felt. "See you tomorrow then."

He started to turn away.

"Casey?"

He stopped, looked at her.

"Don't you even want to know why?"

What man wanted to hear why a woman didn't want to go out with him? Rather than answer, he simply waited.

But the echoing footsteps of someone walking into the garage from the street caught her attention, and she glanced over and waited until the pedestrian had turned the corner out of sight. "This is why," she said quietly. And then she moved closer to Casey, stood on tiptoe, and kissed him.

When the momentary shock wore off, when he realized this was no simple good-bye peck, he took her in his arms and kissed her back.

She pressed herself against him, letting him know in no uncertain terms that *she* wanted him. His pulse rate doubled at her touch. And as soon as it became apparent that *he* wanted her, she backed away, shoving her hands into her sweater pockets and looking at him with an expression he couldn't quite interpret. "What's wrong?" he asked.

"You still don't get it, do you?"

"Not sure I do."

"How much sleep would you get if we kept that up?"

Who cared? Still, he thought it best not to answer.

"I work hard," she said. "And when I'm done? I play hard." She smiled. "Big day tomorrow. See you in the morning, Casey."

And when she turned and walked into the parking garage, all Casey could do at that moment was stand there and watch the sway of her hips, his pulse still pounding from their brief encounter.

Tomorrow was going to be a *very* long day...

THIRTY-FOUR

One advantage of heading into work at zero-dark-thirty was that Bay Area traffic was much lighter, and Casey made it in record time. Even though he wasn't assigned to be there two hours early, he wanted to sit in on the Strangler op briefing because of his part in discovering Francis Dunmore's possible role. Of course there was a good chance that Dunmore *wasn't* the Strangler or even the strong-arm robber from Ghirardelli.

Think positive, he told himself as he walked from the parking garage into the breezeway toward the building's entrance. When he saw Becca and another officer near the doors talking, he slowed. Becca, her long dark hair pulled into a ponytail, was dressed in running gear for the surveillance op. She stood with her back to him. The officer—sergeant, actually—was in uniform, probably working midnights considering what time it was. Casey recognized him from the academy. About Casey's age... Art Sutherland. Nice enough guy, Casey thought, even if he was standing a bit too close to Becca.

It was this last observation that struck him, and though he was too far to hear anything, it appeared they were deep in conversation, probably not even aware he was approaching. And then Sutherland nodded at something Becca said, leaned down, and kissed her.

It wasn't just the quick kiss that bothered Casey. It was the overwhelming sense of familiarity between the two afterward that stopped him in his tracks. Becca never saw Casey there, and he waited until he felt enough time passed that she would have left the lobby, taken the elevator up.

How had he not known she was involved with someone?

Because he never asked. He merely assumed.

And what should he say when he saw her next?

It never occurred to him he'd be running into her ten seconds later as she rounded the corner, apparently not having gotten onto the elevator at all.

"Hey," she said when she saw him as he pushed through the lobby doors. "I didn't think you were coming to this."

"Just wanted to hear the briefing."

"Pride of ownership, eh?"

"Something like that."

She narrowed her gaze slightly. "What's wrong?"

"Look," Casey said. "I know we're not exclusive, but I saw you and Sutherland. In the hallway."

Her brows shot up. "Sutherland?"

Several uniformed officers walked past, giving them a wide berth.

Casey shoved his hands in his pockets, staring at the ground. "I'll admit to being really out of touch, but I just thought—"

"He's my ex."

Not what he wanted to hear. "Ex-boyfriend?"

"Ex-husband."

"Do you have kids?"

"Does it change things?"

"No. Maybe. I—" He realized he was treading on unfamiliar, even shaky ground, especially when she crossed her arms.

"I don't know what you're looking for, Casey, but here's my answer to you. I'm single. I haven't dated anyone since my divorce was final almost a year ago. He and I are still close friends. And no, I didn't think we—you and I—were exclusive either. But I'm also not the kind of girl who—" She smiled at another officer who walked past then waited until the woman was out of earshot before adding, "I can't believe we're even having this conversation."

"I'm sorry," he said.

"Yeah. Me, too. Because I thought I was ready to start dating again. But I think it's apparent *neither* of us are."

And then she walked off.

Casey stood there, wanting to follow her, stop her. Deep down he knew it would be a mistake.

There was too much about her he didn't know.

What if she had kids?

What if she didn't?

Does it change things? He realized that he couldn't answer her question. And until he could with any certainty, she was right. He wasn't ready to go out with her. Probably not with anyone.

"There you are!"

He turned to see Al striding toward him from the elevator.

"Thought you were heading upstairs," Al said.

"Yeah. Got caught up in something." He hit the elevator button, trying to push Becca from his mind.

And failing. At that moment, all he could think of was the image of Becca sitting astride him, dressed only in her jeans and black lace bra. Was that all he thought of her?

"Earth to College Boy…"

"What?" Which was when he noticed the elevator had actually opened. Al was holding the door with his foot. "Clearly I need more coffee."

"At the least."

Once again Al and Casey walked into briefing and found their desks occupied by those working the operation. A table in the back had two empty seats, and Casey took one, while Al remained up front near the door.

Becca walked in a few moments later, eyed Casey and the empty seat next to him, then crossed the room to stand near the window.

Great. Total brush-off.

Even so, several times while the lieutenant and then Edwards spoke about the morning's op, Casey found his gaze wandering in Becca's direction.

She never once looked at him.

"Any questions?" Edwards asked.

"Yeah," said one of the investigators near the front. Casey didn't see who, nor did he recognize the voice. "How is it we think he'll strike here of all places? We're not talking much of a landmark. Maybe a few blocks to the south, but on Stockton Street?"

"Right now, it's our best lead to date, since our team followed him to the Stockton Tunnel last night. Hence the map, in case we end up there."

"Hardly a landmark," the investigator countered. "Not to me, at least."

Al raised his hand. "Take it up with the press. They're the ones who dubbed him the Landmark Strangler."

Edwards said, "Or even better, you catch him, you get to ask why. Right now, we have no idea if he simply has a fascination for watching cars zip through or he's casing the place for something bigger. But there are several spots there that are out of public view. A few alleys, parking garages, the twin staircases leading down to Stockton street from Bush. In other words, a lot of places for us to lose him. So we're going to have a team and decoy there first." Edwards glanced at the clock. "According to our babysitters, he hasn't yet emerged from his mother's house after returning from the tunnels last night. So let's set up at the rendezvous points for your respective teams. And see if we can't get him to pounce on one of our decoys."

A few more questions followed, and once those were answered, Edwards finished by verifying that the street teams—decoys and their backups—all knew where they'd be positioned and where the surveillance vehicles were going to be parked.

Casey remained in the back of the room, watching them file out. Becca left, not even looking his direction.

"Too damned early for this," Al said.

Casey drew his focus from the doorway. "What?"

"Grab your radio. Let's get out of here and get some coffee."

THIRTY-FIVE

"You going to be okay?" Al asked Casey as they walked through the fog from the Sutter Stockton parking garage to the Starbucks on Grant.

"What makes you think I'm not?" Casey replied as they got in line behind business-suited patrons waiting for their caffeine fix.

"Let's see. Ear glued to the tac channel and parking garage practically on top of where they're working." They reached the front of the line. "Two medium coffees, please." Al put a ten on the counter. "She'll be fine. Sometimes these surveillances go on for days before the guy makes any moves."

"I'm not worried about her."

"Bull." Al took the change from the cashier, put some of it in the tip jar. When she turned to get the coffee, Al leaned closer to Casey, saying, "Don't date a cop. Nothing good comes of it."

"You've been talking to my mother?"

"No," he said as he tucked his radio beneath his arm, then picked up both cups of coffee, handing one to Casey. "But you should listen to her. Too hard to separate your feelings and step back. Especially when something big like this is going on."

"I'm technically not even involved in this op," Casey said as he followed Al to the condiment counter.

"So in other words, you came in early just to sabotage any chance you had with the woman."

"Sabotage? You think I did that on purpose?"

"You sure you didn't?" Al set the radio on the counter, turned the volume up slightly.

And as Casey watched him stir two packets of sugar into his coffee, it occurred to him that he wasn't sure at all. A relationship that never took off couldn't be deemed a failure—and Casey hated failing. Was that why he'd come in early?

Al looked over at him. "If you're beating yourself up over it, quit."

"I'm not. I'm just wondering if it's true."

"Maybe it's—"

Al's radio crackled with static as someone keyed it, then spoke. "That him?" It sounded like Zwingler. "He's moving."

Then Becca's quiet voice. "Definitely someone following me."

Al eyed Casey. "You okay?"

"What if something happens to her?"

Al replaced the top onto his coffee. "That, College Boy, is why we don't date the help."

"We're not dating anymore. Sabotage, remember?"

"And she could've said no. But if you're all that worried, we could sit in the car and drink our coffee in the parking garage. We're just a radio call away."

It was still dark out, the streetlights barely cutting through fog. They walked up Bush Street to the garage entrance, since Casey had parked on the second level. Easier access to both Bush and the Stockton Street tunnel below. Radio traffic was sporadic on the tac channel, just Edwards's voice with updates as he followed Becca.

But once Casey and Al were in the car, they heard nothing but static. "Could be us," Al said. "The parking garage causing interference. Or the tunnel."

"What if her mic's out?" Casey said, reaching for the door. "Maybe something's wrong."

"Sit tight, Hotshot. She's got two teams covering her."

"You hear anyone out there? Maybe that's what she's trying to say. They lost her."

Al pulled out his phone then made a call, turning it to speakerphone. "Haynes. What's going on? We're not hearing any radio traffic."

The sound of metal hitting metal filtered in as Haynes said, "Between the fog, the garbage truck picking up trash, and Becca's mic—"

Al ignored Casey's I-told-you-so look. "You have her though?"

"Edwards has her. They were jogging through the tunnel. Should be—"

The radio crackled to life. Becca. "He's on me!"

"Where?" Edwards asked. "I can't see you."

"Brr—"

Casey grabbed his radio then bolted from the car, not even bothering to shut the door. He ran out of the garage onto Bush Street, then turned left toward the bridge, hearing nothing but the whoosh of the cars below as they emerged from the tunnel. Casey's mind raced. Everything he knew about the Strangler was that he'd never strike out here in the open. The stairs, he thought. Twin staircases led from the end of the tunnel on both sides of Stockton Street on up to Bush.

The perfect place to assault someone.

Or kill someone.

He ran to the stairwell closest to him. Raced down, the smell of urine strong, especially at the bottom. No one there or at the entrance on Stockton Street. To his right, car headlights blinded him as the vehicles sped through the tunnel toward him. The sidewalks were empty. He looked to his left. Any number of doorways she could have been dragged into. But Stockton was a busy street. Too busy. When it was clear, he crossed to the middle, looked to the right. A break in traffic, and he raced up the stairs on the other side.

Clear.

He stood there on the top at Bush Street again.

The streetlights barely penetrated the fog. The sidewalk was slick with moisture. He stopped, listened. No radio traffic. Nothing to indicate anyone else was out here.

Then the sound of someone running toward him.

Casey drew his gun, then lowered it as Edwards emerged from the fog.

Edwards saw him, stopped, out of breath. "You see her?"

"No," Casey said. "The stairs are clear."

"I missed her…somewhere around here…Could have sworn she ran up the stairs. Fog…"

Brr "Burritt?"

Edwards turned around, looked up at the street sign. Right behind them. A dead-end and barely wide enough to be an alley.

They ran to the building's edge, peered into the alley. If any of the streetlights had been working before, they weren't now. Casey listened once more, heard something metallic and hollow clanging at the end. Garbage cans. This guy liked alleys and Dumpsters. Places to hide, he thought.

Guns drawn, they raced in. They were nearly to the end of the alley when Casey saw a flash of white. The stripe from Becca's running suit. "Police!"

Becca called out as she struggled with a man in dark clothing. They fell against the garbage cans, knocking them over. Edwards had them covered, and so Casey holstered his weapon, grasped the male by his jacket, dragged him off-balance. Something fell from the man's grasp and clattered to the ground. He turned, swung, his fist striking Casey's jaw. But Becca grabbed the man's other arm, bent his wrist in a lock. He cried out in pain as Casey shoved him to the ground. Becca, still holding his arm said, "Cuffs?"

Edwards tossed his to her, and she cuffed the man's hands behind his back. "Francis Dunmore, you're under arrest."

She held Dunmore by the arm, Casey taking the other side when he tried to pull away. He said nothing as they walked him out. But when they neared Bush Street, Dunmore glanced up at a placard high on the side of a building.

Casey followed his gaze, but it was too dark to see what was written there, and a black-and-white pulled up at the alley entrance. They led Dunmore to the car, the uniformed officer taking custody and searching him before he placed him in the back of the unit.

"Hold up," Casey asked the officer as he walked around to the driver's side. "He dropped something back there. You have a flashlight?"

"Sure," the officer said, then pulled one from his belt, and handed it over.

Casey started toward the back of the alley, then realized Becca was on his heels. He waited for her, his jaw aching from the blow. "You okay?" he asked.

She reached up, rubbed at her throat. "I'll recover. Just didn't expect to end up back here, of all places."

They reached the end of the alley, and Casey shone the light about on the ground in the direction he thought he'd heard something drop. "About this morning…" he said, as he swung the beam around, searching. "I just want to apologize—"

"There," she said, pointing below one of the trash cans. A short baton, the sort a licensed security guard might carry. "That's gotta be what he held up against my throat."

He radioed for a CSI to photograph the weapon, then process it for prints. As he and Becca walked out, he tried once more to apologize.

"Just stop," she said then quickened her pace. He considered following her, but figured she'd been through a lot, needed her space.

Maybe it just wasn't meant to be, he thought as Al walked up. "Got him, huh?"

"Yeah." Which was when he remembered the placard on the side of the building. He swung the beam of light up and read:

ON APPROXIMATELY THIS SPOT
MILES ARCHER,
PARTNER OF SAM SPADE,
WAS DONE IN BY BRIGID O'SHAUGHNESSY.

Al saw the sign. "Dashiell Hammett. Son of a gun. Maybe it was about the landmarks."

Word traveled fast, and by the time Casey made it to the Hall of Justice lobby, he'd received several congratulatory handshakes from officers who were in the building. The other investigators filtered back into Homicide, nodding at Casey, ribbing him for his part. Even Lieutenant Timms came out to shake his hand—just before telling him to get back to work.

In truth, other than his slightly bruised jaw, Casey felt great. How could he not? He'd played a hunch, and it had paid off.

Eventually the talk died down. Zwingler and Haynes showed up a few minutes later, Zwingler holding up a large pink box. "Pony up, Kellog. Your turn to buy donuts."

"How's it my turn?" Casey asked.

"It's tradition. You promote out, you buy the donuts. Figure with this feather in your cap, you'll ace that oral board tomorrow."

"That," Haynes said, "and it really is your turn."

Casey dug some money out of his pocket and tossed it onto Zwingler's desk. "I'm only taking the test for practice."

"That's what they all say," Zwingler replied, opening the box, then pulling out a glazed donut. "But I have *yet* to see *anyone* walk away from a promotion. And after today's arrest, you'd be stupid to turn it down. Timing's everything, and right now you're a superstar." Zwingler lifted his donut in a toast then ate it in two bites.

Casey bypassed the donuts, pouring himself a cup of coffee instead, thinking about what Zwingler said. *Would* he walk away from a promotion? It just never occurred to him that he'd get it.

But maybe Zwingler was right. Landing in the top five on the written portion, and now the arrest of the Landmark Strangler...

Something to think about, he told himself as Al's desk phone rang.

"Krug, Homicide...Great. Thanks." Al dropped the phone in the cradle, then called out to Haynes. "Grab the remote and turn on the TV. Channel two."

Haynes rolled his chair back and did as asked. Everyone turned to the television and listened to the anchor, Sarah Brighton. "...latest poll showing numbers have dropped significantly since Congressman Parnell's office was linked to the murder of Trudy Salvatori. Lacy, have the police issued a statement yet?"

Lacy's face appeared on a split screen next to Sarah's. "According to the press information officer, the case is *still* under investigation, and *no one* at Congressman Parnell's offices is considered a suspect. They're merely looking at every lead that will assist in the investigation. And yet late last night at the Parnell campaign office, there was a very different scene going on. Chaotic even."

A clip filled the screen, showing Parnell emerging from his building with the usual cadre of reporters following after him.

"Congressman! Congressman!" someone shouted. "Do you have anything to say about the latest allegations in the murder of one of your volunteers?"

Congressman Parnell quickened his pace, trying to get past them. "I have every confidence that the police will get to the bottom of this. I suggest we let them do their jobs."

"Sir! Is it true a search warrant was served on your office in regard to the murder?"

"No comment."

"Is it true that the money found in the killer's possession came from your campaign accounts?"

Parnell stopped, then faced the woman who asked the question. Jenn Barstow. Casey about doubled over when he saw her, almost missing the congressman's answer. "*No one* from my office is involved in any way in the death of Trudy Salvatori. And if the unthinkable happens and we find out different, then I will be first in line to assist the police in their investigation. Now if you'll excuse me. I'd like to get home to my wife and children."

He turned and left, his aide ushering him into a black sedan that sped off the moment the door closed behind him.

The picture switched back to the field reporter, who said, "There you have it. Congressman Parnell is neither confirming nor denying that the police are now looking into his campaign office records in the death of Trudy Salvatori. We're told the police intend to release a statement—"

Al grabbed the remote from Haynes, then shut off the television. "Can you say *screwed*? As in we are?"

"How would she have gotten that information?" Casey asked, glancing over at the lieutenant's office, wondering how long it would take to filter back to him. Luckily his door was closed. "It wasn't like we announced it to the world."

"Doesn't matter. That's what it'll look like." Al tossed the remote onto the table, then returned to his desk. "And the first person they're going to suspect is that pretty little reporter you were working with."

"They can suspect all they want," Casey said as his phone rang. Worried it was the lieutenant, or worse yet, the captain, he was relieved when it turned out to be the secretary. "There's a Mr. and Mrs. Gregory in the lobby waiting for you."

"Thanks."

The timing couldn't be better, Casey decided. After seeing that news report, he needed the distraction of work.

THIRTY-SIX

"**M**y boy is *not* this Landmark Strangler. He just isn't."

"Of course," Casey said to Mrs. Gregory. A neutral response was always best when you had no idea where someone was going with their statement. Besides, what was he supposed to tell her? We know who the Strangler *really* is? Your son was just an ordinary hit man? But when she started crying, Casey offered a sympathetic smile, though not quite up to par with the one Al gave. Apparently, though, Casey was getting better, because she didn't look quite as upset. "Go on."

"I told you about that phone?"

Casey recalled her mentioning a phone and wondered if it was the same one they'd found in the truck. There were no texts, just numbers belonging to other pay-as-you-go cell phones. In other words, a burner phone, one in which they were still waiting for the reports on which cell towers it had been closest to at the time of the calls. "A friend of your son brought it, I think you said?"

"With that envelope filled with money. I—I asked my son what it was for. He said it was a job, so naturally I was happy. He was finally working."

"Did he say what that job was?"

She pinched her mouth closed, looking hesitant, and her husband reached out and grasped her hand. "It's okay," Jon said.

"No. It's not." She gave them a broken smile. "I was worried they were going to pin all those murders on him. I heard him, you know. That morning."

"Which morning?" Casey asked.

"When that woman was killed on the jogging trail. I was in the truck."

Jon Gregory's brows shot up. "What d'ya mean you were in the truck? You *knew* he had it?"

"He needed it for the job. I had that appointment, and I thought he could drop me off, come back, and pick me up. What was I supposed to do?"

"Tell him to pound sand, Lin. Look what—"

"Mrs. Gregory," Casey cut in. "What do you mean you heard him?"

"Well, I don't think he realized I could hear the voices."

"Voices?" Casey echoed, suddenly worried she was talking about something in her head. Or her son's. Even Al sat up at that.

"On the phone," she clarified. "My son is—was—a little hard of hearing. An artillery accident in the Middle East. He's been to the doctor, but...what was it you wanted to know?"

"You heard voices..."

She nodded. "On that phone. A man, saying something like, 'She's leaving now. She'll be there in about forty minutes.' And then my son asking, 'What's she wearing?' The man said blue and black. And that's when I heard a woman's voice in the background, saying something like, 'Same as me.' Like they were on a speakerphone, because her voice was as clear as his."

Casey and Al exchanged glances. Trudy had been wearing a blue-and-black running suit, something that hadn't been released to the press. It fit. Which confirmed in Casey's mind that this was legitimate information. "Did you hear any names mentioned?"

"No."

"Anything at all?"

"No. Just that when we saw her, I asked him what was going on. I thought it was like a PI job. That's what he told me."

Casey looked up from his notes. "You *saw* her?"

"Leave her house."

All three—Casey, Al, and her husband—simply stared. Finally, Casey asked, "You saw the murder victim leave her house?"

"Well, I don't know if it *was* the same woman who was killed. But we were parked up the street when that phone call came, and then out she popped from that front door, dressed in blue and black, just like the caller said. And when I asked my son what was going on, he told me not to worry. He was just going to follow her. Like a PI. And then he dropped me off, and—" She glanced at her husband, then broke down again. "I'm sorry. I just—I wanted him to have a job…"

"Can you believe her?" Casey asked after the Gregorys left. He and Al were sitting in the interview room, where he was finishing up his notes. Stalling, he realized. Not wanting to return to his desk, worried that the news report with Congressman Parnell was now common knowledge. "We should arrest her."

"For what? Being stupid and wanting to believe her son was innocent? I don't think it'll fly. Especially since he's dead."

"For being an accessory after the fact. Her son was a dirtbag. And right after someone delivers ten K *and* a cell phone to him, a woman ends up dead—a woman she knew he was following."

Al shut off the light of the interview room, and the two walked back to Homicide. "We'll be better served finding out who was on the other end of the phone during that call she overheard. We know Fife called a burner phone, one that wasn't used after the initial call."

"What about triangulating the cell towers? At least we can get a general idea about *where* the call went to?"

"That, College Boy, is—"

Both stopped short when they saw Jenn Barstow waiting in the lobby, her gaze pinned on Casey.

Al gave a neutral smile. "I'll see what I can't wrangle from the phone company while you, well, do what you gotta do."

He continued on toward the Homicide office, and Casey waited until he was out of earshot before saying, "How did you find out about that search warrant on Parnell's office?"

"A confidential source."

"Yeah? Well everyone seems to think that source is me. So in the future, if you're looking for a statement, you need to go through the press information office." He started to walk off.

"I was wondering if you had a chance to look at those videos."

Casey stopped, faced her, tried to ignore the vulnerability he saw in her eyes over her foster sister's case. But then he reminded himself this was the same woman who had gone after Congressman Parnell last night like a pit bull. The last thing he planned to do was tell her about the Ghirardelli op and the arrest of Dunmore. That would come out soon enough. Just not through him. "We're looking at them," he said as the captain and Lieutenant Timms rounded the corner. "If you'll excuse me," he said, hoping they wouldn't notice. "I have a lot of work to do."

Her faint thanks followed him down the hallway, and he was acutely aware that both Timms and the captain were right behind him.

He barely made it to his desk when Timms called him into his office. This is it, he thought as he walked in, shut the door.

The captain, his arms crossed, glared at Casey. "I'm not even sure where to begin. I've got a US congressman calling me about a threat you made to sic the press on him. Right after he comes here to give a *voluntary* statement to you last night, he gets accosted by the press with information about a warrant you served."

"The press thing was a misunderstanding," Casey said.

"A misunderstanding? Did I imagine the reporter you were talking to just now?"

"I didn't even know she was here until I walked out of an interview with someone else. And for the record, I asked where she found out about the warrant. She said the information came from a confidential source."

"And she didn't mention a name?"

"No," Casey said. "I can assure you, though, it wasn't me."

"Then what were you talking about?"

The feeling that his career was riding on this answer struck him hard, and he glanced at Timms, whose expression remained neutral. "She was asking if we'd had a chance to view the video evidence on the murdered prostitute case. I told her we were looking into it."

"What the *hell* do you think the press information officer is for?"

"The evidence was hers."

"Hers? The reporter's?"

"She's the one who suggested the connection between that past case and the Landmark Strangler. Without her we'd have nothing."

The captain stared as the words seemed to penetrate. "That reporter?"

"Yes, sir."

"Son of a—" He slammed his hand on the desk, then closed the distance between them. "Do you realize that Congressman Parnell has lodged a complaint against us? Against *you*?"

"No, sir."

"Well, he has. And if I so much as find out you have fed one iota of information to the press—if I even *see* you talking to a reporter about this or any other case, about the damned weather, even, I will boot your sorry ass back to patrol. Do I make myself clear?"

"Yes, sir."

"Dismissed."

Casey walked out.

"You okay?" Al asked.

Casey strode past Al without answering, on out the door, down the hall to the men's room. Finding it empty, he paced the floor, then turned toward the sink.

"Damn it!" He slammed his hand against the wall, then caught his reflection, saw the growing bruise on his jaw. Instead, he focused on the drain, almost afraid to look at the mirror for fear he'd smash his fist into it as well. He had enough bad luck without adding a broken mirror to the mix, he thought as Al walked in a few minutes later.

"Thought I might find you in here," Al said.

Casey refused to look at him. "It was like I had everything going for me this morning. Then bam! All gone..."

Al said nothing.

"How do you do it, Al? You blaze through interrogations and interviews, political correctness be damned, then walk out completely unscathed. Nothing fazes you. You never lose your cool. You—"

"I what?"

"You make it all look so easy. I don't get it, Al. I had my whole future planned out. The degrees, the police work, my life. I bust my butt, thinking I'm doing the right thing, saying the right thing, and I get my ass handed to me for it."

"Are we talking about the investigation or the girl?"

Casey glanced at Al in the mirror. "Does it matter?"

"You ever see that cartoon about a book called *How to Understand Women*? It's like three feet high with a gazillion pages. Spot on. When it comes to women, sometimes you need to step back. Take it easy. Don't rush things. If it's meant to be, it's meant to be."

"Pretty sure I screwed it up beyond repair. Becca wouldn't even let me talk this morning."

"You never know with women. Give it some time."

Casey gave a cynical laugh as he faced Al. "Even if Becca decides to overlook my idiocy with her, who's going to want to date a loser like me? I'll be lucky if I'm not booted from Homicide and transferred to midnights before the day's over."

"The reporter thing? I'll admit it looks bad. Not like you were dating her or anything. Maybe wait until everything settles before you start charging up your flashlight."

"After what we saw on the news? The congressman filed a complaint, and I've got my promotional interview tomorrow. How's that going to go over?"

"You're young. You'll recover just fine. And by this time tomorrow, all the world's going to know you were instrumental in catching the Strangler. So you play that card for all it's worth. Congressman Parnell, on the other hand...A shame, too. The guy really was a decent politician. Got things done. Just..." He shrugged. "He got screwed because he was sleeping with someone from his office who had the effrontery not only to embezzle money from him, but to get murdered." Al leaned against one of the stalls. "Talk about dumb luck."

Someone walked into the men's room, one of the investigators from Property. He nodded at Casey and Al, then walked past them to the urinal.

"By the way," Al said. "Tony Salvatori called about the card we left on his door last night. Let's go talk to him and see if we can't at least make some headway on that case."

THIRTY-SEVEN

The drive helped to clear Casey's mind, and he was considerably calmer by the time they arrived at the Salvatori home.

"Thank you for seeing us again, Mr. Salvatori," Casey said when they showed up at his door. "But we have a few more details we're trying to clear up."

"Of course. Please. Come in."

He held the door for them, and they entered. The house was neat, but dark, the heavy floral drapes closed. A stack of unopened cards sat on the table in the entry, undoubtedly condolences, along with other mail, bills, also unopened. Casey wondered what it must be like for those left behind, faced with the day-to-day tasks of living while the police continually reminded them of the dead. "I hope we won't take up too much of your time," he said, pausing in the foyer.

"Would you like some coffee or water or..."

And just as Casey was about to decline, never wanting to bother anyone, Al said, "That would be great. Water." Because that's what Al did best. Always got people to do something else. Or think about something else.

"This way." He led them through the dining room into the kitchen at the back of the house. Here, the white lace curtains were open, the window a beacon of light in comparison to the funereal dark they'd just passed through. The window faced the Valentines' house next door, and Casey glanced that direction, saw the blinds in the Valentines' kitchen shifting slightly.

Undoubtedly Marcie or Devin watching, he thought as Tony asked them what they wanted to drink.

"Water," Al said.

He turned to Casey.

"Nothing for me."

Tony filled a glass with ice cubes and water from the automatic dispenser on his refrigerator and handed it to Al. Then he pulled out a chair at the kitchen table. "Sit, please."

They did so, and Casey opened his notebook. "I apologize in advance, Mr. Salvatori, if these questions seem impersonal, but—"

"No, no. I understand what you must do. Ask away."

"Thank you." And even though he technically had permission, it still didn't make the job of exposing layers of one's personal life any easier. Especially if those layers were revelatory in unexpected ways. "We were wondering about Trudy, about, well—" The man looked as though he was ready to start crying, and Casey couldn't quite bring himself to ask.

Al leaned forward, his eyes sparkling with kindness as he ripped off the first layer. "Was Trudy having an affair with anyone?"

Tony stared at Al for a good while before finally saying, "We worked past all that, Trudy and I. A long time ago."

"But you were getting divorced?"

"What I mean is, the anger was over. We realized we were no longer in love. She went her way, I went mine."

"Who was she having an affair with?"

"That's just it. I don't know. That office manager, I think. Roy Webber."

"And you?"

"Well, I know you heard. My real estate agent. But that was over a long time ago, too."

Al nodded at Casey, who pulled out copies of text messages between Trudy and Congressman Parnell. "Mr. Salvatori,"

Casey said. "Any chance your wife was having an affair with the congressman?"

Tony eyed the messages, staring for a very long time. "She lied to me. I knew she was seeing someone. She never said it was the congressman. It was someone else. Someone who wasn't even working there anymore…It was the only reason we agreed that she would still work there."

"Anyone from his office ever call you and talk to you about it?"

"No." His voice was barely a whisper, probably trying to digest the lies his wife had told him.

Casey, hating this part of the job, glanced at Al, noting his expression was one of compassion. And Casey tried to emulate it as he asked, "How were finances between you and your wife?"

He leaned back in his chair. "It's worse than I thought. She hid a lot of what she spent from me. By the time I sell the house and pay off her credit cards….Not a lot of extra to go around."

"Did you ever see your wife with money she couldn't explain?"

"We had a joint checking account. And savings."

"Beyond that."

"No. Nothing that stands out. What does this have to do with her murder?"

"That's what we're trying to find out."

"I don't understand."

"Mr. Salvatori. Were you ever aware that your wife was skimming money from the campaign accounts at Congressman Parnell's office?"

Tony Salvatori stared at each of them in turn. Then, as the words seemed to sink in, he asked, "My wife? Was stealing money from Parnell's office?"

"We believe so."

"Why would she do that?"

"That's what we're trying to find out."

"You think someone killed her because she was stealing money?"

Al said, "We're still trying to figure things out, Mr. Salvatori." He opened the laptop. "There's a video we'd like you to see. It will only take a minute." He clicked on the file, then turned the screen so that it faced Tony. "Any idea who that person is? The one with the hat."

Tony leaned in close. "It looks like Trudy."

"Are you sure?"

"I think I'd know my own wife."

"Even though you can't see her face?"

"Trudy had a very distinctive walk. And I recognize the purse. I can show you."

He got up and walked to the living room. Casey followed for the simple reason that cops are always uneasy about someone being out of sight. Especially in the middle of a murder case. And when Salvatori opened a closet just off the entryway, then reached in, Casey instinctively slipped his hand beneath his jacket, felt for his weapon. A moment later, Salvatori emerged, holding a large black handbag. He shook it, jangling the keys hanging from a ring hooked to the strap. "You see? Trudy always hung her keys on her purse. Just like in the video."

The two men returned to the kitchen, Tony placing the purse on the table. He reached out, lifted the key ring, grasping a large silver heart-shaped charm among the keys, turning it over. "It's from Tiffany's," Tony said. "Trudy told me the girls at the office chipped in and gave it to her." He let it fall from his grasp, as though it had suddenly burned him. "I thought it seemed expensive."

Casey eyed the picture paused on the screen. Definitely the same heart-shaped key ring. "Would you mind if we had a look inside the purse?"

"Have at it."

He pushed the purse toward Casey, who pulled out her wallet, a makeup bag, hairbrush, and an assortment of papers, half of which he handed to Al to look through, while he searched the other. It was there he found one single stub that had been torn off one of the checks made out to Margie Foulke. Casey set it on the table, sliding it toward Tony. "Do you know anyone named Margie Foulke?"

"No. Never heard of her."

"We believe that was the name your wife was using to collect money. Ten thousand dollars."

Tony sat back in his chair, his jaw dropping open as he took in the amount. "Ten thousand dollars? For what?" He stared at the check stub. "That doesn't make any sense."

"We're still looking into what it means," he said, noting that Al seemed absorbed in something he'd pulled from an envelope.

Al turned a page, his brows rising slightly. "Mr. Salvatori..." He held out the documents. "Why didn't you mention that you and your wife both had recently taken out large life insurance policies?"

Tony stared at the papers in Al's hands. "Honestly? I forgot about them. It wasn't my idea. I—"

"What do you mean, not your idea?" Al asked.

"Trudy wanted to do it. She was worried that if something happened to either of us and we weren't able to sell the house, we'd lose everything."

"And have you contacted the insurance company, yet? About her death."

The man's face paled. "Yes..."

"Didn't forget for that long, then, did you?"

"I swear. It's true. Bev's the one who reminded me."

"Bev?"

"My real estate agent."

Al folded the papers, returned them to the envelope, then gathered up the rest of the papers, replacing everything into the purse. "Are you and Bev still involved?"

"No. I swear."

"You understand we'll need to take this. We'll get you a receipt."

Tony nodded, his yes barely audible.

Casey wrote out a receipt on the evidence-booking form, handed it to Tony, then said, "We'll see ourselves out."

If Tony heard them, he gave no indication, and Casey's last glimpse as they left the kitchen was of a man looking scared.

THIRTY-EIGHT

A
l handed Casey the Salvatoris' insurance policy in the car. "Look at the amounts," Al said.

Casey scanned the pages. The policy listed Trudy as Tony's beneficiary and Tony as Trudy's. Tony was insured for one million, Trudy for half a million. "That's a lot of money."

"See the witness on there?"

Casey read the signature witnessing the designation of the beneficiaries and saw Bev Farland's name. "Is it possible Trudy didn't know about her husband's affair with the real estate agent?"

"Guess it's possible. Depending on who you talk to, it seems almost common knowledge."

"If you were having an affair with someone, you think your wife would've let that woman witness the beneficiary on your life insurance policy?"

"Exactly what I was thinking. So either Trudy forgave the woman, didn't know about the affair, or we've got some forged signatures. Either way, what you're holding there is plenty of motive to want Trudy dead."

"Five hundred thousand reasons, I'd say. Definitely enough to go have a chat with Ms. Farland and find out if she's the female voice heard by our killer's mother."

Fifteen minutes later Casey and Al arrived at the office of Bev Farland Real Estate, situated on Broadway, just east of Montgomery. Bev was at her desk, talking on the phone when they walked in, and she covered the receiver and said,

"Don't suppose you're here to inquire about property, are you?"

"No," Casey replied as he and Al took seats in front of her desk.

"Hey," she said into the phone. "Something came up. Let me give you a call back." She gave Casey a cynical smile. "If you're not here to buy something, then what are you here for?"

Al leaned back in his chair, crossing his arms, waiting for Casey to take charge. He slipped the insurance documents from his folder. "Is this your signature?"

She eyed the paper. "It is."

"And...you forgot to mention that you actually witnessed a fairly new insurance policy taken out on the victim?"

"It was also taken out on the husband. And since the policy was Trudy's idea, it didn't seem something worth mentioning. Had it been the other way around...?" She gave a shrug.

"Trudy's idea?"

"Yes. Tony told me."

"So basically, you have Tony's word that this policy on his now-dead wife was her idea?"

"And later, her word. I was there. Signing it, if you recall." Her smile did not reach her eyes.

Casey wanted to reach out and shake it off her face. "What was the reasoning behind it?"

"Money, of course."

"Were you involved in her murder?"

She stared for several seconds. "You're kidding, right?"

"No, Ms. Farland. We're not. What were you doing between the hours of seven and eight on the morning of the homicide?"

"*I'm* a suspect now? What happened to the guy you chased into the oncoming car?"

Casey glanced at Al, who gave a slight nod as if to say you're on the right track. "He's still dead. Just implying that he might not be the only person involved."

"Wants to share the blame, eh? Imagine that. I was here, in this office, and I have the security tapes to prove it. You're welcome to look."

"If I recall, you told us you were out of town on the day Trudy was murdered."

"I was in LA. But I was here that morning. I didn't find out until after I got back."

"Were you here alone?"

"All morning." Her cell phone rang again, and she pressed a button, silencing the ringer. "What motive could I possibly have to kill the woman?"

"That's what we're here to find out."

"If I had to go to prison for murder, I'd at least make sure it was for something worthwhile, Sergeant, and Trudy Salvatori was not. She was a pain in my ass ever since they listed that damned property. All I needed her to do was sweet-talk her neighbor into cutting down that stupid eucalyptus grove so I could list the place as a bay view. And yes, I could have increased the price tag had it worked, but kill her for it? Uh, no." Her phone vibrated on her desk, she picked it up, looked at the caller ID, then returned it to her desk. "Maybe the person you need to be looking at is Marcie. *She*, apparently, was incensed that Trudy would even ask. Or maybe that Trudy was stupid enough to have an affair with Marcie's husband, thinking she could get him to convince Marcie to cut the damned trees down. I could have told Trudy she was wasting her time."

"Why is that?" Al asked.

"Because Marcie's husband has no say in the matter. The property and the parcel with all the eucalyptus behind it belongs solely to Marcie. I know, because I looked it up. Inheritance."

"The parcel doesn't belong to the city?"

She heaved a sigh. "Every last stinking eucalyptus tree and the ground beneath it belongs to Marcie, and Marcie alone. But she was adamant that as long as she was alive, it was staying in the family."

Al and Casey looked at each other then Casey asked, "How much would something like that be worth? That parcel?"

"Alone? Not a lot, because there's no access or easement to the road. But take a house in front to create an easement?" Her eyes lit up. "We're talking the *last* piece of *undeveloped* property in the city with an ocean view—well, once you raze those trees. That property in the right hands? Unprecedented bidding war." And then a sigh of resignation. "Unfortunately, sentiment got in the way."

"Sentiment?" Casey asked.

"Marcie's. Like I said, she refused to sell—never mind she got into it with Trudy about those damned trees. I'd be a rich woman if it weren't for stupid people." She typed something on her keyboard, then turned her computer screen so they could see the security video of the morning in question. "Here you go. Me, the morning of the murder. The alarm company also has a copy, so in case you think I have some way to tamper with this feed, I don't." Her phone buzzed again, she picked it up, eyed the screen, then said, "Is there anything else? I have a business to run."

Casey looked at Al. "You have anything?"

"Not at the moment," Al said, and they left after instructing her to call if she thought of anything else she might have forgotten to mention.

"Okay, sport," Al said, once they were outside. "If not her voice, then whose? Marcie's? Because she's the only one left."

"Well, she's certainly got motive. Her best friend's sleeping with her husband. Wouldn't be the first spurned spouse to off the other woman."

They walked across the street to where they were parked, the Bay Bridge visible at the bottom of the hill. Casey unlocked the car, and Al opened his door but nodded at the vista below.

"Another million-dollar view. Imagine if you could afford a place looking out at that."

"You think Marcie would kill Trudy over the trees?"

"People have killed for less." Al shook his head. "But if I had to pick a motive? The affair with Marcie's husband seems more likely."

"Good point," Casey said, as they got into the car, then buckled their seat belts. Casey checked his mirror then pulled out. "And add that affair to the fact she's already pissed that her friend's trying to get her to cut down her grandfather's legacy? That could work. But let's say Marcie *is* our female voice. Who was she talking to?"

"That, College Boy, is the half-million-dollar question. And if I had to bank my money, I'd put it on the recipient of that life insurance policy."

Lieutenant Timms was watching for them when they got back, and Casey realized the man looked as though he'd aged several years since that morning.

For that, Casey felt responsible. It had been a long day, and it seemed that with every step forward, they'd taken one back. A new piece of information seemed to fit, then it slipped away the more they looked into it.

And though they now had the cell phone records, unlike the Strangler case, there were no smoking guns like the video of the security guard to save this case.

Not to mention they had an angry congressman defending his campaign trail.

"Close the door," Timms said.

Al pushed it shut, and they both took seats.

"Tell me you can make this case go away."

"Not exactly," Al said. "But we're closer. And if it makes you feel better, we have other suspects besides the congressman."

He nodded at Casey, who pulled out the reports they'd gotten from the phone company. "We finally got the records on that cellular found in Fife's car. It triangulates to within the parameters of Marcie's and Trudy's house. We already know Marcie lied about leaving before Trudy. This just confirms it."

Timms made a notation on a legal pad. "This is the call that Fife's mother overheard?"

"It is," Al said. "A man talking and a woman's voice in the background."

"Speculation on the voices?" Timms asked Al.

"Tony for the insurance. Parnell to silence her about the affair. Possibly his wife if she found out. Some as yet unknown person at his office regarding finances. And then there's the neighbors, Marcie and Devin. Just the motive's a little thinner there."

"What about the real estate agent sleeping with Trudy's husband?" Timms asked. "Any chance she was in collusion with him? Get rid of the wife, take the house off the market, and cash in that policy?"

"Except," Casey said, "the real estate agent has security footage of her at her office, right around that time."

Timms frowned at that. "So you think it's possible that Marcie colluded with Trudy's husband?"

"Possible," Al said.

And Casey added, "She did lie about leaving the house before Trudy. We found the hat Trudy wore in her house, and when we booked Trudy's purse, we found Marcie's ID in it."

The lieutenant tapped his pen on his desk, eyeing the two of them. "Marcie appears to be the common link." He glanced up at the clock. "Bring her in tomorrow morning. Let's get to the bottom of this."

They started out, and Timms said, "Kellog."

Casey stopped in the doorway, faced him.

"This thing with Parnell and the reporter...He filed a complaint with OPR. He thinks you're the source."

"I wasn't."

"It's been a long day. You have the oral board tomorrow. Go home."

Casey nodded. The thing that stuck with him as he returned to his desk was that Timms did not say he believed Casey. Just told him to go home.

Wasn't much he could do about it. Wait it out, Al had said.

Secretly, though, he wondered if he should just skip the oral board tomorrow. Why bother showing up when the captain, a man who had a very big say about who was promoted, was being influenced by an angry politician? Besides, he was only taking it for practice, wasn't he?

He locked his desk, refusing to answer that question himself.

"You out of here?" Al asked, watching him.

"Yeah."

"See you tomorrow."

Casey was nearly to his apartment when he realized he didn't want to go home. He drove to his parents' house instead.

His mother saw him pull up, then met him on the porch, her gaze widening when she saw his face. "Is that a bruise?" She reached up, touched his jaw. "How did that happen?"

"A bunch of us were tackling this guy during an arrest."

She made a noise that implied she knew he wasn't being entirely forthcoming. But she didn't pursue it, instead asking, "What *are* you doing here?"

"Just thought I'd visit."

"What a nice surprise. Are you staying for dinner?"

"Depends. What are you having?"

"Leftovers. Spaghetti. Your dad's playing poker tonight. So it's just me."

He followed her into the kitchen, opened the fridge, then pulled out a beer.

"How was work today?" she asked.

"Fine," he said as he searched through the drawer for the bottle opener.

She walked over, plucked it out, and handed it to him. "You don't look like it was fine. You look stressed. I can't imagine why you wouldn't be. Working as hard as you do. And with that big test tomorrow."

"It's just an interview. And I'm not sure if I'm going through with it."

"Why not?"

"I've got a lot going on."

"Have you talked to Al about it?"

"Why would I?"

"He's supposed to be your mentor. That's why they put you together."

"It's not a decision he can make for me.'"

"Well, I think you should. You know how I feel."

"I know," he said, pulling out a barstool and sitting at the counter.

"Turn on the TV."

"The quiet's nice, Mom."

"Oh, nonsense. Who wants to hear me talk?" She walked over to the small TV on the kitchen counter and turned it on. "I'd rather hear the news."

The last thing Casey wanted to hear was the news, but he also didn't want to worry his mother, so he sipped at his beer, and pretended interest in her reheating the spaghetti in the microwave. She looked up when she heard the sound bite on the arrest of the possible Landmark Strangler. "That has to have a lot of people relieved," she said, watching the newscaster discuss how many murders he was suspected of. Then she eyed Casey. "Weren't you involved in that case?"

"Just peripherally."

She opened the refrigerator, pulled out a bag of prewashed lettuce, then placed a handful on two plates. "Do you want any cucumbers on your salad?"

"Sure," he said, his gaze glued to the television as Congressman Parnell appeared.

"That poor man," his mother said. "Having something like that happen in the middle of his campaign."

"Yeah…"

She eyed Casey. "Are you part of that investigation?"

"You know I can't talk about it."

She reached over and turned up the volume.

Parnell's voice filled the room. "What we have here is a travesty of justice. An overeager investigator using bullying tactics to make his case by threatening my staff. If you look into his history, you'll see that he's recently taken the lieutenant's exam. He's skewering me and my campaign to make a name for himself when he appears before the promotional board. Well, I'm here to say it's not going to happen. He'll have to find someone else to malign. I will *not* let a corrupt police detective dictate the direction of my campaign. I'm here to stay."

"Casey…" he heard his mother say.

He held up his hand, wanting, needing to hear this. Wondering how much of a career he'd have left by tomorrow as the crowd of onlookers applauded the congressman's words. A moment later, someone pushed his way to the front, calling out, "She was my wife!"

And when it seemed the congressman's paid security were going to block the man, Parnell waved them off. "It's okay. This is Mr. Salvatori, Trudy's husband." Parnell reached out as though to shake the man's hand. "Mr. Salvatori—"

Tony Salvatori took a step forward, then swung at Parnell, hitting him in the face. "Maybe if you hadn't slept with her, she'd—"

A security guard tackled him, and the crowd surged forward, everyone shouting at the same time.

"Oh my—" His mother stared at the TV in shock.

Casey's gut twisted as the congressman's men hustled Tony Salvatori from view. He put down the beer, suddenly losing his appetite. "I need to go."

"You're investigating that case, aren't you?"

He nodded.

"Well. Then I'm glad that man punched him. I would have done the same."

"You realize he just called me corrupt on national TV?"

"The only thing *anyone's* going to remember about that interview is that a US congressman was publicly accused of sleeping with that man's dead wife." She reached over and patted Casey's hand. "Makes me glad I didn't vote for him."

THIRTY-NINE

When Casey walked into Homicide the next morning, Al, Haynes, and Zwingler were standing in front of the television, their attention glued to the news, where they were replaying the clip of Parnell accusing Casey of being corrupt.

Al saw him. "You see this?"

"Don't remind me. I just want to fade into obscurity and have this week be over. This month, even."

"What are you talking about?"

"Did you miss the part where he accused me of being corrupt? On TV?"

"Trust me. The only thing *anyone* is talking about right now is that accusation that Tony Salvatori made about Parnell sleeping with his wife. They pretty much cut out most of that earlier speech, going right to the coldcocking of the congressman, while the newscaster is narrating that Trudy Salvatori was murdered."

"Got him good," Zwingler said, turning off the television. "After a show like that, there is no way this guy can run for reelection."

Al walked over to the coffeepot and poured himself a cup. "You ready for that interview?"

"I don't know if I'm going to do it."

"Of course you are. You put too much time into it. And like Zwingler said, you're a superstar."

"So you think Marcie's good for it?" Casey asked. "The murder? Because I'm not seeing it."

"We know a man and a woman were heard talking on the phone with information that ties them into the murder—one or both probably hired Fife. The only women we have left— and with motive to kill Trudy—are Marcie and the real estate agent."

"What if the real estate agent faked that security video?"

"Maybe she did. But I also checked with the airport. She'd have to do some serious driving to get to that plane in so short a time. Not impossible, but definitely difficult."

Haynes glanced over at Al. "What about Parnell's wife? I think she'd have some motive."

Al and Casey both turned toward him, Al saying, "We have her in our sights. But if we can identify the male voice, we can probably figure out who the woman was." He looked up at the clock. "What time's your interview?"

"Five," Casey said.

It seemed everyone cringed at the response. Al gave him a sympathetic slap to the shoulder. "Tough luck, kid."

The last interview of the day was not an enviable position. Quite simply it was difficult to concentrate on anything when all one could think about was the upcoming promotional board. "That at least leaves me time to look into some of those leads."

"Negative, College Boy. The only place you're going to be working is at that desk."

"We're talking nine hours from now. I'll go crazy if I have to sit here that long."

"And you'd go crazier if you got stuck out there on some call, or worse yet, in traffic."

"Besides," Zwingler said. "We have a vested interest in making sure you pass. There's enough bad lieutenants out there."

"He's right," Al said. "So use the time to catch up on reports. We'll let you break for lunch."

"Awful big of you. Except Marcie's supposed to come in this morning."

"Reschedule," Zwingler said. "What if she dives over the table and tries to strangle you or something? We can't have you hurt before the big interview."

"I think I'll be okay. But thanks for your concern."

Although they expected Marcie to show up with her attorney, she showed up alone. The first question out of her mouth was, "Does my husband know about this?"

"We haven't told him," Casey said. "Why? What do you think he'd say?"

"That I need my attorney. Should I call him?"

Although Casey wasn't sure if she meant her husband or their attorney, he had to be careful about how he answered. "That's your decision."

She seemed to think about it then nodded. "What do you want to know?"

Casey opened his folder, took out her ID card, which was now in a clear plastic evidence bag, and placed it on the table in front of her. "Is this yours?"

She looked at it, nodding.

"Where's the last place you had it?"

"In my purse."

"You have no idea where you lost it?"

"I didn't even know it was gone."

"Why would Trudy have it?"

"Trudy?" She looked up at Casey, then at Al. "I told you both. Things keep turning up missing. Little things. My keys. Now this. How should I know? Maybe she took it."

Casey replaced it inside his portfolio. "Have you ever been to the campaign office where Trudy worked?"

"Once. A while back."

"Did anyone ever give you any checks written from Parnell's campaign accounts?"

"No. Why?"

Al smiled at her. "We're just trying to re-create Trudy's last days," he said. "And clear up some inconsistencies."

"What inconsistencies?" she asked.

Casey waited a beat, trying to see how she'd react. "We know you lied about leaving before Trudy. You left after her. So who did you call on your phone?"

"I didn't call anyone."

"You don't have another cell phone that you were using? A throwaway phone?"

"What? No."

"Why did you lie about when you left?"

"I don't know what you're talking about."

"Do you recognize these text messages?" Casey asked, sliding the printout from the phone company toward her. "'She's leaving.' You're talking about Trudy. Aren't you?"

The color drained from her face. "How did you get these? I erased them."

"On your phone, yes. But the phone company has them on their server. So let me ask you again. Why did you lie to us about when you left?"

Tears sprang into her eyes. "Fine! I followed her, okay? I thought she was screwing my husband, and so I hired this guy to rough her up, but I changed my mind."

"Rough her up?"

"Let her know that she needed to leave Devin alone. They were spending all this time together. I just wanted to scare her, not hurt her."

"And who was it you hired?"

"I don't know. Someone named Ben Johnson."

"How much did you pay this guy?"

"A few hundred dollars. A hundred and fifty to take the job, then the same once he confronted her."

"A few hundred? That's it?"

"He wasn't doing very much. Just scaring her. But I lost my nerve and called it off. I—I worried that if Devin found out, he'd leave me. I mean, they were moving, right? Trudy and Tony? All I had to do was wait it out."

"You called it off?"

"Yes."

"And how do we get ahold of this Ben Johnson?"

"I don't know. I found him in this chat room. We did everything online. And then it was by text. Except the one time we met in person. When I paid him the first installment. But you have the number. Can't you just get in touch with him from that?"

"Unfortunately he's not answering it, and there haven't been any messages since your last one to him."

"Can you blame him? I'd be scared too. I *was* scared. After Trudy was killed, I was sure you'd blame me. Even Devin thought so."

"Devin knew?"

"I couldn't keep a secret like that from him. Not after I accused him of sleeping with Trudy. But he wasn't. They were planning a surprise birthday for me. I even called and verified it. A weekend in Napa."

Al smiled at her. "Did you kill Trudy? Or pay someone to kill her?"

"What? No. Of course not." Tears streamed down her cheeks. "I want to go now. Can I go?"

Al opened the door. "We'll be in touch."

She walked out, not looking back.

"Why'd you let her leave?" Casey asked.

"Because we don't have enough to hold her, and we need to find this Ben Johnson person. And to do that, we're going to need to get a search warrant for her computer. Which means we can show up there tomorrow. You can write up the warrant. That will give you something to occupy your time until your interview this evening. You bring anything to study?"

"I've been studying every day. It's like I dream this stuff."
They continued down the hall toward their office. Casey thought about what his mom said. To ask Al. "You think I should do it?"

"Of course I do. Why wouldn't you?"

"What if I pass?"

"Isn't that the object?"

"I was always just taking it for practice."

Al looked over at him. "You sure about that, College Boy? What about the battle plan?"

"I haven't been in Homicide all that long."

"Yeah, but you have to be here for the right reasons. Most of these guys, they're in it for the long haul. Retiring out after doing their time here. I don't think anyone expected that of you. We've always known you were on your way somewhere."

"Maybe I won't be promoted. Parnell filed a complaint on me with OPR."

"Filed, I'll bet, when he thought he still had a chance at being reelected. After that debacle last night—"

"Doesn't matter. It's there. They're going to take that into consideration."

"They'll investigate and find out it's not true. Which means they'll interview that reporter."

"Who won't reveal her source."

"You know what I'd worry about?" Al said, once they reached the office. "Passing that interview. Everything else will work itself out. Trust me."

Work itself out? Why then, was he doubting everything, including that interview?

FORTY

"Devin?" Marcie said, when her husband finally called home. "I've been trying to call you all day. Why didn't you answer your cell phone?"

"Sorry. Just a lot going on here at work. I must have turned the ringer off."

"The police questioned me again this morning."

"Why didn't you tell me?"

"Because you didn't answer your phone."

"What did they ask?"

"About Trudy having my ID. They had it with them."

"What for?"

"I guess for evidence."

"Look, Marcie. You shouldn't be talking to them without our attorney. It's not safe."

"If I take an attorney, they're only going to think I'm guilty. I don't want that."

"What you don't want is to be arrested for murder."

"That's ridiculous. They're not going to find anything." She glanced up at the clock, saw it was nearly five. "Are you working late again?"

"Sorry. A lot going on. But that's why I called. I had to take the car to the shop, and I need you to pick me up."

"Okay."

"And bring the gun. It's in the kitchen drawer."

"Why?"

"You said you thought someone was following you. I want to take you to the range for practice."

"I'm really not comfortable carrying that thing around."

"Don't worry. It's not loaded. And once we get you through this firearm practice, you'll be plenty comfortable."

"I thought you said you had to work late."

"I'm almost finished. By the time you get here, I should be done. We can go to dinner after. There's a restaurant nearby we could walk to."

It had been so long since they'd gone to dinner. Something they used to do all the time. "I'd like that."

She heard a phone ringing in the background as Devin said, "I have to get that, Marce. Call me when you're on your way."

"Okay."

Her phone beeped when he disconnected.

How was it that her life had come to this? Every sound she heard scared the living daylights out of her. It was almost as if Trudy had come back to haunt her.

Marcie's gaze caught on the eucalyptus grove out back, and she crossed the room, opened the door, then stood there on the threshold, breathing in the sweet, almost piney scent of the trees that Trudy had wanted to remove. Even Devin had suggested it for a while. After all, if improving the view increased Trudy's property value, surely it would increase theirs. Which was when Marcie told him that she had no plans to move from her grandfather's house; therefore, it didn't matter.

She closed and locked the door against the chill that swept into the room, regretting the past few weeks, wishing she'd not thought so ill of Trudy, and even Devin. Now there was only guilt, and somehow the smell of eucalyptus only intensified that feeling.

Maybe she should sell the place, she thought, putting on her coat, then heading downstairs to the kitchen to get her keys. Start fresh, where there were no reminders of how she'd maligned the memory of her once good friend over this perceived affair.

She thought about the gun. Even Devin had suggested that this stalker of hers was imaginary. Was she losing her mind?

Maybe she was.

Maybe she shouldn't be carrying around a firearm, loaded or not. But Devin was finally going to take her to the range to practice, and that is what she wanted.

She opened the drawer. The black semiauto was sitting on top of some old bills. What an odd place to keep a gun. Why not in the bedroom, where someone was likely to be attacked? She didn't want to touch it, but forced herself to take it in her hand, wondering how to even tell if it was loaded or not. Now what was she supposed to do with it? Put it in her purse?

Dish towel, she decided, wrapping it, then carefully picking it up so that her finger was nowhere near the trigger.

At the front door, she punched in the alarm code, then walked out, locking the door behind her.

"Marcie!"

She saw Tony on his porch, holding a white envelope in his hand. He was crying, and the only thought that went through her head right then was that she didn't have time to deal with his grief.

Not very neighborly to be sure, but dealing with her own personal crises was stressful enough.

"I'm in a hurry," she said. "I'll stop by later, okay?"

"You should see this." He held up the envelope.

She unlocked her car with the key fob and opened the front passenger door, setting the towel-wrapped gun as well as her purse on the front seat. She wondered how rude it would be to dart around to the other side, get behind the wheel, and drive off. Whatever was in that envelope was not something she wanted to see.

But he walked toward her, his grief mixed with anger, and she found her feet glued to the sidewalk, the envelope beckoning. Before she knew it, he stood in front of her.

"Look at this," he said, handing the envelope to her.

The typewritten address on the front belonged to Tony, the space where the return address would be written was blank. A canceled stamp was postmarked with yesterday's date and showed it was mailed here in the city.

Why she even noticed this, she couldn't say, except perhaps the look in Tony's eye, the shaking of his fingers as he'd handed it to her.

"What is it?" she asked.

"Open it."

She did, pulling out a computer-printed photo of Devin and Trudy kissing. Both were seated at a table with a white tablecloth, a bottle of wine in front of them.

Marcie recognized that restaurant. In Napa. She and Devin had been there twice. The cost of even the house wine was exorbitant.

"Where did this come from?" she asked, turning the picture over. Nothing written on the back.

"Today's mail."

So many thoughts crowded her head, first and foremost that she'd been right. They *were* having an affair.

Her knees felt as though they were giving way, and she leaned against the car. "Did you know about this?" she asked Tony.

He shook his head. "Did you?"

"I suspected. The day she was killed…She came over to our house and was upstairs talking to Devin."

Tony looked away, wiping his hands across his face. "Why didn't you say something?"

"I'm sorry," she told him. "When I asked Devin what was going on, he said they were planning a surprise party for my birthday."

"You believed him?"

Guilt and shame flooded through her. "I—I guess I wanted to believe that they really were planning something for me. It was so much easier…" Her attempt to smile faded when she saw his face, the pain in his eyes, the tears. "I'm sorry."

"It's not your fault. She was leaving me anyway. I just…why would someone send this now? Just to hurt me?"

And what could she say? That by coming out and showing her, it was like someone sticking a knife in her gut, too? And here she and Devin had been making strides in getting their marriage back on track.

Or was it all her imagination? No. Devin had been manipulating her the entire time. Anger surged through her at the thought.

Her phone alerted her to a text, and she knew it was Devin, asking if she was on her way. She held up the photo. "Do you mind if I take this?"

"I—I don't know."

"I think we deserve an explanation."

Tony sucked in a ragged breath, his gaze fixed on the picture. "Okay."

Worried he might change his mind, she walked around to the driver's door and got in.

Tony knocked on the passenger window, and she lowered it. "What if there's some explanation?" he asked. "Maybe someone's just trying to hurt us?"

"All the more reason to let me show this to Devin and find out what's going on."

She tossed the photo onto the seat beside her, started the car, then pulled away.

At the top of the street, she glanced in the rearview mirror and saw Tony standing there, watching her still. It struck her as odd, and she glanced over at the passenger seat, saw the butt of the gun showing from beneath the towel.

She hesitated, wondering if she should go back and explain why it was there.

Then again, why bother?

It wasn't as if she was planning on doing anything wrong. At least that's what she thought until her gaze flicked to that photo.

FORTY-ONE

Casey spent what little time was left before his oral interview finishing up his report on the Presidio case and writing up the search warrant for Marcie's computer. The office was quiet. Most of the investigators were in the debriefing for the Landmark Strangler surveillance and subsequent arrest. The captain was holding a press conference later, and he wanted Dunmore booked on murder charges so that he could announce to the world that they had caught the Strangler.

Unfortunately, all that they had was circumstantial evidence of the current attacks on the three women, including Becca.

But Casey also knew they had served a search warrant on Dunmore's apartment and located some very incriminating evidence, and even now they were interrogating the man on what they'd found. And though Casey would have liked to at least observe—via closed-circuit monitor—the interrogation with the other involved investigators, he knew his time was better spent finishing up the Presidio reports.

That case was still outstanding, a killer still on the loose.

In truth, he hoped that by going over the notes and reports he had written and finishing those he hadn't, he'd find that one piece of evidence or detail that would lead him to the answer.

Who had hired the hit on Trudy Salvatori?

And why?

He had never really liked Marcie for the crime. But the more he looked at it, the more everything pointed to her.

And an unknown male.

Not a lot he could do about it now, he thought as Al and Bishop walked in.

"We got him," Bishop said. "The Strangler."

"*You* did it, Kellog," Al said. "It was the hooker case that broke him. Once he saw the video, it changed the course of the interrogation. West had him in the palm of his hand."

"Where is West?" Casey asked.

"Still in there, finishing up the interrogation with the captain for his press conference," Al said, picking up a file folder from his desk. "Going over the finer details, aka the rest of the nails in Dunmore's coffin." He eyed the report Casey had just finished. "Get any studying in?"

"I wanted to finish this first."

"So it's done. Go get a cup of coffee. Take a break. You deserve it." Al tapped the stack of note cards sitting on Casey's desk. "You have less than half an hour. Use it wisely."

Casey eyed the cards that he'd studied so diligently each night, feeling confident that he'd ace whatever questions they threw at him. Even so, he picked them up, went over them again. Funny, but until this very moment, he hadn't been nervous. And now that the interview was nearly on him, his stomach started knotting. There was a lot riding on this. He told himself that he wanted this, wanted to promote, prove to himself—to his parents, to Al, to everyone in Homicide and Robbery—that he could do this, that he was cut out to supervise.

Time flew. A glance at the clock told him he was due upstairs in five minutes. He secured the cards with a rubber band then tossed them onto his desk.

He was slipping on his suit coat when Al and Lieutenant Timms walked in from the adjoining office.

"You ready?" Al asked.

Casey took a deep breath then let it out slowly. It helped, and he grinned. "Ready as I'll ever be."

"Good luck," Timms said, shaking his hand.

"Thanks, sir."

Timms left, leaving him alone with Al. The silence grew, and Casey gave a pointed look at the clock. "I better get up there. Any last-minute advice?"

Al studied him a moment. "Look 'em in the eye and be sincere."

"That's it?"

"Not sure you need much more than that. You got the Strangler. The rest should be easy."

"Thanks. For everything. For making me the investigator I am."

Al made a scoffing noise but then shook hands with him. "Making you less of a pain in the ass, you mean? Good luck, College Boy. I'm sure you'll knock 'em dead."

Casey walked out, wondering if he shouldn't have worn his black suit instead of the charcoal gray. Like a suit color would make a difference.

Nerves. Funny what they did to a man. At least he looked calm on the outside. And as Al said, he had the Strangler cases beneath his belt. Surely that was worth something. But as Casey took a seat in the waiting area where the orals were being conducted, he wondered if being in Homicide and solving some high-profile case was any more of an advantage than that of these other candidates who had far more years of street experience. Maybe it was like Al said. He'd promoted too fast.

"Quit second-guessing yourself," he whispered to the empty room.

He thought about what he was going to say when they asked that all important question, "Tell us about yourself." The answer was supposed to be a spin on one's career, what many in law enforcement called the I'm-a-god speech. His spin was that everything he'd done in his career led to being a good supervisor. Even so, he wished he'd brought his note cards, just to go over it one more time. Then again, the last thing he wanted was for someone to walk out that door and see him studying them. And no sooner had that thought crossed his mind than the door swung open. A sergeant he barely knew from patrol walked out, his black suit fit to perfection, the burgundy-and-blue stripes of his tie contrasting sharply against his crisp white shirt.

The man eyed Casey, nodded, then continued on past him, and Casey's heart started thumping at the realization this was it. His time was near, the moment he had to prove to everyone that he had what it took to be a good lieutenant.

"We'll be right with you," a woman said from inside the room, just before she closed the door, undoubtedly for everyone to tally and compare notes on the candidate who had just left.

Be calm...

And surprisingly, he was. His heart rate slowed, and he went over his intro speech in his head, making sure he knew both the long and short version in case they threw in some time limitation.

About ten minutes later, the same woman called him into the room, asking him to sit at the table, facing the woman and three men, all lieutenants, two from outside agencies. Introductions were made, and then the woman said, "Tell us about yourself."

"I currently work in Homicide—"

"Kellog..." the lieutenant from Oakland PD said, and Casey tried not to let his gaze drop to the man's tie. He couldn't help it. It clashed with his shirt. Purple and yellow. The guy's wife must be out of town, or she'd never let him walk out of the house in that thing. Color-blind, he thought as the man said, "Didn't I just see you on the news recently?"

It was a moment before his words registered, and Casey worried he was going to bring up Parnell's accusation of him being corrupt. "Possibly. We've had a few high-profile cases."

"Right. The Landmark Strangler case. Were you involved in that?"

"Yes, sir," Casey replied, realizing his I'm-a-god speech was being derailed by the notoriety of the homicide case. "We made the link from an older case."

The Oakland PD lieutenant nodded. "Good work." And then they started peppering him with questions about supervising, never giving him the opportunity to say what he'd prepared. It didn't seem to matter. They were all leaning forward, their attention on him, some even nodding in agreement as though he'd hit on the right answer. He was feeling really good about this. And then that Oakland PD officer asked, "You're supervising a problem employee. One who always seems to be the square peg trying to fit into the round hole. What do you do to make him fit?"

"What sort of problem?"

"You decide."

It was one of those standard rhetorical questions that oral boards favored to see his thought process in action. He kept visualizing someone trying to pound that square peg into the hole. Only he couldn't get his mind off the man's tie.

Color-blind…

And suddenly, all he could think of was the hat they'd seen in Marcie's living room.

He slid his chair back and stood. "You know, that's a really *good* question, and if I had time," he said, looking at his watch, "I'd answer it."

"Is something wrong?" the woman asked.

"Possibly. It just occurred to me that I may have overlooked a very important detail in my murder investigation."

"The interview's not over. Can't it wait?"

"That's just it. I don't know." He started backing from the room, realizing from the looks on their faces that he had completely blown any chances of passing this interview. He stopped, thought about shaking their hands, but figured it wouldn't do any good at this point. "Sorry to waste your time, but duty calls."

He turned and left.

"What the hell?" he heard the Oakland PD lieutenant say.

The woman followed him. "Sergeant Kellog!"

"Sorry, Lieutenant," Casey called out, not bothering to stop. "I may have made a terrible mistake on a case."

"But the oral interview…"

He hurried down the hallway, took the stairs to his office. By the time he reached his desk, he was breathing hard.

Haynes seemed surprised to see him. "You aced the interview that quick?"

"Not exactly. Where's Al?"

"The morgue. Should be back in a few."

Casey grabbed his keys and two portable radios, then hurried out the door. Al was just walking out of the morgue when Casey got to the lobby.

"How'd the interview go?" Al asked as Casey handed him his radio.

"I walked out in the middle of it."

"What the hell for?"

"The Presidio murder. Which is where we're going."

"And what? It couldn't have waited the fifteen minutes for you to finish?"

"I'll explain in the car," he said, calling the op center to have a couple of black-and-whites stand by just up the street from the Salvatori and Valentine houses.

Traffic was fairly thick, and he turned on his emergency lights, making a sharp right turn into an alley, then coming out on the next street over, which was less crowded. He ended up taking side streets, bypassing the busy intersections. He was just a few minutes away when his cell phone rang. It was Becca.

He was shocked to hear from her. Recovering, he said, "Can I call you later?"

"You may," she said. "But right now I'm with Mr. Salvatori."

He realized she was one of the units sent out to stand by. "I wanted everyone up the road."

"And we were," she said. "Until Mr. Salvatori called us. He saw Marcie taking off with a gun on her front seat. Pretty upset by the sound of it. Something about a photo of Devin and Trudy sitting at a restaurant, far too close for casual acquaintances."

"Thanks for the call."

Al overheard. "Guess Trudy had more than the congressman on her list of conquests. So where do you think Marcie was on her way to?"

"If I had to guess? Wherever Devin is." And then he turned on his lights and siren and made a U-turn, heading to the construction site at the Marina District.

FORTY-TWO

Marcie slammed on her brakes and blasted her horn at a car that zipped in front of her from the adjoining lane. As usual, commuter traffic choked the streets and undoubtedly frayed the nerves of every driver on the road.

As if Marcie's temper wasn't already stretched taut.

Her fingers itched to pick up that gun, aim it at the jerk in front of her—and anyone else who got in her way.

She pictured the headline: MAD HOUSEWIFE SHOOTS DRIVER IN ROAD RAGE INCIDENT ON WAY TO KILL HUSBAND.

This was all Devin's fault. She should've told him to find a ride home on his own. She hated driving in rush-hour traffic. Okay, maybe she shouldn't have made that one stop first. That delay certainly didn't help matters. But she was seeing red, not thinking about how crowded the roads were becoming.

Finally, though, she arrived. She parked near the fence, careful to keep the gun wrapped as she walked to the gate of the construction site, which was still unlocked. Most of the workers had left by now, and she didn't see anyone on the grounds. Just as well, considering, and she walked around to the side of the building, to the door that Devin texted her would be unlocked.

He wasn't in his ground-floor office, and she called his cell phone. "Where are you?"

"Top floor," he replied. "Come on up."

"I thought that level wasn't done yet."

"It's getting there. At least we have windows now."

"I'm on my way."

Her footsteps echoed on the polished concrete floor as she crossed the expansive lobby to the elevator. The once-dated bank building had been transformed into modern, upscale offices, with the top two floors renovated into penthouse offices with bay views that would turn a hefty profit when they were sold or leased out.

Her husband was counting on that money, since his business had invested far more into it than they could afford.

A risky venture with great rewards, he'd told her, and that was the thought she carried with her as she gripped that towel-wrapped gun. She pressed the elevator button. The door slid open. She stepped on and rode it up to the top.

The elevator opened to a vast, empty space, the floors unfinished and covered with sawdust and metal shavings. Steel framing indicated where offices would eventually be placed, but at the moment one could see all the way across the entire floor to the far side, where her husband stood over a table set up on two sawhorses.

He saw her and waved. She walked over, her heart slamming into her chest with each step. How was it she'd managed to be so calm downstairs, but not here?

"What took you so long?" he asked.

"I needed to make a stop first." She glanced at the table, saw blueprints laid out, weighted down by a toolbox on one side and a large wrench on the other.

"For what?"

"Why did you lie to me?"

"About what?"

"Tony seems to think you and Trudy were having an affair. He wanted to know if I knew about it."

"We've already had this discussion."

"That was before I saw this." She reached into her purse and pulled out the photo, placing it on top of the blueprints. "That's *our* restaurant."

He glanced at the photo. "So Tony got the letter?"

She'd expected him to deny everything. Come up with excuses. "It's true?"

"Of course it is."

"How could you?"

"How could I what?"

"Send the letter to Tony!"

He gave a casual shrug. "I needed to make sure you saw it. I knew he'd show it to you."

"But...why?"

"Easy. I don't love you. It's your fault that Trudy's dead."

His words hit her like a blow to her gut. Her heart thudded, and her legs turned to lead weights, too heavy to move. "Why did you need me to see that picture?"

"Same reason I needed you to bring the gun." He nodded toward the bundle in her hand. "And why I had the security camera installed in the kitchen. So there'd be proof that you were angry enough to come kill me."

"I wouldn't kill you."

"Well, that's just it. You only *tried* to kill me. I was fortunate enough to get the gun from you before you could."

"You're insane."

He lunged toward her and grabbed the gun, throwing the towel to the floor. He aimed it at her. "Calculating, yes. Insane? No."

Move, she willed herself. But she couldn't take her eyes from the gun. "It's not loaded."

"You're sure? It feels like it is."

Marcie saw the elevator from the corner of her eye. It seemed so far.... "Devin. Think about what you're saying. You don't have to do this. I'll give you a divorce. Whatever you want."

"The house?"

"Is that what this is about? Because I won't sell my house?"

"Do you even know how much it's worth? How much those damned trees behind it are worth?"

She edged toward the table. "Did you kill Trudy?"

"Her death was an accident."

"Accident...?

He took a step forward. "It should have been you."

Fear and adrenaline ripped through her. She grabbed the pipe wrench and threw it at him. Then she turned and ran.

He didn't shoot. But she realized that if he was going to make it look like she was trying to kill him, he'd have to be closer.

She darted around a ladder, keeping it between her and Devin.

"There's nowhere to go," he said, circling the ladder as she did, looking at her through the rungs.

"Think about this, Devin. You don't want to go to prison..."

"Me? You're the one on camera getting a gun out of the kitchen drawer. You and your imaginary stalker." He side-stepped the ladder, and she turned and ran. He was on her in a second, slamming her to the ground. She heard a ringing in her ears, smelled and tasted fresh sawdust as she tried to suck in air through her mouth as he forced her face to the floor, then pressed the barrel of the gun into her ribs. He yanked her by the arm to her feet, then toward the sawhorses. "Trudy might not be here anymore, but I think she'd want to finish this."

"Why would Trudy want this?"

"She set it up. We found out how much the property was worth. Those damned trees..."

Her grandfather's trees. She wanted that to be her final thought. The trees behind her house. The last good place...

FORTY-THREE

Casey heard the gunshot as the elevator opened on the top floor. He and Al stood on either side, their weapons at the ready, Al calling for backup on the radio.

No cover, Casey thought, shoving his foot against the door to keep it from closing. But Marcie and Devin seemed to be locked in an embrace, unaware they were even there. Blood streamed down Devin's arm as the pair struggled.

"Police!" Casey shouted.

Devin looked up, saw them. "She has a gun. I'm shot!"

Then Marcie, crying. "I didn't do it!"

And before Casey or Al could make a move, Devin swung Marcie around, putting the gun to her head, her body as a shield. "Come any closer, and I'll kill her."

Casey froze, his weapon trained on Devin.

Al whispered, "You have a shot?"

"No." Casey scanned the room, saw there were a few places that might offer some rudimentary cover. "Split up. Divide his attention."

Al looked around then nodded. "Slow. That gun moves our way…"

"Got it."

They stepped out, each moving the opposite direction.

"Stop!" Devin said. "I *will* kill her."

Casey knew very little about negotiations, except that their job seemed to be to keep the suspect talking. Keep his mind off the hostage. "You don't want to do this, Devin."

"Yes, I do. I've wanted to for a long time." Marcie started sobbing. He shook her. "Shut up," he said. His attention on her, Casey and Al sidestepped away from the elevator. "You had to ruin everything. From the beginning. I couldn't catch a break because of you."

"I'm sorry…"

"Yeah. You are now." He looked at Casey. "She hid. That's why Trudy was killed." Al made a step to the side, and Devin turned that way. He held the gun up closer to Marcie's head.

Casey knew he needed to keep Devin's focus away from his partner. Al had the best chance to come up behind him. "We know it was an accident. You didn't mean for Trudy to die. It was the phone calls."

"Calls? You're trying to confuse me."

"The one to the killer. You told him that Marcie was wearing blue. She was wearing purple."

Al, still circumventing the room, waved his fingers as though to say, "Keep talking. It's working."

"And then the call to your attorney. About the hat. You said it had a blue flower. It was purple."

"I didn't know…" He lowered the gun slightly.

"How could you?" Casey asked, glad to see Marcie's sobs quieting. That's what they needed. Calm. "You see red as green. Purple as blue. You'd have no way of knowing the color, unless someone told you. Like the hat. When Marcie told you the flower was purple."

"None of that matters," Devin said, raising the gun again, Marcie flinching as he put it to her temple. "Trudy's gone. I loved her…"

The emotion on his face struck Casey. And with it a flash of insight. "You didn't know about her and the congressman? She was having an affair with him."

"No. She loved me."

"She was using you. Whose idea was it to kill Marcie?"

He hesitated, looked over his shoulder, a sense of panic in his eyes when he saw how far Al had moved. But then he turned back to Casey. "She loved *me*."

And then Al said, "Was it before or after she found out how much Marcie's property was worth?"

He turned, forcing Marcie with him so that they faced Al. "After. But—" His throat seemed to seize, and he looked down at the top of Marcie's head. "What have I done? Oh, God—" He lifted the gun.

Casey fired. The shot echoed throughout the room.

Devin staggered back, then crumpled to the ground, the gun flying from his fingers. Marcie stood frozen, tears streaming down her face, her gaze fixed on Casey.

"You're okay," he said, then moved forward, past her, his aim still on Devin.

He was still alive, bleeding from his hip. Casey kicked the gun toward Al, who picked it up and covered Casey while he hand-cuffed Devin. "You have the right to remain silent. Anything you say can and will be used against you…"

FORTY-FOUR

The last person Casey expected to see in the lobby when he and Al showed up for work the next morning was Jenn. She was wearing her glasses again, and he realized he liked them on her. Wasn't sure how he ever thought they didn't fit.

"Sergeants," she said in greeting. Then to Casey, "Is there somewhere we can talk?"

Al glanced down the hall. "I'll wait over there. Give you two some space." He walked over to reception.

Casey, worried that someone would see them together, led her to one of the interview rooms. "What can I do for you?"

"So formal?"

"You befriended my mother with the express purpose of getting to me. So you'll forgive me if I'm a little suspicious about why you're here."

He expected her to deny it. Instead, she said, "I wanted to thank you for taking the time to look into Bella's murder. But also to apologize for putting you in that position with your superior officers. That's why I came. I hope you don't mind, but I went to your lieutenant. I couldn't reveal my source, but I thought it might help if he knew it wasn't you. I didn't want to get you in trouble."

"Nothing I can't make up for at this point."

"I'm glad," she said. And then, surprising him, she stepped forward, put her hand on his shoulder, stood on tiptoes, and kissed his cheek. She looked up at him, her face mere inches from his. He breathed in the floral scent of her hair, felt the light touch of her fingers burning through his jacket. It took every ounce of willpower not to move, not to take her in his arms and kiss her right back. Every second she remained there was testing his willpower.

But then she stepped back and smiled. "If you're ever up for that drink, you have my number."

She waited a beat, then moved past him and toward the door.

He realized he didn't want her to leave. She was halfway across the lobby when he called out to her.

Jenn stopped, looked at him.

She's the press. "Take care."

"You, too," she said, and this time he let her go.

Al was still waiting for him at reception. "Things go okay?"

"Yeah. She talked to Timms, I guess."

"Good for her," he said.

The moment they walked into Homicide, Lieutenant Timms called them into his office. "I suppose you saw the reporter on your way in?"

"In the lobby. She said she talked to you about her, uh, source."

"She did. Which I appreciate. But that's not why I've called you in. Apparently the congressman withdrew his complaint."

"Why?" Casey asked then realized how idiotic that sounded. "I mean, I'm glad, but what made him change his mind?"

"Social media backlash, from what I hear. Apparently some news reporter discovered you walked out of your promotional interview to save Marcie Valentine. Once it hit the airwaves, Parnell's public statement about you trying to get ahead at his expense seemed more like self-aggrandizement on his part. Rumor has it he'll be announcing his resignation from the race any day."

"Gotta love social media," Al said.

"Which," Timms said, "brings me to my next point. Good work last night."

"Thank you, sir."

"Walking out of your oral board to handle that case—not something you see every day."

"I wasn't trying to be disrespectful."

"No one thought you were. In fact, once the captain heard about it, he thought we should reschedule your interview. They're finishing up the slate of candidates today and could tack you onto the end."

Casey glanced over at Al, who gave an encouraging thumbs up. "Thanks. I appreciate it."

Casey and Al walked out to find Zwingler and Haynes discussing a case they'd picked up the night before, a homicide in the Mission District. The robbery investigators were in their corner, discussing a spate of strong-arm robberies in North Beach.

It all seemed so normal. So much going on. So much more to learn.

And that's when he realized he was about to make a big mistake. He walked back into the lieutenant's office just as Timms was picking up the phone. "Sergeant?" Timms asked, eyeing him.

"I appreciate the offer, sir. But I think I'm where I need to be right now."

Timms held his gaze a moment then nodded. "I'll let the captain know."

"Thank you."

When Casey returned to his desk, he saw the look of approval on Al's face. And then Zwingler pulling a dollar from his pocket. "Liar's poker. Last donut. Who's in?"

The End

ACKNOWLEDGMENTS

As usual, I owe a debt of gratitude to others in helping me with this book. Since it has been a while since my last visit to San Francisco Police Department, I am grateful to Lieutenant Pat Correa (ret.), San Francisco Police Department, who not only let me question her endlessly about police procedures specific to San Francisco but allowed me to put her on speed dial—or rather speed text—to ask even more questions as they cropped up. To Sal Towse, of San Francisco, who helped me scout out locations in the city and was patient with my fictional scenarios. To Kim Ostrom, aka Kimberly Cates, who let me bounce ideas off her as we sat in Panera working on our respective books. To Allison Brennan, suspense author extraordinaire, who happens to have a background in political offices and was able to answer my questions about finances in campaigns. And last but not least to Susan Crosby, my longtime critique partner, who knows me so well, and even more important, knows my writing so well, pointing out all the right places that, well, needed work.

I would also like to thank Shirley Arnett for her generous donation to the Anaheim Library for the character auction. Shirley bid on and won a character name to be used in this book. She chose to include Kevin V. Melton, artist/illustrator by night and caregiver extraordinaire by day. Shirley and Kevin, I hope you are happy with the role I created.

ABOUT THE AUTHORS

ROBIN BURCELL
Robin Burcell spent nearly three decades as a police officer, hostage negotiator, and criminal investigator before retiring to write fiction full time. An FBI-trained forensic artist, her drawings have been used to solve a number of crimes, including homicides and bank robberies. She is also the award-winning author of ten novels to date, including *Face of Killer, The Bone Chamber, The Dark Hour, The Black List,* and *The Kill Order.*

CAROLYN WESTON
Carolyn Weston grew up in Hollywood during the Depression. She played hooky from school in movie theaters and libraries, honing the craft that would make her books so remarkable. During World War II, she worked in an aircraft plant and then did odd jobs around the country before writing *Poor Poor Ophelia,* the first Al Krug/Casey Kellog police procedural, which became the hit TV series *The Streets of San Francisco.*

Made in the USA
San Bernardino, CA
10 October 2016